D1535331

Where We Lived

Where We Lived

A FICTION

CHRISTINA FITZPATRICK

HarperCollins*Publishers*

WHERE WE LIVED. Copyright © 2001 by Christina Fitzpatrick. All rights reserved. Printed in the United States of America. No part of this book may be used or reproduced in any manner whatsoever without written permission except in the case of brief quotations embodied in critical articles and reviews. For information, address HarperCollins Publishers Inc., 10 East 53rd Street, New York, NY 10022.

HarperCollins books may be purchased for educational, business, or sales promotional use. For information please write: Special Markets Department, HarperCollins Publishers Inc., 10 East 53rd Street, New York, NY 10022.

FIRST EDITION

Designed by Jeannette Jacobs

Library of Congress Cataloging-in-Publication Data is available upon request.

ISBN 0-06-019769-2

01 02 03 04 05 ❖/RRD 10 9 8 7 6 5 4 3 2 1

These stories are for
my mom,
in appreciation for all she has given me

CONTENTS

Where We Lived

Tanya

WHERE WE LIVED

MISTY MALONE'S MOTHER WAS A HOOKER. They lived two doors down from me in a flat-roofed house that was black with pink trim. My house was the same, but it was white. Our whole neighborhood was full of these houses—trailer homes without wheels. The street we lived on, Scarsdale, was long and narrow, full of potholes and sand; it led to no other streets, only woods littered with junk. The woods was a dumping grounds for things that people wanted to get rid of: a couch with missing cushions and ripped-open arms, a rocking chair that no longer rocked, three-legged tables and desks, and even a stove that had missing burners and knobs.

When Misty and I were friends, when we were seven, we used to play in the woods building magnificent rooms out of the furniture we found. Together we moved the couches and tables and chairs together so that they could form one giant living room, one larger than the space of either of our houses. We didn't have the strength to move the stove, so we left it where it was dumped and moved part of a kitchen sink we found, brown and rusted, next to it. We tried to make walls out of the trees, picking certain areas where the trees clustered together and shadowed our view. We spent hour after hour, day after day, out there getting dirty and sweaty, just to create a house, a make-believe house.

We left the woods when it got too dark, when the sway of the trees became eerie and the sudden snap of a branch made us nervous. Then we went to her house, never mine.

I had a brother who was mean, really mean. My mother was a nurse's aide and she worked at the hospital as much as she could—double shifts sometimes, three in the afternoon to three at night. My brother, Ian, who was seven years older than me, was supposed to be my baby-sitter. But once my mother was gone, friends of my brother's, the neighborhood boys, came over. They sat around the TV, on the floor and couch, eating popcorn and chips and drinking beer out of cans. Whenever I was home, I was never quiet enough for Ian—our house was so small. I was always flushing the toilet, running water, or letting dishes clank too loudly in the kitchen. So . . . he put me in the closet. It was always the living room closet, which smelled like the dust and dirt of our vacuum cleaner mixed with the smell of my mother's perfume, the sweetness which lingered in her jackets and sweaters. Sometimes he left me in there for hours, locked in, fidgeting with the doorknob, my hands desperate and sweaty, and then I'd start screaming and banging—the darkness, the frustration, seemed never ending. And he'd laugh and so did some, not all, of the others.

Of course, sometimes his friends weren't over and sometimes he didn't lock me in the closet. Sometimes he just licked his hand and slapped it on my face or he peeled the dead skin off his feet and put it in a glass of my milk where it would float undetectable for a sip or two. Or he just called me things: frog face, moron, douche bag, dunce.

I feared my brother, hated him, and whenever I heard his laughter, even in the presence of my mother, I instantly stiffened.

Misty was the only one I talked to about this, about what Ian did to me. When we were alone in the woods, I told her how long ago I used to be able to hold my brother's hand when we crossed the street together or sit in the car with him, side by side. It was once all right. "But then he got older and meaner or something," I said one time, not looking at her but at my hands. We were in the woods sitting at a broken table that we had propped against a tree—the dining room.

Misty said, "You don't have to like your brother just because he's yours, Tanya." She shook her head. "You don't have to." Misty had a brother too, Mattie, but he was only two years older. Misty told me that Mattie said something once about her mother which wasn't true. "Something really bad," she said and moved in her seat. The wobbly table tilted. "He's a liar," she said.

Misty's mother worked at night just like my mother, but she went in at ten and came home much later. Misty told me her mother was a waitress at a restaurant that was a few blocks away—it was called The Corral.

The Corral was supposed to be like a steak house—it looked like one from the outside. It was a long brown building with white shutters around the windows and ruffle curtains that you could see from the outside. The sign out front was written in western-style letters and there was a wooden horse underneath it which looked like it was eating grass. Directly across the street from the restaurant was a motel called the Gables which rented rooms by the night or by the hour.

Misty's mother let us wear the wigs she wore to work. They were always too big, falling forward on our foreheads, but we still had the illusion of being beautiful with all those fake blonde curls or jet black strands hanging down past our shoulders. We wore her jewelry too, which was very different from my mother's—it was lighter, full of color and rhinestones. Misty and I wore as much as we could so that with each movement we made there was this fabulous tinkling sound.

The first time I ate over their house, Misty's mother bought us Chinese food for dinner. She was still in her bathrobe when the deliveryman came. I was sitting next to her on the couch wearing a wig, the long blonde hair covering all of my back. Misty was in the bathroom, so her mother gave me the money to pay the deliveryman. "Give him a two-dollar tip," she said and walked into the kitchen so that the deliveryman wouldn't be able to see her—her tangled hair, the mascara still under her eyes, and her bare feet, which were callused from the shoes she wore.

I stood there in the living room staring at the wad of money she had given me. I had never seen so much money—it was probably a hundred dollars. The deliveryman knocked again.

Misty's mother said, "Tanya, honey, you gonna get it?"

I said, "Yeah," and opened the door. The deliveryman was Asian, presumably Chinese, with a little mustache. He kept staring at me, at the wig, but he said nothing. I felt self-conscious when he watched me count the money—my bracelets kept clanking and the money was in a crumpled ball of ones, fives, and tens. When I went to give him his tip, the two dollars, he backed away. "No, no," he said.

I stepped forward. "Yes, yes."

But he wouldn't take it. He walked back to his blue car parked in front of the house and I stood there watching him with the brown bag of food at my feet.

When I went back into the kitchen, I gave Misty's mother her change. Instead of putting the money in her purse like my mother would've, she put it in her robe pocket.

We ate the Chinese food in the living room right out of the white cartons, no plates. Misty's mother kept telling us to be careful with the wigs—"Don't touch," she said, pointing at our greasy teriyaki fingers. Together we watched a rerun of *Bewitched,* and Misty's mother kept humming its theme song as we ate.

Whenever I ate over at their house, Mattie didn't come out of his room and Misty's mother never went in there to get him. I knew what he looked like because I had seen him walking to school. I liked Mattie from a distance. I liked his white-blond hair, his pale face, and the way his head was always tilted down. I often hoped he might come out of his room when I came over and watch TV, but he didn't. His bedroom was directly connected to the living room. Through that closed door, he must've heard us: the rattle of our bracelets, the television voices, and then our own voices—his mother's the loudest, so raspy and deep.

Once he came out when Misty's mother was getting ready for work. She was wearing this long black dress that had glitter butterflies all over it. Her wig was short and red. She was looking at herself in the full-length mirror which was in the corner of the living room. Mattie came out of his room and went down the hallway to the bathroom. On the way back, he stood in his doorway staring at his mother. Still looking at herself, she said, "Mattie, there's pizza in the fridge for you."

He didn't say anything. He just stared. Misty and I sat together on the couch. He didn't look to me like he was angry or sad—he looked expressionless, like he was watching something happen that was happening over and over again. Misty said, "What are you looking at her like that for?"

He looked at Misty and then his gaze fell on me. He said softly, "Hi," and walked back into his room, letting the door shut.

Misty's mother sat down in the chair next to us and picked her cigarettes up off the coffee table. "He's a jerk," Misty said to her mother. "I wish he didn't live here."

"Does he eat?" I whispered.

"In the middle of the night." Misty shrugged her shoulders. "When my mom's gone."

Her mother didn't say anything. She put a cigarette in her mouth.

I looked at Misty. "Is he mad at you guys?"

Misty was playing with a pair of beads around her neck. She kept pulling them tighter and then loosening them.

Her mother said, "Somebody said something to him at school—they tease him." She was trying to light the cigarette in her mouth, but the matches were wet or something—they wouldn't light. She kept striking the match again and again, her lips tense. "Boys who grow up without any men, just women, they come out different." She took the cigarette she couldn't light out of her mouth. "There's two ways they can go. They can either love women to death, become sissies sometimes even, or they go the other way, they don't like women." She picked up a lighter and put the cigarette back in her mouth. "They think we're bitches almost." She lit the cigarette and inhaled. "They think we keep the men away. Every time they hear some other boy talking about fishing or camping or whatever—they get angry. We . . . ," she said and looked at Misty, who was half listening, half watching TV. "We took that from him, that's what he thinks."

When she said this, I thought of my own father. He lived in California. My parents divorced when I was three and Ian was ten. I never really had a clear memory of my father the way that Ian did—I didn't know what I was missing. I had seen fathers in my neighborhood, in their driveways or front lawns. I saw fathers who yelled a lot and drank beers, fathers who had wide leather belts and red irritated faces. I saw fathers I didn't want.

But according to Misty's mother, all boys wanted their fathers. That night she said, in the direction of Mattie's bed-

room, "You ain't missing much." Then she looked back at Misty
and me, shrugging her shoulders. She kept smoking, and Misty
and I remained quiet. I kept my eyes fixed on Mattie's closed
door. On the other side, I imagined a boy standing there with
his arms wrapped around himself and his feet wide apart as if in
a stance. But the boy I saw wasn't Mattie, it was Ian.

Shortly after that night, my brother hit me in the face with a flyswatter. It was in the morning; I was eating cereal in the kitchen.
He just walked into the room, opened the refrigerator, picked
up the flyswatter on the counter, and hit me. My mother was
home in her bedroom, sleeping soundly with earplugs in her
ears. But there was nothing for her to hear anyway: I didn't cry
and he didn't laugh. We were silent—there was just the drip of
the bathroom faucet which we could hear all the way in the
kitchen. I put my spoon down. "Why do you hate me?" I asked.
"I wanna know why?"

"I don't hate you," he said. Our cat jumped on the table
and he started petting it. "I just think you're ugly and stupid,
that's all."

I got up from my seat, put the bowl of milk down for the
cat, and walked to Misty's house. It was late April, still cold, and
I didn't have a coat on. I went right into her house without
knocking. Misty was sitting on her couch with her pajamas still
on. It was Saturday morning, cartoons were on the TV. She
immediately noticed the red mark the flyswatter had left on my
cheek. She said, "What happened?"

I stood there with my arms wrapped around myself and my lips
pressed together. I stared at the TV in front of me. *Tom and Jerry*
was on—Tom was trying to eat Jerry between two slices of bread.

Misty kept looking at me. When I finally looked at her, she
said softly, "Your brother."

I nodded and sat down next to her. Together we ate an

entire box of dry Frosted Flakes. The sugar along with sitting still for so long made me feel restless, dizzy.

Misty asked, "Do you want to race?"

"OK," I said, watching her put on her sneakers.

We raced inside of the house—that's where it started. We raced from the kitchen to the living room, down the hallway into her room, out her bedroom window—there were two windows, one for each of us. From the sill, we climbed up onto the roof, where we ran back and forth. With the sugar and the adrenaline running through us along with the cold air against our faces, it felt so good to be moving so freely above everything: the houses and treetops and streets.

We ran faster and faster, letting the tips of our sneakers get closer and closer to the edge. Our feet against the gravel of the rooftop must've sounded like pounding from inside the house, and even the ceiling must've shook.

"What the hell are you doing up there?" Misty's mother called out to us.

Together we stopped, skidded almost, with our mouths open, panting. We walked to the edge of the roof, where the front of the house was, where we knew she was. Misty's mother was barefoot standing next to this rusted car hood that sat on their lawn. She had her arms folded, her hair was tangled and messy.

She said, "What are you, an idiot? Get the fuck down from there!" She was yelling directly at Misty, not me—but in standing so close, I felt it, the harshness, the anger. "I was sleeping!" Misty's mother yelled—she was so loud that I looked over at my house, worried that my mother or Ian might hear her. "I need to sleep, can I just have that? That one thing?" She wasn't just yelling now, she was ranting aloud to herself. Still trying to catch my breath, I looked down at Misty's mother and saw the difference between her and my mother. She was angry because we had woken her up, not because we were running around on a rooftop like maniacs, not because we could've fallen off, crippled ourselves, or worse.

"You better get the fuck down," she said again. As she walked toward the front door of the house, I heard her mutter, "Dumb asses," and then she went in, letting the door slam.

We walked slowly across the roof back toward where we had climbed up. I concentrated on my footsteps, trying to make them as gentle as I could. When we were almost down, balancing on the sills of Misty's bedroom windows, Misty grabbed my arm. "We're not going back in there," she said. Her eyes were glassy and her nose was running. She still had her pajamas on. We jumped down from the window to the ground. I could feel the pressure, the pain of falling, in my feet.

We walked down to the woods and sat on the couch. She sat on the right-hand side and I sat on the left. It was one o'clock in the afternoon, the sun was out, but it was still a cold spring day. We didn't say much. We kept our arms wrapped around ourselves and watched squirrels run through the trees. When one squirrel jumped on another, we laughed, but it was a strange sort of laughter, nervous and self-conscious, like we were afraid if we laughed too loud, someone might come and stop us.

How anyone found out for sure about Misty's mother, that she was a hooker, I don't know. No doubt someone from our neighborhood had gone, someone's father, had walked into The Corral through that windowless door. It was a bar, not a restaurant, and Misty's mother did indeed serve drinks. But the waitresses were "friendly." They sat at the tables, had a drink or two, and if things didn't go right, they would move to another table. When things went right, they went to the Gables.

The Gables was a motel that had giant high-backed chairs on

its balcony, as if anyone would ever sit out there and bother to look out at the view of passing cars, telephone poles, and yellow-lined parking lots. And the men who went there into the rooms, the rooms I have never been in, I imagine to be lonely men, not bad men; men who went there with the simple hope of unbuckling their belts, kissing and sucking and moaning until the emptiness of our town, our world, drifted away from them like chimney smoke across a winter sky.

To the people we lived with, however, the ones who shopped at Walgreens and Food Mart, who stood in lines at the Springfield Community Savings Bank, who had kids with taunting voices who sat in Mattie Malone's fourth-grade lunchroom, and even the ones who lived right there on Scarsdale Street, to all of them, The Corral was the epitome of everything disgusting and dirty that loomed in our town.

Yet Misty's mother, so skinny and small, with her child-size wrists and curveless square body, had a toughness about her—she would not lie. She said to anyone who asked, "I'm a waitress," and if they asked, "Where?" she looked right into their eyes: "The Corral."

I was allowed to be friends with Misty for only three months: April, May, June. The last night I was over her house, we watched *Poltergeist*. It was the first week of summer vacation and it was already hot. The windows were open—the curtains moved in the breeze; they were a sheer pink.

Poltergeist was our third scary movie for the night. Misty's mother had gotten cable that week—we couldn't get away from the TV. When the movie ended, it was no longer daytime, but night. Sitting in that dark house, we jumped when we heard any noise, whether it was the twitter of a cricket or the sudden crash of dirty dishes settling in the sink. Misty's mother wasn't home and Mattie was in his room, the door shut, and the light underneath leaked in. I couldn't even look at his door, because if I did, I kept imagining myself opening it and finding not Mattie, not a room, but a giant white limitless space.

It was ten o'clock, time to go home, but if there was ever a moment when I did not want to be locked in a closet, it was then. Besides Misty didn't want me to go. She was scared and kept biting her thumbnail. "Sleep here with me," she said. "Your mother won't even know."

I thought about it for a minute and shook my head. "No, she won't know. You're right."

We slept in the living room on the couch: Misty on one end, me on the other. Above the couch, there was a picture of the Eiffel Tower—it was cartoonish and pastel, but it looked eerie to me that night, as if at any moment it might turn itself upside down. Neither one of us wanted to sleep in her bedroom, though. We wouldn't even go in there to change. Instead Misty gave me one of her mother's nightgowns to sleep in—it was in a cloth bag on the coffee table. We talked for a while against the silence of the room and then somehow we fell asleep—the heat of summer, the hours and hours of sitting too close to the television, had made our eyes grow heavy.

In the middle of the night, there was a banging on the front door, the living room door. I woke up immediately. Misty wasn't there on the couch—earlier in the night I had woken up and seen her walk sleepily into her bedroom. The knocking frightened me, but by then, I was no longer haunted by the fantasy of demons and ghosts. I was afraid of what was really there: an actual person.

I stared at the door, but didn't move. Then I heard, "Tanya, are you in there? Tanya?" It was my mother.

I got up and opened the door. "Thank God," she gasped and pulled me to her. My mother was still wearing her uniform—it felt scratchy against my face like the texture of a stiff curtain. When she let go of me, I stood in front of her, half asleep, in my white cotton underwear and black lace nightie. The spaghetti straps were of course too long, not even covering me. My mother said, "Where's your clothes?"

I rubbed my eyes. "I don't know." I looked around the darkened living room. "I don't know where my clothes are."

I can't clearly remember my mother's face or even how she stood in that doorway, but I know that there was a pause. I imagine that somehow she must've zoomed forward in her mind envisioning me, years from then, fifteen maybe, in the same black nightie, saying those same words, "I don't know where my clothes are," but I would be wide awake, sneering at her, mascara smudged under my eyes.

Without waiting for me to look for even my shoes, she yanked me by the hand out of the house and slammed the door shut. Her grip on my hand was tight, painful. She pulled me alongside of her, I was half running to keep up with her gait, as we moved through the grass of our neighbor's yard to get to our house.

In the morning, my mother was standing in the doorway of my bedroom. She looked as though she might've been standing there all night. She said to me, "You can't go over Misty's house anymore."

I was still wearing the black nightie. I sat up in my bed. "I won't sleep over again without asking."

"No." Her voice got louder. "You're not going to go over there at all. And . . . and she can't come here."

"That's right, she can't come here," my brother said, appearing behind my mother. He must've heard us talking. The house was so small that from across its width with doors shut, you could still hear conversation. "Tell her, Ma. Tell Tanya what you told me last night," he said. He had a box of crackers in his hand. He pushed past my mother and stood in the middle of my bedroom.

"Ian," she said, "shut up."

"Tell her."

"You're the one that was supposed to watch her. . . . You're the one."

"Misty's mother's a hooker," Ian said, "a hooker."

I glared at him. "She's a waitress."

"I told you not to tell her," my mother yelled and walked over toward Ian.

I screamed at my mother, "She's a waitress!"

My mother wasn't listening. She was standing over Ian with her hand inches from his face. "I told you not to tell her." Her eyes were glassy and her voice seemed to weaken. "What the hell is wrong with you, Ian?"

He looked at her hand. "Go ahead. Slap me."

She put her hand down. A lawn mower was buzzing next door.

I said, "She isn't a hooker."

My mother looked over at me. "You don't even know what a hooker is."

"Yes, I do," I said angrily. I was mad at her the way that my brother always was. I was angry that she was saying this, making it up, lying. She was trying to take Misty away in the same way that she took the house from me by leaving it every day. I had grown to distrust my mother. I never told her what Ian did to me, not because I feared Ian so much as I feared her—and what little she would actually do to save me.

"I know what hookers are," I said and looked at both of them: my mother standing over Ian and Ian sitting in my desk chair. He was holding one of my Barbies and pushing in her face with his thumb. I glared at my mother—I wanted to hurt her. "Hookers are women who stand on street corners, they get in cars with men. They do it with them for money. I know that. I'm not stupid."

My mother stared at me. My brother ate a cracker.

She walked back through the doorway and out of my room. She moved slowly like she wasn't exactly sure where she was going to go, what she was going to do. My mother turned to me, but she was looking at Ian too. "You aren't to go over there anymore." She paused. "I'm sure Misty is very nice, but. . . ." I stared at my mother and thought, *As if you would even know, as if you have ever met her, as if you're ever here.* She continued, "She's not going to be like you." She shook her head. "You're not the same." Then she gave me this strained look as if she was doubting herself, as if she was suddenly realizing that Misty and I weren't that different.

One week later, Misty came to my house to find me. I hadn't left the house or the yard all week. I had been locked in the closet four times. When she came, showed up on my front steps, I wanted to leave with her, go to the woods, hide. But Ian was watching me— he was really watching me now. He was in the backyard with his friend, Louis Larson, and another kid. They were smoking pot and laying in the sun. I knew he would know if I left.

I stood on my steps in front of Misty. She was wearing a blue pair of shorts and a red T-shirt. Her hair was up and I thought that her mother must have pinned it that way, because she could never have done it herself. She said, "There's a new couch in the woods—it's long and it's got wooden arms and legs." She wasn't looking directly at me. She was tracing the edge of the step with her foot. It was like she knew there was something wrong, a reason I hadn't come over in one week, but she didn't want to bring it up. She just wanted to start up again like we were before. "It's a really fancy couch and it hasn't been rained on yet."

"I can't," I said.

She waited a minute or two. I could hear the sound of my brother and his friends on the other side of the house. They were talking and laughing.

"Why?" she asked me.

"My mother's mad at me."

She bit the corner of her lip. "I have your clothes at my house still."

"I know."

The voices in the yard got louder, they were up moving toward us, coming around the house. I looked at Misty—I wanted her to run. Ian came around the corner first. He didn't say anything until he was standing right next to us. "You're not supposed to be talking to her."

I didn't say anything.

Misty had never met my brother. She was staring at him. He wasn't wearing a shirt, just cutoff corduroys. He looked skinny, his ribs stuck out.

"She can't talk to you anymore," Ian said to Misty.

Her eyes got glassy. Her face looked so small with all of her hair pulled back. She started to back down off the steps.

"She can't talk to you because your mother's a hooker."

'My mother . . . my mother's a waitress."

I couldn't look at Misty, or Ian. I looked between them at a sprinkler that was twirling in someone else's lawn.

"Your mother's not a waitress," Ian said, putting his hand up like he was holding a tray high in the air. "She's a hooker." He stood with his legs wide open and tilted his pelvis.

Misty's chin began to tremble. "My mother's a waitress!" she screamed and tears came down her cheeks.

I just stood there. I had not thought that whole week about whether or not Misty's mother really was a hooker. I had thought about me, about Ian, about my mother. But now watching Misty, the way her hands at her sides went to fists and let go, and then went to fists again, I realized something: She knew it was true.

My brother and his friends stood in front of her, their eyes puffed up and round from the pot. She kept crying. I expected her to turn at some point and run out of the yard. But she stood there for what felt like a very long time and then she slowly walked out of our yard. I watched the blue and red shape of her walk slowly down the street past her house. I looked at my brother. He was watching her too, rubbing the side of his jaw.

"You probably shouldn't have done that," Louis Larson said. He was standing behind my brother with his arms crossed, looking down at the grass.

My brother swallowed. "I know."

Shortly afterward, Ian and his friends went into the house and I stayed outside. I sat in the backyard, drawing in the dirt with a stick. If someone had come and asked me what was wrong, I couldn't have explained it. The sun felt hot on the top of my knees and I could smell chemicals, pesticides, drifting over from our neighbor's yard. The cat came over and brushed up against my leg, but I wouldn't touch him. At that moment I couldn't have touched anyone or anything. It wasn't Misty or how my brother had hurt her that upset me, it was that he had actually felt bad for her. It was the way he had stood silently in front of his friends, his bare foot grazing the top of the grass, as if he was embarrassed at what he had done. But day after day, he felt nothing for me.

What I was coming to understand was that he had never turned into some sort of evil, mean thing. He was a person and he chose to do the things he did to me.

At some point while I was outside, my mother came home. I didn't even hear her car pull up. She said, "What are you doing?" in this sweet playful tone.

I stared at her. Everything felt hazy—I had been thinking

too hard and the sun was draining. I threw the stick I was holding at my mother. It hit her in the arm, soft though, not hard
the way that I wanted it to hit.

She said, "Hey, what's wrong with you?"

"I hate you," I said.

She looked at me, her mouth open. "What?"

"I hate you."

She started to walk toward me, but I didn't want her anywhere near me so I started to yell to keep her at a distance. "He
locks me in the closet, he spits on me, he calls me names, and he
hurts me! You leave me here." I was starting to get choked up;
it was hard to breathe and talk so loud and fast. I said weakly,
"You leave me."

"He locks you in the closet," she said as if she hadn't heard
me right. I glared at her. She said, "You . . . never told me that."

"How can I?!" I was pulling up grass with my hands, not
looking at her. "If I tell, you'll say something and he'll do it
more. I'm always alone with him, by myself." I looked up at her,
eyes narrowed. "I know you know. You've always known. You
just act like you don't."

"Tanya, I didn't know," she said. She had her hands out in
front of her and her cheeks were splotchy and red.

"You don't care. You won't let me see Misty—I like it at
Misty's. And now I'm stuck here with him and he won't stop
hurting me." I looked away from her toward the house. "He's
just going to keep hurting me and you don't care, all you want
to do is work and I hate you for it and I hate him and this house
and the way I never get anything. I hate . . . "

My mother was crying, but she wasn't looking at me. She
was off somewhere else. "Why . . . ," she started to say and
stopped. "I'm trying so hard." She put her hand over her mouth
and then on her chest. She looked at me. "I can't be everywhere.
I can't be here and there. I only have one body." She pointed at

herself. "I only have this. I have to work! I have no choice. And you kids are so angry." She swallowed. "God, the two of you."

She came over to me and sat in the dirt. She touched my hair and I sat there with my neck stiff like I didn't want her touching me. She whispered, "I didn't know."

For a while I continued to sit there, rigid. But then just because I needed to, I leaned into her. She put her arms around me and I pressed my face against the white collar of her uniform.

For the rest of the summer, I didn't stay at home when my mother was at work. I stayed with Marilyn O'Connor, a widow who worked with my mother at the hospital—she and her daughter, Mia, watched me. Sometimes I slept in their extra bedroom, a bedroom that some dead aunt of theirs used to live in. At night in that room which smelled so sweetly of vanilla, I never dreamed of my brother. I dreamed of Mia's dead father, of her aunt, both of them roaming through the big peaked house.

I rarely even saw Ian. My mother made him get a job at Burger King and told him if he didn't like it, he could leave.

That September, she enrolled me in school under Marilyn's address; I was put in their district. Each afternoon after school, I went back to Marilyn's house; sometimes I stayed there for days. Within two years, my brother moved out. He was sixteen and he had fallen in love with a girl. They moved into a motel apartment downtown. Even then, though, with him gone, I wasn't allowed to be in that house, in that neighborhood, alone.

For years it went like this. I spent my time in Marilyn's neighborhood, Wilbraham. If you went through the woods at the end of our street, walked farther and farther, climbed over a chain-link fence, you were in Wilbraham. It was a place of regular-shaped houses, sidewalks, and curbs. It was a neighborhood that had more girls than boys—girls with names like Emma and Gwen, Patience and Hope.

Of course, I still saw Misty, but it was from far away. She was often with some other girls who lived farther down our street. One summer when I was twelve, I remember seeing her sitting on the roof of a gold Camaro in front of her house. They were smoking cigarettes and drinking Coca-Cola straight from a two-liter bottle. From where I stood, I couldn't tell what Misty really looked like, if her face had changed. Her hair was longer, to her waist almost, like one of those wigs we used to wear. As I stared at her, my mother followed my gaze—we were in our front yard, about to get in the car. My mother said to me, "Misty's getting kind of chesty, isn't she?"

"Yeah," I said, and we laughed, but the laughter was a nervous kind, not taunting. To the both of us, Misty in her tight tank tops and cutoff jeans seemed to embody a period of time in which my mother had failed me, and so we were always awkward and shifty-eyed whenever Misty appeared in the distance.

That same year, when I was twelve, I saw Louis Larson at the movie theater and I asked him about Misty. At first he didn't answer me. He was staring at my friend who was standing next to me, Gwen. Gwen was tall and thin, with hair that fell down past her bra line. She aspired to be a model and boys always liked her for that—it was as if they already considered her to be one. I suppose it was also her face that captivated them—not just its beauty, but its gentleness, its serenity. She had the face of someone who seemed incapable of ever yelling at someone or hurting them.

Still looking at Gwen, Louis said to me, "Misty's got a boyfriend. Tom Bailey." He raised his eyebrows as if that was supposed to mean something to me. Tom Bailey was the one who owned the gold Camaro. He was seventeen, with a black mustache and a leather trench coat he wore practically year-round. "Mean guy," Louis said, and I nodded as if I somehow already knew this. "They fuck all the time," he said. Gwen looked at him and turned and then looked at him again like she wasn't sure he really had said that. Louis continued, "Tom's even got pictures of them doin' it." We were standing in line at the concession stand of the movie theater. "I've seen some of them, the pictures," he said as we moved a little bit forward.

I didn't ask him anything else. I just pretended to be looking up at the prices on the sign in front of us. The lights were bright and the smell of the buttery popcorn turned my stomach.

"How's your brother?" Louis asked.

"He's good," I said. "He's working and he's got a better apartment on Richfield Street." My brother was nineteen by then.

"Still with that same girl?"

"Yeah."

"I like her," he said, approvingly.

"I do too."

Louis stared at me. I felt in that moment like he was going to say something to me, about my brother or the closet. I didn't want him to say anything, especially in front of Gwen. I started fidgeting with the velvet rope alongside of us and Louis, somehow sensing my discomfort, looked at Gwen and smiled.

But my brother and I were getting along by then anyway. He was older. On my eleventh birthday he bought me three sweaters that his girlfriend must have picked out and a silver necklace with a unicorn on it. He even told me once that I looked pretty—we were standing next to his car, it was summertime, it was dusk, my mother stood next to us barefoot.

I was even visiting him at his apartment sometimes. One night in particular, we sat at the kitchen table alone eating coffee cake. His girlfriend was behind us washing dishes.

I said, "This kitchen is bigger than ours at home."

"Yeah, that house is so small," he said. He had no more cake left on his plate, but he still had his fork in his hand. "I think," he said abruptly after a long pause, "I think that's why I used to act the way I used to." He swallowed. "It was really small in there."

I nodded. I knew what he was trying to say.

His girlfriend turned the faucet off. "Do you want more cake?" she asked me and lightly touched the back of my head.

I looked up at my brother and not at her. "No, I think I'm OK." I shrugged my shoulders. "I think so."

When I was fourteen I started seeing Misty regularly again. She was not my friend. Her brother, Mattie, as antisocial as he once was, was now throwing parties at their house. These parties lasted late into the night, and no matter how loud the music got, the police never came. Gwen was the one who wanted to go to the parties. She liked the boys in my neighborhood. She liked their greasy long hair, their jean jackets, their construction boots with red laces, and their bodies: so long and lanky. She wanted to be with them, have a beer, talk. We used to sleep at her house, sneak out the window in the middle of the night, and then walk for twenty minutes in order to reach my neighborhood. We had to pass my house to get to Misty's. My mother would be home sometimes, her Toyota in the driveway. Looking at my house from the outside, from the night, I'd imagine my mother sleeping alone and feel strangely sad.

The parties at Misty's didn't make me feel much better. Their house, which was still black and pink, was creepy to me. Everything looked the same: the couch, the chair, the television, the coffee table. Even the loose threads and broken potato chips on the carpet seemed to be the same ones, in the same spots, as before. I also started to notice things they didn't have that my mother and I did. There were no photographs, no knickknacks, not a single book. The only thing on the walls was the pastel picture of the Eiffel Tower which had scared me so many years ago. It was cracked now.

Whenever I saw Misty, we always locked eyes. We never pretended we didn't know one another, but we didn't speak to each other either. If I was in the kitchen standing with Gwen and some other boys and I saw her coming toward us, toward the refrigerator, I moved quickly out of her way without her having to say anything. There were usually only about thirty kids at the party, but because the house was so small—the living room and kitchen being the only places to stand in—it was easy to stay on the other side of the room, away from her.

When Gwen saw Misty for the first time, she stared at her in such an obvious way that I nudged her—"Stop!"

Misty, for fourteen, was short but she had this grown-up teased blonde hair and noticeably large breasts. Her makeup was too heavy, disfiguring almost—she wore foundation that was a few shades too dark and thick black eyeliner that made her eyes look smaller.

"Who's that?" Gwen asked.

"Misty," I said, "she lives here."

"She's the one whose mother's a hooker?" Gwen said, making a face which seemed mildly exasperated, but mostly amused. Instantaneously I took offense. Yet the offense I took was not out of respect for Misty, it was out of respect for myself. Gwen had a perfect family: a father, a mother, a little paperboy brother; she had no sense of what Misty's life, what my life, might be like.

There were all sorts of stories that I heard about Misty in that house. She slept with over fifty men. She had a notebook, they said, listing each guy, and then there was a series of stars next to the name, a rating. One boy insisted that she didn't take showers, that she was dirty. She had a rotten tooth, someone else said, and it was falling apart in the back of her mouth.

Gwen asked me one night, "Why is her mother a hooker any-way? What do you think happened to her?" Gwen apparently still believed that there was a solid reason, an answer, for the way people were or the things they did. She persisted, "Have you ever seen her? Do you know?"

"No, I don't know," I answered stiffly and gave her a look so that she knew I wanted the conversation to end.

The truth was I hadn't seen Misty's mother in quite a while. I had heard that she had been leaving them for longer and longer periods of time, sometimes days, sometimes weeks. Where exactly she went I do not know. Sometimes I saw her in her beat-up Volkswagen driving by, but her figure in the passing car was shadowy during the day and nonexistent at night. I never saw her in the yard, at her mailbox, or in the driveway. She had become a ghost in my mind, like the ghosts I believed as a kid once owned the furniture in the woods. When I was seven kneeling next to Misty, I used to examine those old tables with their legless chairs and think of how they once looked, whole and polished. I'd even imagine the people who used to sit in the chairs with their legs crossed and their hands flat on their laps. But those ghosts were of course different from Misty's mother—they only left behind broken objects.

The last time I went to a party at their house, Misty was about to be beaten up. The night before, Misty had cut off another girl's hair. They were out alone drinking Bacardi 151 in the woods and the other girl had passed out. Misty cut the girl's hair off, all of it, an inch or two off the scalp, with a pair of scissors she mysteriously had in her bag. Louis Larson claimed there were still clumps of hair mixed with dead leaves in the woods. "I saw it," he said.

The girl who lost all that hair was Lisa Bailey and her brother, Tom, was the one who was going to beat Misty up. He was the guy who was once her boyfriend, the mean one.

At the party that night, everyone was talking about Misty. They were making bets as to when Tom would show up: 11:00, sometime before 12:00, 12:30, someone else even had 11:52. Among all of this, I kept watching Mattie. He was drinking beers really fast. I was right next to him, standing next to the wall, and he was below me in a chair. He had on a T-shirt and his arms looked very thin. He still had that frail look to him, but now as a teenager, it softened him, it made me momentarily forget the bitterness to his voice or the sharp distant way he often stared. Mattie said, "She's such a fuckin' idiot. It's her own fault." His face was tight, irritated.

Where I stood in the living room was right next to Mattie's bedroom, which was the first door before there was a short hallway that led to Misty's room and then the bathroom. I kept looking in the direction of Misty's bedroom—I imagined her sitting in her bed, her feet tucked underneath her, waiting. She was waiting for some guy to come into her house, open up her bedroom door, and drag her out into the yard. There he would kick her and punch her and hurt her any way he could and no one, not even her brother, was going to stop him.

Gwen said to me, "Can you imagine having all your hair cut off?" She touched a strand of her own honey blonde hair as she said it. "Isn't that the worst?"

I looked at her—she was standing at my side—and then looked back out in front of me without answering. I was reaching this point with Gwen where I felt superior. I thought the things she said were simplistic and stupid; it was like she wasn't paying attention to anything. She must've saw that, the annoyance. Gwen said to me, "What?"

"Nothing," I said and started to walk away from her. "I have to go to the bathroom."

I didn't go to the bathroom, though, I went into Misty's bedroom. First I knocked on the door gently so she would know it wasn't Tom, and then I went in. She was on her bed, sitting against the wall. I said, "Hi."

"Is he here?" she asked. She had her hands close to her face.

I shut the door. "No, not yet." Her bedroom light was off and it was hard to see. The only light was from the street lamp outside. Loose papers were blowing around on the floor—one of the windows was cracked and cold air was coming in.

It seemed natural to just go over and sit on the edge of her bed, but then I was afraid of her a little bit so I stood awkwardly in front of her. She had the same bed that she had when we were kids, a small twin bed. I leaned against its white wooden frame.

In the middle of the silence, she said, "He's gonna beat the fuck out of me." She paused and swallowed. "I saw him once get in a fight with this kid in the parking lot behind Burger King. I don't know what the kid did—something—but Tom kept punching him and the kid was just standing there trying to catch his breath. He had his mouth open and you could see blood on his tongue. Even when the kid was down on the ground, Tom kept kicking him in the ass, right in the ass, and the kid kept trying to breathe."

I pressed my lips together and sat on the edge of the bed.

"He's gonna kick my ass, he's gonna." She had her hands inside the sleeves of her sweatshirt and she was rocking back and forth.

I said, "He . . . he used to be your boyfriend, though, right?"

She laughed bitterly. "So?"

I felt stupid—I felt like Gwen, asking questions that didn't belong. I said, "You gotta get up, you gotta hide."

"He'll fuckin' find me," she said and then I realized she was crying softly into her sleeve.

I touched her arm, but she pulled away. "Don't touch me."

I stood up. "Get up," I said and pulled her by the arm. She

let her hands out of the sleeves of her sweatshirt and smacked my hand away. So I smacked hers and we kept going like this, smacking at each other's hands. But it wasn't playful, it wasn't like two little girls stuck in the back of a station wagon smacking at one another. We were hitting each other hard, scratching a little bit; it was like we were trying to shake out all that nervousness, the fear.

"What are you just sitting there for? Get up!" I yelled at her. But she wouldn't; she seemed exhausted leaning back away from me. But this time when I pulled her arm, I got her to her feet. "Where's your shoes?" I said. "Where are they?" She didn't answer. "Where are they?" I said louder.

She pushed me back. "Where the fuck am I gonna go? Where?"

I stood there, the wind was coming in through the window harder now—whistling. "The roof." I shook my head. "They won't find you on the roof." I went over to the window and opened it. "Put on your shoes."

Slowly she picked up a pair of slippers that were under the bed and started to put them on. I was getting irritated, edgy. At any moment I felt like the door was going to blow open and Tom was going to be there. "Come on," I said and pointed at the roof.

She crawled through the window. I watched her slippers on the sill. When she was finally on the roof, I picked the blanket off her bed and followed her. "Here," I said when I got up onto the roof. She was shivering. I pushed her forward toward the middle of the roof. "You can't stay on the edge," I said.

"I know. I'm not stupid."

I kept pushing her. "Get near the middle and lay down." She had the green blanket draped over her. Some of the loose black gravel from the roof was sticking to the blanket. She was dragging her feet, and I said nervously, "Stop that, you're making too much noise."

We stood in the middle of the roof for a few minutes. It didn't seem as big as it once had when we were kids; everything, it seemed, was getting smaller and smaller. Above us the sky was starless. It was the kind of night where you could still see the clouds moving, drifting.

"Go back down. They'll know if you're gone," Misty said.

I looked over at the driveway. There wasn't a gold Camaro. "He's not here yet."

"Go back down," she whispered. She had pulled the blanket over her head now so that she appeared perfectly cocooned in it. "I don't want you up here with me."

She sat down and I stood above her. I had my arms wrapped around myself and the wind blew my hair in my face. To the right, I could see my house and my mother's car. Misty was biting her thumbnail—I could hear it. I walked back toward where her bedroom window was. I didn't say good-bye or anything. I just left.

Tom Bailey arrived at twenty after twelve—about a half hour later. When he walked through the door, everyone sort of looked at him without looking directly at him. It wasn't like the movies when the bad guy comes and the music gets lower and everyone stops talking, but there was a feeling, an energy, once he got there. He had that same trench coat on that he always wore. His hair was long, in his face. I saw him talk to Mattie and then go into the hallway to Misty's room.

"She's not fuckin' in there," he said, coming back into the living room.

"Yes, she is," Mattie said, annoyed. He was leaning back in the couch smoking a cigarette.

"No, she's not."

"She didn't come out here. Check the closet."

"If you're lying to me—"

"Why the fuck would I lie to you?" Mattie was sitting up now, slightly turned toward Tom. They stared at each other.

"She didn't come out," Louis Larson said. "I didn't see her."

"She's gotta come back." Mattie put out his cigarette. "Where else is she going to go?"

There was a silence. Gwen looked at me from across the room—she was twisting her gold necklace between her fingers. For a moment, I worried that she knew where I had been, what I had done.

Tom said, "Then I'll wait for her." He walked across the living room. He moved slowly with a slight strut. When he passed Gwen, she looked down at the rug as if she was afraid that if she made eye contact, he might touch her.

Staring at Tom from across the room, all I could think about was how much I hated him. I hated the way he held his beer, the shape of his lips when he took a sip, and even his boots I hated, so narrow and pointed. It was so easy to hate him, to hate an actual person, rather than the place, the world, we lived in.

Tom must've caught me looking at him. I was glaring at him or so I thought. Perhaps though from across the room, I looked like I was trying to be sexy or "come hither" with my narrowed eyes and lips curled up so tight. He got up and started walking toward me. The living room was not that large, but it felt like it took him a very long time to get to me. He squatted down in front of my chair. He was so close I could see the baby hairs around his face and the veins at his temples. His lips were chapped. He pushed a lock of hair out of my face and twirled the hair softly between his fingers. He was not quite touching me, but he was.

I couldn't move or speak. I was so frightened that I wasn't even sure if I was still holding the beer I had or if it had slipped out of my hand and rolled onto the carpet.

Louis Larson and a few other boys came over to us. The music was turned down. I can't remember if it was a motion they made, or if they said, "Hey, get away from her." But in any case, those boys saved me. Tom walked away, he went in the kitchen.

Then Gwen came over. She put her hand on my arm, and in that moment, I felt strangely special in a way I did not deserve.

Misty was still on the roof, lying under a blanket, waiting. It was mid-November, cold. When I was up on the roof I had thought of staying, but it was only for a moment. Because I was afraid, afraid of getting too cold, of being found with her, or worse, not being found. Sitting up there with the darkness, the night, all around us, I would've felt the same frustrated terror I once felt sitting on a vacuum cleaner in the closet with my hands on the doorknob—when can I leave, when can I get out, when will things really be all right?

Gwen

DRAMA

I DIDN'T WANT TO BE JUST plain old Gwen Driscol, a fifteen-year-old nothing; I wanted to be something more: a supermodel. So I went to the mall. I entered a contest. I won. It was the 1994 Look of the Year Contest, and I made my mother drive me forty minutes just to get me there. We arrived late, we had to race through the parking lot, my mother dropped her keys. But then I got up there on that stupid stage where they usually put the Easter bunnies and the Santa Clauses. I walked, back and forth, like a lady with a tail. Tight denim skirt, fuchsia heels, eye shadow. The judges looked at me and I looked at them and I knew it. I knew it, knew it, knew it. What I wanted was finally here: excitement, fame, drama.

When I came off that stage, the banner across my chest, my mother was standing among a bunch of old ladies who were eating ice cream cones. The cascading water fountain nearby was loud. I shouted, "I won!"

My mother said, "Yes, yes you did." Then she smiled in a

way that seemed too composed and calm. My mother was always doing this: being regular. She was a woman with straight blonde hair, glossy pink lipstick, and strapless square purses—purses she held tightly under her arm as if within them you might find all the wild emotions she never expressed. My mother seemed lifeless in comparison to the people I saw on *Days of Our Lives,* on *Oprah,* on *Current Affair.* She was a housewife, a cleaner, a person who seemed to think that anything bad in the world could be wiped away, sponged at, dabbed.

On the car ride to the mall, before I won, she had said, "It's not winning that matters, Gwen. It's the experience."

I nodded as if I agreed, looking out the window at a cluster of brick factory buildings, their skinny chimneys tall and puffing. But in my mind, I was not in the realm of those smoke-filled skies—I was somewhere else. I wasn't picturing *Vogue* covers, or runways, or beaded purses full of money. If I won, I'd leave home, leave Springfield. Move to New York. There, I'd have all sorts of things, like a soap-opera-star boyfriend who'd wear mascara and face powder. I'd abuse him, smash plates. The *National Enquirer* would have photographs of me and him at a dinner table: the soft candlelight, the silverware gleaming, I'd have too much lipstick on, I'd be yelling, and he'd sit there across from me, upset, his mascara running, his face a perfect shade of beige ivory. The caption would read: "What's Her Problem?"

My mother would call me. My father would call me. They'd say desperately, "Please honey, just come back."

In the car, imagining all of this, I said to my mother, "We're late." I pointed at the speedometer. "Drive faster, Mom. Please, faster."

When my mother and I got home from the contest, my father was in the kitchen sitting at the table. It was the first week of September, still warm, and he didn't have his suit on—he was wearing a T-shirt and plaid boxers. Without looking up from the newspaper he was reading, he said, "Hey, critters."

I said, "Dad, I won!"

He ignored me, his face close to the paper. I knew what he was reading about without even looking over his shoulder. There was this girl who had recently been killed. Everyone was reading about it. She was older, twenty, and she had once lived in our neighborhood with her mother. The police found her, naked, on the floor of her one-room apartment. The faucet was on, the radio going, a kitchen knife next to her. Her name had been Emma Jacobs.

My father kept smoothing his hair with one hand as he read. He said to my mother, "That girl was lying there for a whole day, right in the doorway, before anyone found her." He put his hands lightly on his lips. "I can't believe that."

My mother was taking off her coat. "Did you hear what Gwen just said? She won." She was smiling now, looking more animated, which bothered me. Why wasn't she like that when we were at the mall?

My father folded the newspaper on his lap and smiled. "What did you win? A math contest?"

"No." I was pacing back and forth, turning and twirling in front of him. I had my jacket off, the banner was clearly visible.

"A spelling bee?"

"A modeling contest!" I shouted back at him. "Bomb Modeling Agency is going to call me. I'm going to New York."

My father looked at my mother, his eyebrows raised.

"If they call," she said. She was standing in front of the refrigerator pouring herself a glass of Coca-Cola. I glared at my mother. She said, "You never know with these people, you never know."

My father took a sip of my mother's Coke. "Maybe you'll get a sweatshirt or something." He looked at my mother. "Dean's kid won a modeling contest. She got a sweatshirt."

I shouted back at them, "*I'm* going to New York!"

My father rubbed the bridge of his nose and my mother stood next to him, the ice in her glass clinking.

The next morning on the way to the bus stop, I told my little brother, Duncan, what was going to happen when I became a supermodel. We were walking down our street, down Linwood Lane. "I'm going to live near Central Park," I said. I described the apartment I would have: the giant windows, the balcony out front, and the roar of cars, taxis, and trucks beeping down below. I pictured myself on that balcony looking down. "I'll wear gauzy dresses and scarves, all sorts of scarves."

Duncan was twelve, old enough to get bored with me, but he listened with his book bag on his shoulder, his blond hair curling in the moist air. He said, "I hate scarves. Stupid people wear scarves."

I made a face at him, but he didn't look up. We kept walking. It had rained the night before and there was a muggy morning fog. Houses appeared in the distance, piece by piece: a chimney, a rooftop, a porch, a front door.

Duncan said, his voice soft, careful, "You're not really going to go?"

"If they call me, I am. They said they would call me." I was looking down at the ground. I noticed Duncan's sneakers—one of his shoelaces was untied. "Mom and Dad don't want me to go, though. They're going to try to stop me." I didn't really think that of course. But I wanted to believe it and I wanted Duncan to believe it too.

He said, "Mom won't stop you. Dad might." Duncan smiled. "Perhaps he'll shoot you."

I looked at him and he looked at me—we started laughing. Duncan and I were always making fun of my father behind his back. He had been in Vietnam, he had been a soldier. Yet it seemed impossible to us that our father, with his soft green eyes, his hunched shoulders, his navy blue suits, had ever held a gun or gotten dirt on his face. He never talked about Vietnam and we weren't allowed to ask about it. A restriction that I couldn't remember anyone really telling me; it was like we had been born knowing it: You can't ask.

Duncan kept laughing as if he couldn't stop picturing my father with a gun. When he noticed I had stopped laughing, he got quiet. We walked in sync. There was only the sound of our feet on the pavement and the rolling click of a rock that Duncan kept kicking. "Will I be able to visit you?" he asked, looking forward, not at me.

I said, "Yes, of course you will," and I heard the way my voice sounded. Very serious. It wasn't often that I thought about how one day I would inevitably live without my brother, in another place. Just the thought made me feel suddenly cold, uncomfortable. I zipped up my jacket. He was still kicking the rock.

"When you visit, you'll have to look more stylish," I said. "You'll have to brush your teeth, your hair, your eyebrows." He rolled his eyes at me. "Your hands, you'll have to scrub them good." Duncan was a paperboy and his hands, his fingertips, even his arms were always stained with ink.

When we got to the bus stop, Duncan and I stopped talking about me leaving. He ran over to the cluster of boys he knew and I went over to my friend Tanya. She was standing next to a mailbox, pulling the red flag up, then down. The moment she looked up at me, I wanted to tell her about the modeling. I wanted to scream it at her. But then I knew not to—she wasn't like Duncan, she wouldn't smile. She'd just shrug her shoulders, stare off.

I said, "Hey," to her and she said "hey" back. We stood side by side.

The morning fog was thinning out, and from where we were I could see down the street, past the rows and rows of houses, a dog sitting in the middle of the street. But what caught my eye was the same thing Tanya appeared to be looking at, the Jacobs house. It was a three-story house, mint green, with a wraparound veranda. Two days before there were reporters camped out on the front lawn, waiting for Mrs. Jacobs. On Channel 40, I had seen her on the news. I saw part of the house in the background, her blue car behind her. They asked her, "Do you think you'll ever get through this, this tragedy?"

She did not answer. She stood there in a long brown ski jacket, her face was very pale, and her eyes were unblinking, as though nothing could shock her. Looking at her on the television screen, I didn't feel much for her. I didn't. I was only thinking of Emma Jacobs. I was thinking of how no one would've ever known who she was if she hadn't been murdered. I was thinking in a very strange and twisted way, Will everyone ever think of me that way? Will they care? To be famous like Emma Jacobs meant you were really a part of the world, it meant you mattered.

Four days passed and Bomb had not called me. I decided to call them. The woman who answered said, "Did you get your 1994 Bomb Look of the Year sweatshirt yet?"

No," I told her. "I'm not getting a sweatshirt, they're supposed to call me. That's what they told me."

"Who?"

I paused. I didn't know. The woman I had spoken to, one of the judges, had somehow become in all my excitement rather faceless, ageless—I couldn't even say if her hair was brown or blonde. I said, "All I can remember is she had on orange."

"Well, whoever it was, will call you. Don't call us, she'll call you." The receptionist paused. "OK?"

When I got off the phone, I said to my mother, "They're trying to screw me out of my prize."

We were in the kitchen. She was in front of the stove, bare-foot. She looked at me. "Honey, what did I tell you?"

"I know what you told me," I said, irritated. It was as if in warning me, she had jinxed me.

"I'm not surprised." She paused. Her thoughts seemed to be immersed in dinner, in the meat loaf she was making. She said, "Isn't it enough that you won?"

I rolled my eyes.

Duncan was sitting at the kitchen table. His geometry book was open in front of him. I watched him make dots on a sheet of graph paper. He turned a page of his book and said, "Did you see the news today?"

I didn't say anything—I was still thinking about Bomb. They had to call me, they had to.

Duncan said, "They had Mrs. Jacobs on TV again." I looked up at my brother, at the pencil in his hand. "She was crying in front of the police station. I guess she had just seen some more photographs of, you know, the body."

My mother put a bowl in the sink—it made a crashing sound. She said to Duncan, "Did you deliver all of your papers today?"

He nodded, and then said to me, "They can't find the guy who killed her. He's loose somewhere. He could be anywhere. He could be in our basement."

My mother said, "All right, shut your mouth." She wasn't looking at my brother, but at the meat she was kneading in the bowl. She was concentrating on the bread crumbs, the tomato sauce, the meat between her fingers.

My brother pressed his lips together and looked up at me. I stared back at him. It's not that we never saw emotion in my mother; it just seemed as though we never saw enough.

She did have occasional sudden moments of anger, of sadness. Once she and I were alone in the house and we were lying side by side on my parents' bed. We weren't tired or anything—it was late afternoon. Rain was coming down on the roof. She started telling me about my father—how she met him. She told me how on their first date they went out for dinner and my father couldn't butter his bread. His hands were shaking so badly that his knife kept clinking over and over against the butter plate. "I thought it would never stop," she said, but she didn't laugh afterward like I thought she might.

I sat up and turned toward her. I was only ten at the time, but I could sense that there was a sudden shift in the conversation that had started out so light and happy.

My mother swallowed. "Your father was in Vietnam when he was eighteen." She told me about the platoon he was in, the villages he had walked through. She said that once my father saw what he guessed to be a grandfather walking with his grandson out of a field.

She put one hand under the pillow and said, "The grandfather was calling out to your father in English. He was trying to tell him something." My mother paused. "But then someone behind your father shot the grandfather. Then the grandson. Your father said, he said, that the little boy didn't have a shirt on and they shot him in the chest." My mother shifted so that she was not on her back, but lying on her side. She said, "Your father went over to the bodies, saw their faces, saw their hands. They were still holding hands."

The sound of rain on the roof grew softer, a light tapping. My mother looked at me. "For years, your father's own hands shook and shook." Her voice became louder as if she was bringing the story to a close. I stared at my mother, her head against the pillow, her lips quivering. I watched her eyes shift from one section of the ceiling to the next. At that moment, I felt as though I knew more, not just about my father, or my mother, but about drama, the power of it: It could make someone fall in love with you.

On the seventh day that I had been waiting for Bomb to call me, something happened. Something I had never feared or expected. Something dramatic.

Duncan was delivering papers on his bicycle when he crossed Woodland Road without looking. A car hit him. Or actually the car hit the front wheel of his bicycle and then he flew off his bike, over the car, onto the pavement. His head cracked open.

One of the neighborhood boys ran eight blocks to our house to tell my mother. He was panting, only six years old, in a blue jacket and jeans. He said, "The ambulance came to take him, but his head, it's all broken up and bloody." He held in his hands, as proof, a tiny piece of my brother's bicycle.

My mother stood in the doorway, looking at him. She had on a blue sweater with pearl buttons. She closed her eyes and then the phone started to ring. She went to answer it and I stood in the spot where she had stood. I could tell whoever was on the phone was telling her the same thing. She said, "Yes . . . OK . . . yes . . . all right . . . Mercy Hospital, OK." She was pulling on one of her pearl buttons—it fell off and rolled somewhere that my eyes could not follow.

When my mother got off the phone, we just looked at one another.

At some point, we got in the car. I don't remember walking across the lawn or putting on my jacket. I just remember being inside of the car, the doors already closed, the sun coming down over the trees. My mother's hands kept shaking and she couldn't really get the key in the ignition. She started to cry with her keys still in her hands and her hands against her face.

"Do you want me to drive?" I asked in this tone that wasn't

appropriate—I was being light, conversational. "I can drive. Let me drive. Give me the keys. . . . " It seemed to me, if I kept talking then it wouldn't be real, if we stayed long enough in the driveway, Duncan would emerge from one of the sunlit trees or someone would come over to the car, knock on the window, and say, "They made a mistake. Different paperboy."

I said again to my mother, "I'll drive. Just let me. What, you don't think I can drive?"

"Shut up!" my mother screamed and then I saw a cat run across the street.

"All right, you drive," I said softy, as if it was all in that one moment I came to understand what was actually happening.

In the emergency room of the hospital, my father, my mother, and I sat. My father arrived shortly after we did. My mother did not call him—I don't think she could've dialed the numbers. My father's footsteps as he moved down the hallway toward us were loud, echoing.

The doctor came out and stood in front of the three of us. I noticed that there was dirt on the cuffs of his white lab coat and I thought: He's not a good doctor, he's not a good doctor at all. The doctor only made eye contact with my father even though he was talking to all three of us. Duncan was unconscious, he said, in a coma. They couldn't tell when he would wake up. "It could take minutes, weeks, months, or more." He talked about bruising, about damage, about spinal fluid. "The swelling is what we're worried about. With swelling, parts of the brain can die." He swallowed and said, "We just have to wait."

Once the doctor left, my mother said to my father, "It was your idea for him to get this paper route, your idea." Her pink lipstick was smeared and she had pulled three more buttons off her sweater.

My father stared at her and stood up slowly. He turned away

from her and then back toward her. "Oh for Christ sake, don't you blame this on me. Don't you even try." He paused and then his voice got louder, as if he had thought about what she said and realized how horrible it was. "I wanted him to get a paper route, that's all." There was a magazine on a table in front of him. He picked it up as if he'd read it, but then he threw it back on the table. "What the fuck did you say that for?"

A woman nearby pulled her small daughter closer to her.

My mother didn't say anything to him. She was staring distantly ahead, completely removed, as if she was not in a room with any of us.

The rest of that day I can't quite remember. The room was light blue. There was a vending machine in the corner of the room. E10 had generic potato chips in a silver bag.

For the next four days, the three of us moved from room to room of our house silently. There was a heaviness between us. To move, to get up, to turn off the TV, we had to push a little harder against gravity, against air. All we felt was the waiting. Waiting to know if we would ever be able to be happy or if we would spend the rest of our lives feeling like we had lost, like nothing that would come to us would ever make us feel quite right again.

Mrs. Jacobs sent us a card. At first my parents didn't open the card, as if they feared superstitiously that opening it might do something, might change our fates, might make us just like her. The purple envelope remained on our coffee table for weeks. My mother finally opened it after my brother came home—after he woke up. It said: "My thoughts are with you. When they can be."

Whenever I saw Mrs. Jacobs from that point on, I always waved and she waved back. We never actually said anything to one another—we didn't have to. It was like there was a feeling we shared, a mutual understanding, that moved between us, between our waving hands.

When I went back to school after Duncan woke up, the boys

at our bus stop asked, "Is his face distorted? Is it fucked up? I heard he lost an eye—it fell right out onto the pavement. Is he brain damaged? Can he even talk?"

My friend Tanya kept telling them to shut up, but I didn't say anything. I just stood there looking blankly out at their little flushed faces, their zippered jackets, their book bags, their eyes so wide open and curious. I felt the way I imagined my father might feel if someone said, "Exactly how close were you standing when they shot the grandfather? Did the grandson scream? Did you feel the sound of the bullets?" I felt the way Mrs. Jacobs must've felt, a microphone in front of her, "So tell us, how does it feel to know that your daughter was brutally murdered? What's it like?"

Standing at that bus stop surrounded by those kids, I came to understand that no one, no one, should be asking those questions. They were stupid questions, inhuman ones. Pain is pain. Leave it alone.

Duncan came home three weeks after he woke up. He was OK, no brain damage, no real "brain trauma." His head was shaved and bandages covered most of his scalp. His left ear had deep red scratches. When we were leaving the hospital, I said to him, "You look like a space creature."

He shrugged his shoulders and said flatly, "I am a space creature and I am here searching for tin." As he said this, a woman passed by and stared at him. We laughed.

For the next two months, I stayed home a lot with Duncan. I bought him a red beret to cover his white stitched-up head. He wore it reluctantly, but only around the house. He was tired a lot and sometimes he just stared out in front of him distantly. I would watch him, trying to imagine what he thought about, what moved behind his eyes.

One afternoon during his first week back, Duncan and I

were sitting together on the couch. My mother had sent the curtains out to be cleaned and the window in front of us was bright and bare. We looked out at the houses, the trees, our yard. My mother came into the living room and started cleaning the coffee table. I noticed the way she kept glancing over at Duncan and me and I realized that she was only cleaning the table so she could be in the room with us.

A few minutes later, my father came home and he sat down on the chair opposite us. It was weird. There was no TV, no music, no newspaper crinkling. Just us. We weren't really looking at one another—we were just sitting there. Everything felt slow, deliberate.

There was a piece of lint on Duncan's beret and I pulled it off so gently that he might not have even known I was doing it. He turned to me. "Did the agency ever call you?"

I said no.

My mother was arranging magazines in a fan on the table.

My father said, "I'm glad they didn't call you." I looked at him. It was dark in the room—the sun was coming down but it wasn't quite dark enough to turn a light on. My father said, "If you left, I would've missed you so much." My mother had stopped cleaning. She had her hands on her lap and she was sitting on the floor looking up at me. She smiled.

I blushed. I felt strange, embarrassed. They were looking at me too softly. "I didn't really want to go anyway," I said, shrugging my shoulders, and I meant it. Modeling, the mall, my mother standing among all those old women, seemed so long ago, so far away—so small and foolish.

We sat together in the living room for about ten more minutes. The house grew dark. My mother stood up and turned on a light. "Are you ready for dinner?" she asked.

The three of us looked at one another. We nodded yes.

Emma

LISTEN

EMMA WAS SITTING AT THE BIG RED TABLE in the front room of the ABC Daycare waiting for someone to come get her. It was a little past 6:00 and she was the only one left. Usually her teacher, Miss Walsh, felt sorry for her, being the last to go home. But today Miss Walsh kept tapping a pencil against the edge of the table while she looked from Emma to the window outside and then back at her watch, which was hidden under her sleeve.

"Who's picking you up today?"

Emma shrugged her shoulders. There were four people who picked Emma up from school: her mother, her father, her Uncle Bill, or her Auntie Dottie. But there was no real order to it—each of them came on all different days. Her mother didn't pick her up that often because she was always working and working way past five o'clock. Usually it was her aunt or her uncle every day.

Her father was only used as a last resort. It wasn't that he didn't want to pick up Emma, it was that he wasn't allowed to. He was separated from her mother and he wasn't allowed in the house anymore. If he came over, he had to stay in the driveway. There was a restraining order against him. It was all because one day he got drunk and was yelling. Then Emma's mother got mad and threw his favorite maroon leather jacket with the silver buckles outside in some mud. She kept stepping on it and yelling at Emma's father. That's when he hit her in the eye.

Emma wasn't there, but she heard about it.

Sometimes Emma tried to picture exactly where they were standing in the yard when it happened, what her mother was wearing, how her hair was done, how loud did she scream? Even that jacket Emma thought about. She hadn't seen her father wear it since that day, and she wondered if he wouldn't wear it anymore because the very look of it upset him.

Other times Emma just thought about the police car—how it must've looked sitting in front of their pretty mint green house. Were the sirens going?

But right now she wasn't imagining any of that—she was just sitting there.

Miss Walsh put her black bag on the table and started digging around inside of it. "Maybe your aunt is coming today?" she asked as she pulled a small mirror out of her bag.

"I don't know," Emma said. Miss Walsh put on lipstick and Emma watched. The lipstick was a dark red, a color Miss Walsh didn't wear usually. "I don't think my aunt's coming. I think she works."

The last time Emma saw her aunt she hadn't said anything about picking her up. But that was a few days ago. Emma had stayed at her aunt's apartment last week because her mother had gone to Boston on business. Uncle Bill lived with Emma and her mother, but he wasn't allowed to watch her at night because he wasn't very good at it. He was always falling asleep with his clothes on and getting sick in the toilet. Uncle Bill was a drinker just like Emma's father.

So when Emma's mother went away, Emma usually went to her aunt's. They'd stay up late, past ten o'clock, painting their toenails red, curling their hair, and watching *Buck Rogers*. Aunt Dottie really liked Buck Rogers.

Miss Walsh was brushing her hair—it was down now and she didn't look as smart as she usually did. Every time Miss Walsh looked in the mirror, she pushed her lips out a little. Emma asked, "Are you going on a date?"

Miss Walsh laughed. "You're only six years old. How do you know what a date is?"

"My aunt goes on dates," Emma said, "with men who look like Buck Rogers."

Miss Walsh smiled and kept working on her face, powdering it. A car door slammed outside. Both Emma and Miss Walsh looked up at the same time, staring at the door. Some guy walked in. He said, "I've been waiting for you at that restaurant for forty minutes." He was talking to Miss Walsh, not Emma.

Miss Walsh stood up. "Her parents haven't come."

"Where's your mother?" he said. For a minute Emma thought he was talking to her, but he wasn't. He was talking to Miss Walsh about her mother. Miss Walsh worked with her mother at the daycare and they lived together in a house which connected to the classrooms.

"My mother, I forgot, has this big bingo thing tonight," Miss Walsh said. "She left a little while ago."

"You could've called," he said, with his hands on his hips.

It was then that Emma realized that this guy was Miss Walsh's date. He was wearing a gray suit with shiny shoes. His hair was combed back like the guys that worked at the gas station, but his face was really clean. He was all right looking, but he wasn't great—he didn't look anything like Buck Rogers.

"I didn't think to call," Miss Walsh said. "I was talking to Emma."

"Still," he said, and looked at Emma. "I hate waiting. Don't you?"

Emma nodded. "I hate it a lot."

He didn't say anything after that. Instead he walked over to Miss Walsh and kissed her on her forehead—it made a loud smacking sound.

Miss Walsh said, "Emma, this is Frank. Frank, this is Emma." Frank smiled and then started walking around the room. He kept touching all the toys: the blocks, the plastic race cars, the dolls with moving eyelids. Miss Walsh was watching him and so was Emma.

Frank looked up at them, raised his eyebrows up and down.

Miss Walsh said, "Have you been drinking?"

"At the restaurant, I had two or three." He shrugged his shoulders. "I was waiting for a whole hour." Miss Walsh's face looked suddenly sad even with all that makeup on. Frank kept looking at her like he was waiting for her to say something. Then he said, "If I wanted to drink I would've stayed there, but I didn't. I wanted to see you so I came."

Miss Walsh smiled a half smile, one that made her look both happy and not so happy. Frank picked up a toy that was on the shelf behind him. It was a plastic tiger. He put it up to his face and squeezed it. The tiger went squeak, squeak.

Miss Walsh laughed.

This whole time Emma didn't know if she should be acting like she was listening or acting like she wasn't. So now she just looked directly in front of her at the bulletin board where all the brown construction paper turkeys were, the ones the class had made out of the shape of their hands. Then she said, not looking at Frank or Miss Walsh, "My father drinks sometimes too. He gets drunk."

Frank smiled. "Sometimes that happens." He was playing with a small stuffed bear now. He kept throwing it in the air and catching it.

Emma watched the bear go up, then down. She said, "But it happens all the time, not just sometimes." Emma paused. "My father's a chef and he tells me that people who cook for a living need to drink a lot." This actually made sense to Emma because she figured that if he didn't drink, then being around all that food would make him keep eating and eating all the time and there wouldn't be any left for the other people, the people out at the red-and-white-checkered tables in the restaurant.

Frank said, "Well, I don't know anything about being a chef, but a lot of people like to drink a lot. It doesn't mean they're bad. It doesn't." He looked over at Miss Walsh. "What do you think, Barb? How do you feel about it?"

Emma made a face at the name Barb and so did Miss Walsh. "Don't call me Barb. I hate when you do that. My name is Barbara, which I understand is hard a word for certain people to say under certain conditions." Frank smiled and said, "Bar-brah." Then he started saying it over and over again until Miss Walsh looked at Emma and said, "There is nothing wrong with drinking. It's just that certain people drink too much. They can't control themselves."

Emma looked at Frank who was still mouthing the word "Barbara" across the table. She said to Miss Walsh, "My father can control it. Like in the car, he never drinks whiskey, just beers."

Miss Walsh sighed and got up from the table. She said, "I'm going to go call your mother right now, OK?"

Emma nodded and watched Miss Walsh walk into the office and shut the door. Then she glanced at Frank, rubbing her stomach. "I'm hungry."

"Tell me about it," he said, and looked over at the room that connected the daycare to Miss Walsh's house. It was the kitchen for both the house and the school and kids weren't allowed in there. He got out of his seat and said, "I'll try to find something."

A few minutes later, he came back and leaned in the doorway. He had a glass of red wine in his hand. Emma knew about red wine because she had seen some at the restaurant her father worked in. She said, "Is that merlot?"

"No, it's a sangiovese." He raised his eyebrows. "Do you drink wine, Miss Emma?"

Emma shook her head. "No, I don't drink."

He laughed. "That's a good thing." Then he sat down at the table with her. Emma noticed for the first time how his legs were too long for the chair; he looked like he was going to slide right off. He put the glass of wine on the table. He pointed at the pictures of pilgrims and Indians on the bulletin board. "Which picture did you draw?" He was trying to be nice.

But Emma didn't answer. There was something so weird about sitting in the middle of her classroom talking to some strange man drinking wine. It was like from this point anything could happen and this frightened Emma. What if no one showed up?

She pictured herself watching TV in the house she had not yet been in, Miss Walsh's house. She pictured sitting in a stiff old lady rocking chair, the TV on, the lights out, and the unfamiliar smell of oatmeal in the air.

Frank started asking her questions about school, but she didn't answer so he slapped his hands on his knees and looked around the room. Miss Walsh came in and said, "I called your mother's office. They said she left to come get you a while ago." Miss Walsh sounded sort of worried but then she said quickly, "I'm sure she'll be here any minute." She walked over toward them and then stopped. "Is that wine? Are you drinking wine, Frank?"

"Yeah, there was some left in the kitchen."

She held up her hands, exasperated. "I can't believe you." She shook her head and her face got angry again. "You can't wait, you can't wait another hour, you have to have a drink now?"

He pointed at the glass of wine in front of him. "Yes, it appears I'm having another one."

Miss Walsh shook her head and looked down at the carpet. Emma just watched. She had seen this conversation before and she was waiting to see how it would end; it could end in many different ways. Miss Walsh said, "You can't drink that in here." Her voice was getting louder. "It's a daycare."

He picked the glass off the table. "It's after six, Barb. Anything goes after six in the ABC Daycare."

"All right, don't be an ass," she said.

"See, you can even swear at the ABC Daycare." He looked at Emma. " It's after six. A disco ball could come down off the ceiling, the lights flashing, it could be madness."

Miss Walsh's face was very red. "If her mother comes in here and sees you with that—"

"If she comes, if," he put his finger up, "I'll hide the glass up my sleeve."

Emma heard the way he said *if*—he didn't think she was coming. Emma was beginning to wonder too. What if her mother was in an accident? She pictured cars honking at an intersection, the red Chevrolet turned over, glass on the pavement, the radio on low, and then there was a hand, a pretty little hand with rectangular nails and a gold ring on one of its fingers; that was the only thing sticking out of the car.

Miss Walsh looked at Emma, then Frank. "How could you say something like that—*if* her mother comes," she repeated, eyes narrowed. "You're going to upset her. Look at her."

Emma felt like she was going to cry and she was trying to hide it, but it wasn't working. She rubbed her nose.

Miss Walsh came over to Emma and rubbed her back. She kept yelling at Frank. "Why don't you think before you speak? Can you do that?" She looked down at Emma. "Your mom's coming," she said softly. "It's probably traffic or something."

Frank got up and went into the kitchen. Emma heard the splash of the wine go down the drain. He came back into the room with a plate. "Emma, I put some pizza in the oven for you earlier, but I forgot about it." He put the plate down in front of her. Emma looked down at the pizza. It was burnt around the edges and there were black olives on it.

She took a bite of the pizza and he watched. Miss Walsh had walked away from the two of them. She was standing near the window. It was dark out. Emma kept eating the pizza even though it didn't taste as good as she wanted it to. Frank was watching her, not Miss Walsh. He was looking at her funny, his lips pursed together, eyes serious. He was sorry.

But Miss Walsh was still mad. She had taken a pack of cigarettes out of her bag and now she was smoking and blowing smoke out the window with the pumpkin pictures all over it. Frank went over to her and touched her arm, but she kept looking out the window. He shook his head. "I don't think sometimes."

"That's always the problem," she said, holding her cigarette close to her face.

Emma wanted to tell Miss Walsh that she knew he hadn't meant it—to hurt her. Just the way she didn't think her father ever meant to hurt her mother. It just happened. It seemed people often did things and then right after—like a second later—you knew what you did. But you couldn't take those things back because they were already outside floating around, climbing into people's heads through their ears, and then crawling down into their hearts where they might burn for a very long time.

Frank turned away from Miss Walsh and came back to

Emma. He sat next to her. He said, "You know, it's good that you're so smart, that you know so much." Emma didn't say anything, she just stared at him. "Because other kids, you know the normal kinds, they don't know anything you know and they won't for a long time. But when it comes, when the trouble starts, it won't ever end and they won't know what to do. But you will, Emma. You already do."

Miss Walsh kept smoking and then she put her cigarette out. Her eyes became soft. It was like she was seeing him all over again, like he had come back again through the front door. Miss Walsh looked like she was going to go over to him and touch his arm or something, but instead, she headed toward the kitchen. She gave him a look in the doorway—one that said, Follow me. And so he did.

Emma couldn't see them from where she was sitting, but she could hear them—they were whispering. They talked for a while and then there was just this soft wet sound like rain dripping on leaves. They were kissing. Emma could hear it and it reminded her of how her parents used to kiss. They used to kiss in front of the giraffes at the animal park. They used to kiss in grocery stores, in malls, in Shoe Town, in the hardware store next to some rakes. They used to kiss at the drive-through window of the bank, in the living room when it was late and dark, everywhere, they used to kiss.

The nursery school door opened, Emma's mother walked in. The chimes on the door were ringing and ringing.

Emma screamed, "Mommy!"

Miss Walsh came out of the kitchen. Her lipstick was a little bit out of the lines but she looked OK. "Hello, Mrs. Jacobs," she said, a little out of breath.

Frank didn't come out. Emma pictured him standing against the wall, listening.

Emma's mother said, "I'm sorry that I'm so late. The traffic

was crazy." Miss Walsh and Emma's mother started talking
about traffic for a few minutes. Emma just stood there and
stared at her mother—the gray coat, the black high-heel shoes.
She was here, she was.

When they finally got in the car, Emma said, "I thought you
weren't coming."

"Of course I was coming. Why wouldn't I?"

Emma scratched her head. She didn't know how to answer.
She didn't know how to say that she thought her mother might
not come because she might at some strange moment stop loving her. Emma said, "You could've called. No one likes to wait."
She looked out the window. "No one does."

"I'm sorry." Her mother's voice was low. A few minutes
later, she said, "I wasn't in traffic, honey. I lied. I did get out of
work late, but what really happened was I got upset. I don't
know what started it, but I had to pull over. I sat in the middle
of the Stop and Shop parking lot . . . crying. And somewhere in
the middle of it, I lost track of time."

"You were crying? Why?"

Emma's mother sighed. "Because my hair looks bad, because
I hate work, because your father is . . . is . . . your father . . .
because I don't spend enough time with you lately, you're with
your uncle and your aunt and whoever else, like a goddamn doll
we pass around, and . . . and . . . I was crying because I'm
scared . . . I get scared sometimes."

They were silent for a moment. There was only the sound of
the car moving along in the darkness. Emma said, "I think your
hair is pretty."

Emma's mother smiled, but then her face went back to the
way it was. She said, "It's just that everything gets so much
harder the older you get. More complicated." She was staring
right out the windshield. "Things can be good for a while, but
then always . . . they change."

Emma nodded. She was starting to understand the word "change." It was in the green leaves that went orange, in their house with the new locked doors, and even in their faces that went sad-happy-sad every day of their lives.

The car pulled into their driveway. Her mother turned the car off and Emma went to open the door. Her mother touched her arm. "Can we just sit here for a minute." She patted Emma's hand. "Just for a minute." Emma let go of the door handle and her mother swung her bare feet onto Emma's lap. She had her back against the door of the car and her eyes were closed. They sat very still.

"Hear them crickets?" her mother asked without opening her eyes.

"There aren't any crickets," Emma said. "It's November. They're all dead."

"No they're not," Emma's mother shook her head. "There's some in the car, they live in the car. Listen."

Emma could hear the car, the light rattle of the engine settling down—it was a small tinkering sound. "I hear it."

"Crickets," her mother said. Her eyes were still closed.

Emma listened awhile and then she said, "I think they're pink, the crickets, from the way they sound."

Her mother opened her eyes and smiled. "They must be."

Emma smiled too. Something about this moment made her feel all right. It was like all that trouble that was always rumbling around, prowling around the places she and her mother went, couldn't get in. And in that car, with their eyes shut, in that stillness, it was just the two of them and the sound of something so soft and lulling.

Mia

STRAW WOMEN

Emma and I were walking barefoot along the boardwalk in our silk nighties and matching robes. We were thirteen. We kept bumping into one another and laughing.

The wind blew crumpled paper, plastic lids, and loose sand across the wooden boards at our feet. All of the shops we passed—Tina's Boutique, Sea Me Café, Fudge Haven, Marimar's—were closed. It was past midnight. We had just snuck out of our motel room, number 16, the room Emma's mother had rented down on E Street in the back of Hampton Beach's main strip. The motel was called the Sands, an old motel, with rusted railings painted white and silver sea horses on each door.

"Mia, I'm so fuckin' drunk!" Emma said, shouting above the wind. But then she stopped walking, not saying another word, and stared at herself in the glass window of a nearby shop. Beneath her reflection, there were seashell necklaces, earrings that dangled, and a pair of white lacy socks.

I was drunk too. Drunk enough to stop and look at the socks as if they were something I wanted, as if within their soft fabric I might find something I had always dreamed of.

Earlier that night, the two of us had been to a party full of older boys before our curfew struck at eleven o'clock. We drank wine coolers, Purple Passions. Their sweetness still ran through us when we got home, when we changed, when we sat there on the edge of the double bed we shared, restless and bored. That's when we decided to sneak out to the boardwalk.

"That guy talking to me at the party, did you think he was cute?" Emma asked me.

"No," I said. "He looked like, he looked like, I don't know, like . . . "

I looked at her and she looked at me. We said in unison, "Like a dirty rat bastard!" Then we started laughing again.

My mother had a special affection for using that phrase: dirty rat bastard. Emma had heard it, I had heard it, and we would continue to hear it for years to come. My mother liked to say "dirty rat bastard" whenever she told us a story late at night. The television would be off, the living room dark, a soda can in my mother's hand. She'd tell us about an ex-boyfriend, or a guy she had met, or my own dead father who she continuously missed and missed. Sometimes her stories were funny, sometimes they were sad, but they almost always ended with her head shaking as she said: dirty rat bastard.

"My mother would kill us if she saw us," I said to Emma, looking down at myself. We were both wearing our slinkiest nightgowns, silky thin, with spaghetti straps. Emma's was mint green. Mine was powder blue. In the right light they were the same color, but only in the right light.

Above us the shop signs flashed: blue, yellow, green. There were pictures of palm trees, bikini ladies, starfishes with faces. In my drunkenness, the signs looked blurry and strangely bright. I said, "I like it here so much," and Emma nodded.

After all, it wasn't home. It wasn't Springfield, Massachusetts, with its dull straight streets, with its plastic factories that
spit out black smoke which grazed across our skies while we sat
Indian-style in empty parking lots, fiddling with pieces of shattered glass, feeling listless, tired, bored.

Here on this boardwalk so far from home, it seemed like
anything could happen. The two of us sensed this somehow. We
kept talking, nervous and giddy.

That's when a male voice from behind us called out, "Hey,
hey."

Instantly, I pictured the person behind us to be Hacky Sack
man, the eighteen-year-old townie who played Hacky Sack by
himself in front of the Coral Cove Gift Shop. He had long blond
hair down to his tan bony shoulders, ribs sticking out, and oh,
so skinny. How we loved him.

But the man who approached us was not Hacky Sack man.
It was an older, gray-haired man in a navy blue windbreaker.
His eyes were bright and glassy. "I could be yours," he said,
walking alongside of us, keeping our gait. We made faces at one
another, ones that said, Oh, gross.

We were not scared.

He said, "You both look so pretty, are you sisters?"

We laughed, happy drunken laughs, revealing purple-stained
teeth.

"The place I'm staying," he started to say and then stopped.
"Where are you ladies staying?"

I said nothing, waiting for Emma; she would think of
something. After all, where we stayed was privileged information. Only the right boys with the right hairstyles, long and
loose, and the right bodies, tall and skinny, could know—but
they couldn't come inside, of course. Our room, our own private room attached to number 17, Emma's mother's room, was
ours alone. That's where we stared at our own naked sun-

burned bodies in the superstar mirror with the giant bulbs aglow.

"We are staying at the Driftwood," Emma lied.

The man smiled at Emma. "I'm staying at the Ashworth, the Ashworth by the Sea. Ever been there?"

"No," Emma said.

I agreed, shaking my head. The Ashworth was the most expensive hotel in Hampton Beach, with its giant looming skyscraper size in the midst of rows and rows of motels with plastic starfish and ruby red mermaids on their blinking signs.

"I have a Jacuzzi. Ever been in a Jacuzzi?" His voice was rising as if we were moving farther away from him even though we were walking side by side. "You wanna come over, get in the tub?"

I didn't say anything. I just tightened the belt of my robe.

Emma said, "We don't have our suits," smiling. A red sheen across her face.

"You can wear your chemises in the water, that's fine."

The two of us eyed one another. What was a chemise?

Then we stopped walking. The boardwalk had ended and there was just a streetlight in front of us. Two cars passed by. "Hey baby doll," a yellow car called out to us. Then there was the sound of the waves suddenly audible, the wind having died down.

It was then standing on the corner of Ocean and L Street that I turned and looked directly at the man talking to us: his gray hair parted to the side, the whoosh of bangs, stubble all around his mouth, and his eyes, so deep-set. Sad.

I looked at Emma and she looked at me. Then we started laughing right in his face. It was as if we could see beneath his windbreaker, into his white wooden house, into the living room where he sat on his couch with his shirt off, a fan blowing the stiff summer air in his face.

Why would we talk to him anyway? Why? Didn't he know that we knew we were pretty? Maybe not for sure, staring in that big motel mirror: my eyes are blue, yours are green, which are better? Yours. No, yours. Emma was short, curvy for thirteen while I was tall, lanky, flat-chested—all legs and bony kneecaps. But we knew we were pretty. Everyone told us so: the voices that came out of passing cars, the women's faces in fashion magazines, and even the Springfield boys with their callused hands and jagged bitten-down nails. Emma and I knew, although we weren't always sure; and if we could have chosen between being pretty and living long, we would have chosen being pretty. There was nothing like it.

But the man we were laughing at didn't seem to think we were so cute anymore. He looked down, his hands in his pockets.

Emma said, "Why would we get in a tub with you?" She was looking at me as she said it, not him, and there was laughter in her voice as if she expected him to laugh back or say, smiling, "I don't know."

He didn't say anything, though. He just stood there, his mouth tense.

Emma stared at him, her face growing more and more amused—she seemed to think his silence indicated a powerlessness. "You're a pervert," she said to him. "Nothing but a pervert." She looked over at me. "He's like eighty, what's he thinking talking to us?"

I smiled nervously—he seemed too close to us. I said, almost in a whisper, "I know."

Emma said, "I don't want to take a bath with him. Do you?" Her face was serious, but her eyes had a playful shine to them.

"No," I said. I found myself taking on the same casual, taunting voice Emma had. "I don't really want to take a bath with him either."

Still he didn't say anything. In the midst of his silence, I started getting taken up with it all—the power we had over him. He backed away from us, his brown eyes gone watery.

Emma wasn't going to let him go though—she took a step closer to him and said, looking directly into his eyes, "Poor pathetic piggy pervert." Slowly, she pulled up the hem of her robe, revealing an inch or two more of leg. She whispered, teasing him, "You can peek but you can never touch."

He stood there rigid. In his eyes, it was easy to see, to know, he hadn't touched a person in such a long time—not a hug, not even a reaffirming rub on the back. Nothing.

"Gonna cry?" Emma asked, her hands on her hips.

That was when he moved forward quickly, closing the sandy space between us. He said, "You dumb bitches." His voice was deep, guttural. It seemed in that moment that with his fists clenched he might pounce forward on top of the two of us. But there was only a steady silence—just his jacket snapping in the wind. With his eyes still focused on the two of us, he walked backward slowly. The red streetlights were blinking behind him. When he got to the other side of the street, we turned away from him, walking fast, bumping into each other. Emma was snorting in nervous laughter.

Once we got back to the Sands, I locked the door. I had this slight paranoia that he knew where he were staying, perhaps he had been following us all day. Emma was a little shaken too. She pulled the shades, and then without saying a word got into bed, her back to me—it was as if in those eight blocks that we ran back to our room, she had suddenly come to realize how close we had come to being hurt.

I turned the light off and laid down beside her. Under the covers, the cotton sheets felt strangely soft against my tanned legs and I could not for some reason keep my eyes shut. I sat up on my elbows and swallowed. "Emma, what if we see him tomorrow on the beach?"

Emma moved so that she was facing me. "It'll be daytime, people all around, he won't come near us." She sounded so sure, matter-of-fact.

"What if tonight he had done something? What if he didn't walk away?"

Emma remained quiet for a minute. "He wouldn't have been able to come after the both of us at the same time. He would've went for just one of us." She stopped like she was picturing this happening. "If he grabbed you, you were closer to him, then I would've hit him or kicked him or something."

"Barefoot?"

"Yeah."

"But wouldn't you have gotten scared, so scared that you couldn't move?"

"No," Emma said without pausing, "I wouldn't have."

"You wouldn't have panicked and run away?"

"No, Mia," Emma said, sounding tired, like she didn't want to talk about it anymore.

I looked over at Emma but I couldn't see her even though we were lying so close. It was too dark. I listened to the sound of the wind outside and then I said, "I wouldn't have either. I'd never leave you like that."

Later that night after Emma had fallen asleep, I cried. I could hear her soft snores, the air passing through her lungs. Alone in that dark room, I kept thinking of the man's voice, the blur of his jacket and face, and it scared me the way that nothing else had ever before. So I cried, in the way I once used to be able to, without hesitation, without letting the feeling dwell in my chest for days and days.

The next morning we woke up to the sound of Emma's mother's knocking, boom, boom, boom, on the door. I opened the door and she came in smelling like coconut—her black hair pulled back tightly away from her little heart-shaped face. She said, "Get up, girlies. It's time to turn golden." Then she pulled the shades. The sunlight came streaming in, making the white walls brighter than bright. Standing in that square room looking at Emma's mother with her white shorts and blue bikini top it seemed as if the scariness of the night before had never happened; it was as if I had dreamed it, but of course, I didn't.

On the beach, with sun hot on my shoulders, I sat on the other side of Emma and her mother, sipping orange juice through a red and white striped straw. They were lying close together on their stomachs, the sides of their faces against the flowered blanket. Meanwhile I sat up, alert, scanning each umbrella, each towel and blanket, for him, the man, the one I was still certain might come for us, might hurt us.

After a half hour or so, I finally laid back down; yet even with my eyes closed, listening to giggling sand-castle children and the squawks of seagulls, I kept wondering, Will he come for me, will he? But that thought fell away, into the lulling heat of summer, into the smell of hotdogs and mustard, the crinkling of potato chip bags, the buzz of airplanes over my head, and the blue sky above us, so wide open and ready. Listening to Emma's mother's radio full of tooting jazz horns, I would've never guessed that one of us would six years later die, be killed, under that same August sun and blue morning sky watching.

It happened to Emma. Not me.

Emma was murdered when I was nineteen, about to turn twenty. She was found in her apartment, dead on the floor, her bed unmade, the clock radio blaring fuzz and static.

The man who lived upstairs from her was the one who killed her. He was tall, black, and thin, with dreadlocks that were beaded: red, white, red, white. He didn't break in, he didn't crawl through a window. He simply knocked.

It was six o'clock in the morning. Emma went to the door in her bathrobe, eyes squinting no doubt. It was August, it was Sunday—the local church bells were about to ring and ring.

The police, they say there was a struggle. Emma must have tried to close the door, but he pushed his way in. Things were knocked off her night-stand, CDs spilled onto the floor. Her jewelry box broke—the miniature ballerina fell onto the carpet, its plastic hands in the air. They found rug burns on Emma's heels and calves—skin under her nails. "She was a fighter," the police said, "she really fought."

If I were to imagine these moments, which I often do, I think of Emma fighting him with her eyes wide open, jaw tense, ripping at his ears, his clean brown ears, pulling on them. In her head, she may have even been thinking how his ear might at any moment detach from the rest of his head like a piece of Play-Doh if she just yanked hard enough. But then he must have tightened his fingers around her neck, knocking the air right out of her.

He didn't strangle her, though. He stabbed her to death.

And where was I? It's a question I must ask myself. It's as if I believe that I had some cosmic connection to her—shouldn't I have been able to feel her terror? Shouldn't my hands have gone cold or my neck become suddenly red and splotchy? Shouldn't something have happened to me?

That night, though, that morning she was killed, I was nowhere near Emma. I was eighty miles away in Boston, in a nightclub called The Red Room. The disco ball kept twirling and twirling.

I was with my newfound friend, Rae. A girl who went to the same college as me in Boston. A girl who sometimes looked very much like Emma. Her face did, at least. Something about the black hair, the blue eyes, the square jaw, and her skin so white, veiny.

Rae and I had spent most of that night in the nightclub bathroom, the handicapped stall. Cocaine on a house key under our noses. Then we drank shots, pink and sweet, our eyes popping right out of our heads.

That night some guy kept talking to me, was it Roberto, Wren, or Demetrius? Who can remember? He was saying he liked me, thought I was pretty, and smart—really smart, so quiet. But I couldn't pay attention, my eyes were shifting around that dimly lit room: the purple velvet couches, Rae laughing and holding on to some guy's neck, a guy with sunglasses falling down, and then there was all that smoke. But none of it mattered. It was the feeling—like electricity going through me—that I loved. It made me think that I could do anything, go anywhere. Always.

My mother called me at eight o'clock the next night to tell me that Emma was dead. I was still asleep. I remember picking up the phone, my eyes on the darkened ceiling, my head flat on the mattress—my pillow had fallen off the bed. I listened to my mother's voice, heard what she said, but I felt nothing—just thirsty.

After I hung up, I stared out the window; the streetlights were on. A boy was bouncing a basketball on the sidewalk. I stayed up for two hours and went back to sleep.

The next morning on the bus ride home, I kept thinking of Emma, but not as though she was dead. I thought of her in terms of time, in terms of how her hairstyle, her jewelry, her lipstick, had changed year after year. I thought about Hampton Beach. I thought about that night when we were thirteen. I heard her voice say, "Dirty rat bastard," and I laughed a little into my wrist.

I kept looking out the window—calm, collected. There was the cloudy blue sky, the stream of cars and trucks, a handprint on the glass. Slowly, though, as more and more of the green exit signs flashed by, I started to get a sick, tight feeling in my stomach; I was getting closer and closer to a place I pictured to be gray skied and foggy.

I had not been home in over a year and I hadn't talked to Emma for a while. It was not because we weren't friends; we stayed best friends until I left. I had wanted her to come with me to Boston when I moved, but she wouldn't. She said, "This is where I come from, my home, where I belong." And I felt a little angry with her for not coming; I thought it was weak of her to stay in Springfield. Didn't she know you couldn't stay in the same place forever?

Within the two years that I was gone, things became awkward the way things can only become awkward when you've left someone, when you feel like you've gone somewhere that they could never go. I no longer felt the level of comfort I once felt with her. I could sit on her bed, put my head on her pillows, but I never let her see the terror I felt in having left home, in having chosen a new life that seemed drastically distant and alone. Emma seemed to already know this, though. She knew how close I was with my mother, she knew about my father too—how he had killed himself when I was ten. Often when I was younger, I talked to Emma about his death, how it had instilled a darkness in me, a darkness which only my mother had the power to illuminate. Emma always listened, always nodded; she'd say, softly, "yeah."

All of this I thought about as I sat on that bus looking out the window. I hadn't thought that hard about anything in a while. I was sober, I was well rested, and the motion of the bus seemed to lull me into a place inside myself that I had not been to in a very long time.

I went to the wake. I went to the funeral. There was a large crowd for each. The newspapers had her high school picture all over it: blue background, pink sweater, white pretty girl teeth. The headline read: AREA WOMAN SLAIN.

Throughout each ceremony, I stood alone. Not with my mother, not with Emma's mother. I was silent and I did not cry. Emma's uncles and aunts were there, her father, who I had never seen before—their eyes were all eyes which I could not look into. I looked at their foreheads. All of them probably looked at me from a distance and thought I looked so thin and washed out from grief—not from the nightclubs or the parties. What no one understood was that I had already begun grieving long ago, over the loss of Emma and my mother and anything I once recognized as home.

As I stood in that funeral parlor, my eyes squeezed shut, all I could think about was how I had left Emma. In that falsely brilliant room full of creamy carpets, creamy walls, creamy broken faces, I thought about how I had left all that was once mine for a life that was completely alone, completely self-run. A life I obviously did not know how to run. I got wasted every night.

Back in Boston, Rae and I went out constantly. We spent hours getting all dressed up, tying our hair back, making our lips perfect and red, so that we could go to rooftop parties, dangle our legs over the edge. We rode around in speeding cars with men we didn't know, men with strange accents, men who called us "sweeties." There were even times when we slept in strange apartments, our faces against pillows that smelled like perfume. But we always made it home, always landed safely in our apartments. We still had the chance to look out our bedroom windows, watch the sun sink down.

Yet the question was: Why did we do those things? For what reason?

In that funeral parlor, the reason seemed obvious. I felt it in the way the room spun, not too fast, not too slow, a whirl. I felt it when I heard a woman next to me whisper, "Emma," and then rub her shaky hand across her face. The answer was all over the fake warmth of that room, lurking in the embroidered chairs, in the rows and rows of grief: Rae and I did such stupid things because we were afraid of our lives, of the turns they hadn't taken yet. We put ourselves in dangerous situations so that our fears weren't something we weakly imagined or worried about—they were instead actual experiences we bravely endured.

That I understood only now—because Emma was dead. But at the same time, I could not treat her death as if it were real; I dealt with it in that compartment of my mind that dealt with all the imaginary things I often worried about. I hid it there. I stood right in front of Emma, loomed above her white sound-less face, but I made not a whimper, not a tear. It was like I was waiting for her death to take hold of me, waiting for it to wrap its hands right around my neck, pull me somewhere.

I only stayed in Springfield for three days. The last day, Emma's mother called me to tell me that she needed to see me. I sat in their kitchen; the air conditioner wasn't working right, it was hot. Over a cup of tea which I did not want, Emma's mother described the pictures she had to look at of Emma sprawled on the floor naked. She went into great detail about the blood, about the shape it made on the carpet.

At the kitchen table between us sat Emma's broken jewelry box, the blue satin trim still intact, the broken ballerina lying inside of it. I kept looking at my hands, unable to look at the box or Emma's mother. Then, finally, as if she noticed my atten-tion fading, she put her fist down on the table, her teacup trem-bling. She said, "This is real, Mia. Do you see that this is real?"

I looked right at her, feeling somehow invaded. "I know that."

"No, you don't!" she screamed. "But you better figure it

out or this is going to take you out, it's going to take you right out!"

I stared at her distantly as if I was observing her from another room. Her way of grieving wasn't my way of grieving. I didn't find any use in going over and over the details of it all: the knife, its size, the number of wounds, the color of Emma's stained bathrobe. I really didn't want to hear it, and Emma's mother was jolted by that, angered. She yelled something else and I flinched. I thought she was going to hit me.

I looked down at the floor. I could see the frayed hem of her pajamas, her pink slippers, the chipped nail polish on her toenails. She began crying, and she continued to cry for such a long time that I didn't know what to do. I thought about leaving, I thought about touching her arm, but I felt awkward and strange, like I was living out something that other people were watching on a screen.

Finally she wiped her face, began patting the sides of her hair. She looked up at me and I said, "I'm sorry." I touched her hand, felt the moisture of her open palm, and then I left abruptly as if a bell had rung. The pink-and-white curtains on the kitchen door fluttered as I walked out.

I ran and ran down their street, past parked cars, past twirling sprinklers that hissed. When I got home, I was out of breath. My mother was sitting at the screened-in porch, a newspaper in her hand. When I came in, I turned away from her, facing the door, hearing the click as it shut.

She said, "Honey," with such concern.

I heard her coming toward me. "Emma's mother is freakin' me out!" I screamed as if my voice might keep my mother at a comfortable distance. "She's going crazy, crazy!" I was leaning against the door, my lips trembling.

My mother came up behind me, her hands on my shoulder, her nose against my hair. She said, "I don't blame her. I can't imagine what I'd do if something like that . . . if it happened to you." She held on to me tighter, feeling me shake. Then she said softly, as if she were merely talking to herself, "That dirty rat bastard."

And then there was something in that, in that little phrase, that made my nose twitch and the heat rise in my face. I started to cry and I did not stop even when my mother put me to bed. I woke up in the middle of the night crying, I took a shower crying. It seemed as though it would never end.

When I got back to Boston, I lived outwardly like nothing had happened. It was September, classes began; but still, I went out with Rae every night. The only thing that changed was the cocaine. I couldn't stand to do much if it, only a line or two, just enough to keep me walking, talking—never more. The elation it once brought me was gone, replaced by a nervousness, an edgy speediness that made me think too fast, too hard, about Emma.

But Rae . . . she did cocaine all night, every night—to the point that her hands permanently shook. People on subway cars and street corners often stared, but I don't know if they knew the shaking was from drugs; her hands were so pale and thin, delicate looking, the type of hands that inherently trembled.

I watched Rae's hands instead of looking at her face when I told her how Emma was killed. First they quivered on her lap, then at her neck; finally she put them beneath her legs, sat on them. I told her about the stab wounds, all six of them. I showed her how big the knife was with my hands. I gave other miscellaneous facts: Emma had black hair, she was five foot two, her apartment was very small. I became like Emma's mother, repeating data like a machine. I even mentioned to Rae that night that Emma and I were walking on the boardwalk, but again the story had no thoughts, no feelings. Just movement.

"Do you think you're getting better?" Rae asked me only a month afterward. We were sitting together at a bar, it was eight o'clock, the beginning of our night. We weren't drunk yet; Rae wasn't high.

I said, "What do you mean?" I took a sip of my gin and tonic, which did not taste good. Across from us, in the dim pinkness of the room, a middle-aged man was smiling at us. He smoked a cigarette which was very long.

"I mean, is it getting easier?" Rae asked, putting her hand on the bar as if it were my arm. "Are you feeling better?" In her tone, she was pleading with me to talk to her. To tell her what lurked inside of me. But I wouldn't. Not in some bar, in some smoke-filled room, where a strange man was presently smiling at us, pining for us: *Oh honey, do I like you.*

Besides, the question was stupid: Are you feeling better? It was as if she thought I could take some thermometer out and measure the heat of my heart. People who never experienced real grief always shocked me that way. Didn't they know it didn't go away, not for a long time; it just sat there hard like metal, an indestructible gray.

"No," I said, "I don't feel better."

Rae moved her straw around in her glass, the lime swirling. She looked up at me. It was then in her eyes that I was able to see what she saw: I was very sick.

But of course so was she. She was always so nervous and needy, full of a certain kind of fretful sadness that reminded me of my father. Perhaps that's why I spent so much time with her; her weaknesses were endearing, they made me feel important. At parties I protected Rae from men, kept her from going into strange rooms with them. Even though we were always endangering ourselves to some degree, I was the one who drew the line, the one who said no; even before Emma died I had been like this, keenly aware that there were men, lonely and lost, who yearned for girls like us, ones who were so desperate to touch us that their passion turned to anger, their love into hate, their caresses and kisses turned into beatings and stabbings and screams.

I always had a strange sense of that. Ever since I was thirteen, ever since that night on the boardwalk.

In late October, at a party, a girl I didn't know said to me, "I heard about your friend. Did they find that guy who did it yet?"

Instantaneously my eyes started to tear—I stepped away from her, embarrassed. But she couldn't really see my reaction. We were in a kitchen and the light wasn't on; there was only the faint stream of brightness from the adjoining hallway. I turned away from her and touched the buttons on the microwave in front of me. "Who told you that?" I was trying to keep my voice controlled and regular.

She said, "Rae did, she told all of us."

I pressed the "cook" button on the microwave. The light went on, a humming started, and I thought right then and there: I'm going to kill Rae.

In my mind, those people had no business knowing about Emma. Emma was a part of me, a part of a world that did not belong in some abandoned apartment with candles everywhere. It cheapened Emma somehow, it made her into a story that a bunch of sniffling strangers could talk about as they waited for their turn with a two-inch straw.

I yelled at Rae that night. I made her come outside with me so that I could scream at her in private. We were standing on a sidewalk on Newbury Street, a late-night drizzle coming down on us.

I said, "I can't trust you, can I? I can't fuckin' trust you!" I was screaming at her, and it seemed as though I just couldn't stop. Even when I realized she was crying, I kept going, yelling.

Then finally I ran out of breath, and she said, "I was worried about you. I told them that I was worried about you."

"They don't fuckin' need to know that!" I screamed back at her. We were standing two sidewalk squares apart from one another. I stepped closer. "They don't fuckin' need to know anything about me!" I knew, even then, that none of those people were our real friends. They were just people that we got dressed up for and stood next to.

I screamed, "I'm not some fuckin' story for you to be telling!" Then I lost my breath again and said softly, "And neither is Emma."

Rae shook her head, her face was shiny—whether it was from tears or the light rain I could not tell. I turned away from her and looked through the window of a hair salon. I could see a fan of magazines on a table, a telephone with a red light on a desk.

Rae said to me, I had my back to her, "I didn't do it on purpose. I didn't do it, I didn't do it because I wanted to talk about you. I did it because I wanted to help you and I don't know how." I could tell in her voice she was shaking. She took a few steps closer, I heard the heels of her shoes on the cement. I would not face her.

She said, "Me and you, we're not like them anyway." What this had to do with anything, I don't know, but that's what she said. She was always doing that, redirecting conversations into weird places; she'd talk fast, hands and fingers moving, foam at the corner of her mouth.

She said, "We're not like them," and then I heard the crinkle of paper and without turning to look, I knew what she was unwrapping. Right there on the sidewalk, she was snorting. When she finished, she said loudly, a renewed urgency inside of her, "We're strong women," or at least that's what she wanted to say, but she was slurring. It came out, "We're straw women."

I nodded and stared into the salon window, where I could

faintly see in the reflection of the glass my shoulders and face, with Rae standing somewhere close behind me. I could not see her clearly, but I knew that her jaw was tense and her hands were balled up into fists. She always looked like this when she talked about being strong. She believed that we were strong because we had left home, because we instinctually had something inside of us that made us leave what we had for a place that was new and more difficult.

Straw women. Those words saddened me somehow. And it was apart from what I felt for Emma. It was something else, some darkness that I had felt for years and years. Long ago, that night that Emma and I got away from that man on the boardwalk, was perhaps the first time I realized it—how small and fragile we all were. In that hotel room, as Emma slept next to me, I had cried and cried, terrified of something I could not identify.

Even then, at thirteen, I had known that danger existed. I knew that girls' dead bodies were constantly springing up all over the place: on the side of a road, in a woods, in a swamp, at the bottom of a Dumpster, behind a big tree. But I hadn't ever thought before that anything could actually happen to me: I was different, I was special, I had a purpose.

But that certainty left me that night on the boardwalk, and it was permanently gone now as I stood there still shaking over Emma.

"Yeah, me and you are straw," I said to Rae, but she didn't seem to catch the fact that I had changed the word.

She pulled me by the arm over to some steps so that we could sit. The rain was coming down harder now, pitter-pattering on the awning above us. She said, "You're the only one I care about here. You know that, don't you?"

I was looking in front of us at the rain and the cement. I said, shrugging my shoulders, "Yeah," and then I looked at her sideways, at her knees which were right next to mine. It was then that I should have told her that she mattered to me too. But I didn't.

Because I was afraid. Because I knew with a certain knowledgeable anguish that Rae was just like Emma—she was falling apart, dying. I could see it in the flakiness around her nose, in the way she did line after line without stopping, without resting, without caring. That was what life seemed to be about at that point: watching people get destroyed.

Two months later, three months after Emma died, I went out with Rae for the last time. We were in the Ritz Carlton. I was very tired, irritable. We were standing in the hotel foyer with this guy named Elton who we had just met at a party. He was in his early forties, tall and thin. He had an unshaven face with razor-sharp cheekbones. He looked exactly like the kind of forty-year-old who would hang around with a bunch of twenty-year-olds. Earlier that night, he had invited us to come up to his room— he said he had an ounce of coke.

So we were standing there in the middle of the Ritz waiting for him to get his key—he had lost it. I remember the lighting most. How bright it was. There weren't many people in the foyer; it was early in the morning, six o'clock. The lack of hustle and bustle made us stand out more: me in my long leopard print coat, and Rae in her leather pants and T-back shoes against the chandeliers, the blue-and-gold wallpaper. We had another girl with us too; she was blonde, she was annoying. She was sitting in a high-back navy chair. She took her shoes off, which embarrassed me—it made me feel even more like trash than when the tall-hatted doorman opened the door and said, nodding his head, "Ladies."

Elton had been at the front desk for more than fifteen minutes now. They appeared to be asking him for more forms of ID. The blonde girl called out to him from the chair she was sitting in: "Elton, I want some orange juice." She sounded childish and whiny.

He turned around and said, "We'll get some." His voice was hushed like a whisper, but it was loud enough to carry across the room.

She uncrossed her legs. I could see her underwear—it was pink. "Elton," she said, and waited for him to turn. "Elton, do you think it'll be fresh squeezed?"

Before Elton could answer, I pulled on Rae's arm. "I wanna leave."

She said, "Why?"

I shrugged my shoulders. It wasn't really the blonde girl and it wasn't Elton and it wasn't the cocaine. I simply wanted to go home, sit on the corner of my bed with the lights on, stare. I wanted to be alone for the sake of being alone. It had nothing to do with Emma anymore. I had grown sick of thinking about her, actually. Over the past few months, she had been running through my head every day, every second, and it seemed with those few lines I shared with Rae, Emma stayed a little longer; it was never her face or her voice I thought of, it was simply a blurred picture of her and the carpet she died on.

"You can't go," Rae said. "I wanna talk to you about something."

She could've meant anything: her hair color, her mother, or the way she felt when she woke up in her bed, so headachy and small. But I didn't want to talk about any of it, and I really didn't want Elton touching me up there in that room, his nose on the back of my neck, his hands on my waist.

Rae looked at me and then to the left at some distant point, "Stay."

Elton had his key now and he was standing in front of the elevator. I could see him pressing the illuminated button over and over again.

MIA • STRAW WOMEN

I turned away from her. Behind us, one of the bellhops was looking at us and I felt suddenly foolish. Foolish in a way I would have never felt if Emma had not died. I was now strangely able to see the pathetic stupidity of everything Rae and I did. We went out and did mindless things in order to pass the time, in order to pass the nights away. That way we wouldn't have to sit home alone and think about the things we missed, the things that hurt us—the things that made us who we were. We were afraid of that, pretty and all dolled-up in tank tops and high heels, we were afraid to admit that all of this was not fun. Strangely, it hurt.

Rae said, "You're not really going to leave, are you?"

I took a while to answer her. I felt strange and distant, disconnected. It was as if I was looking at myself from a higher point—everything that was happening now seemed to have happened to me before. Here I was with my black-haired best friend and only a few feet from us was an older man who wanted to take us to his hotel room. And then Rae was saying, "You aren't going to leave?" which struck me as the same conversation that Emma and I had had at the Sands: I wouldn't have left you with him, would you have left me?

It was then at that moment, staring back at Rae—her jaw going back and forth and her eyes looking more swollen than blue—that I felt ready to admit what I had known all along when I was thirteen and right there as a twenty-year-old: Yes, I would leave you. Whether it was Rae or Emma or anyone. If I had to, I would leave. Which I suppose sounds coarse, heartless. But it wasn't. It was the simple, pained acceptance that I couldn't save Emma, I couldn't save Rae, I could only save me.

I looked up at Rae. She was standing in front of me, waiting, gazing down at her trembling fingertips. I watched her for a minute, feeling like I should say something, tell her I was sorry, kiss her on the cheek. But then I couldn't do that—it might make me cry.

So I just turned. I walked away. There was a stretch of carpet, a black suitcase, a potted plant. When I reached the exit, the set of glass doors, I didn't turn back toward her, I didn't pause to see if she would follow. I just pushed.

for Erina and Liz

Mia

MISSING

Missing: *adj.* **1 not in its place; lost.** 2 (of a person) not yet traced or confirmed as alive but not known to be dead. 3 not present.

MIA'S MOTHER, MARILYN, was picking through her husband's shoes. They were still—four months after his death—lined up along the wall behind her bedroom door. There were Francis's white Nikes, the ones he used to go jogging in. The ones that he wore during a manic moment in which he thought he could quite easily jog from Springfield to Plymouth to visit his sister for "a spot of tea." Marilyn smiled, rubbing the soft canvas, tracing the Nike slash, and then pressing her fingernails in between the grooves of the soles. She could smell the faint odor of talcum powder, Gold Bond, even now.

But there was no point in smelling old jogging shoes or

pressing his white oxford shirts against her face. Nothing meta-physical was going to come about, no special energy, no notes left in pants pockets that might say: This is where to find me.

He was dead. Two months after he had stopped taking his lithium—one sunny May morning—he jumped off a bridge and, there in the Connecticut River, he stayed. The police never found his body—the river's current was particularly strong—the water pulled and pulled him somewhere else. At first, there were always moments when she would imagine him on the bank of the river, lying in high grass, gasping for breath. But it had been a long time now and that didn't happen anymore.

Marilyn put the shoes down and leaned against the wall with her eyes shut. She said under her breath, her voice faintly humor-ous, "Francis, you dirty rat bastard." Then she shook her head. She was not having a good day. Earlier that afternoon, the phone woke her up. She had worked a late shift at the hospital and her head felt so heavy, like it could never leave the pillow. She reached one hand out blindly, searching for the phone. "Hello," she said, in a throaty voice.

"Mrs. O'Connor, is this Mrs. O'Connor?"

"Yes, yes it is."

"This is the Springfield Police Department."

He seemed to pause for too long. Marilyn said, "Yes?"

"We . . . we found a metatarsus in the river last week. Well, a fisherman did over in Chicopee." She remained motionless under the giant green comforter. "A metatarsus is a foot bone . . . part of the foot." She rubbed her jaw, which ached from grinding her teeth throughout the night. "Chicopee is as you know very close to the section of the river where your husband jumped . . . where the bridge is. We think that it might be your husband's." He paused and said, "We need a shoe."

After the phone call, Marilyn tried to remain as calm as pos-sible, but then there was Aunt Abbie. Aunt Abbie was Marilyn's aunt, who had been living with them for the past three years. She was sitting in the living room watching a soap opera. Her pink satin hair cap was still on from the night before. Marilyn sat down on the couch and told Aunt Abbie as clearly as she could about the phone call.

Aunt Abbie said, "Why do you have to bring in a shoe? Just tell them size eleven." She shook her head. "Leave it to the police to waste your time."

Marilyn looked irritated. "They need a shoe with an imprint of his foot. They need the shape, I guess—I don't know." She leaned back into the couch. "It's just, this is all so crazy. It just feels like this . . . shouldn't be happening."

They were quiet for a moment—there were just the voices of the television.

Aunt Abbie finally said, "Well, this is happening, it is." The flatness of her voice bothered Marilyn, but this was the way Aunt Abbie was. There was a seriousness to her, a severity. Aunt Abbie sat day after day in a black leather chair that was *hers*. No one else could sit there, not even little Mia, who was only ten years old. They weren't to touch the books either, the ones she had stacked on the floor next to her chair. Aunt Abbie often fell asleep reading those books without even knowing it: her mouth open, tongue out a bit, and her heavy glasses slowly sliding off the bridge of her nose. Sometimes the voices of the television would wake her up. She'd straighten her glasses and say to herself, "More foolish ass shit, more and more." At the age of seventy-two she had taken to swearing frequently.

Francis used to hear her sometimes. He'd come into the living room and point at the person on the television—no matter who it was—and say, "Dirty rat, dirty fucker."

She'd smile and say, "Motherfucker, dirty motherfucker."

They'd keep going like this until they were out of breath, giggling uncontrollably at nothing.

Nowadays when Aunt Abbie swore, there was a softness to her eyes.

Aunt Abbie said to Marilyn, "Are you going to the police station now?" Marilyn nodded. "On the way back," Aunt Abbie asked, "could you pick me up some fudge swirl? I've been dying for some."

Marilyn felt the heat rise in her face. She stood up, tightening the strap of her bathrobe, and went into the bathroom. As she closed the door, Aunt Abbie called out, "Marilyn, for Christ's sake, who else's foot would be floating around?"

Marilyn let the door click shut. She whispered angrily, "What's wrong with her?"

Aunt Abbie called out again, "It's him."

Marilyn stood in front of the mirror pop-eyed and said softly, "I cater to you, cater." She splashed cold water on her face. "Little bitch." Water dripped from her chin and nose. "Take you to the salon." She wiped her face quickly and reached for her makeup bag. "Hot Locks, have to go to Hot Locks," she said, mimicking her aunt's hoarse voice, while she smoothed powder over her face. "Take you to church." Every Sunday she dropped Aunt Abbie off at St. Catherine's Church, watching her finger the four dollar bills she placed in the donation envelope before she got out of the car.

Marilyn smeared dark pink lipstick over her lips. "Then to the cemetery." She brushed her shoulder-length ash blonde hair in short quick strokes. "Get you your flowers."

Aunt Abbie brought her dead husband, Uncle Patrick, flowers every week. It had been five years since he died, but still she bought flowers for him and the arrangement went like this: seven lilies of the valley, two orchids, four daisies, and one red tulip. No deviations were allowed.

"Ungrateful. That's all," Marilyn said, piling all of her makeup back in the bag. She tried to open the door quickly, but the corner of the door got caught on the bathroom rug. She slammed the door shut, threw the small circular rug into the bathtub, and then reopened the door. Standing in the doorway, a bit out of breath, she said, "Alone, want to be alone, please."

She felt her eyes start to burn. She looked away from Aunt Abbie and saw her Mia in the corner of the living room. She was still wearing her jacket and her book bag was on the floor next to her.

"Honey, you're home from school already?" Marilyn tried to steady her voice. She went over to Mia and crouched next to her. She stroked Mia's hair. Through the thin brown strands of hair, she could feel the bump on the top of Mia's head that she had had since she was a baby. Somehow the feel of that bump, of that slight curve, made her feel more in control.

"Why don't you go for a walk with Aunt Abbie?" She rubbed Mia's leg. "OK?"

Mia wrinkled her forehead. "What's wrong?"

"Nothing, honey. Nothing." Marilyn forced a smile and looked over at her aunt.

Aunt Abbie nodded. Then she shut her eyes and opened them slowly as if to say that she knew everything Marilyn had been feeling, standing in that bathroom alone.

Mia sat on a bench with Aunt Abbie. The park they were in was called Look Park. It wasn't all that big—there were six swing sets, a slide that had dirty words written on it, a few benches, and a dirt path that went in snaky shapes all down the western bank of the river. They were sitting on one of the benches which faced the river.

Aunt Abbie had a romance novel in front of her. She had only been reading for a few minutes when she said to Mia, her eyes still in the book, "Your mother is going to the police department today." She put the book down on her lap and looked at Mia. "They found a foot and it's probably your father's." She started fingering the beads around her neck. "She doesn't want you to know, but I'm telling you anyway." Aunt Abbie stared at Mia for a while like she was expecting her to cry or something, but Mia didn't.

She said, "They found his foot?"

"Yeah," Aunt Abbie said softly.

They were quiet for a minute, and then Mia made a face. "That's really gross."

Aunt Abbie blinked back at Mia and waited. It was like she expected Mia to say something else. Aunt Abbie rubbed her finger along the spine of the book in her lap. "They don't know for sure right now that it's his, but . . . it is."

Mia remained quiet. She thought about her mother coming out of the bathroom today—so angry and sad—so this was why. Mia knew that she was supposed to feel the same way, but she didn't. To her finding that foot meant as little as finding some wristwatch or sock of his. It didn't matter. Because she didn't believe her father was inside of it. "Inside of it" was not the right way to say it but that's the only way she could really express the idea. He was outside of it, moving around, sweeping through places he wanted to be. She had seen this sort of thing—people leaving their bodies—in movies and cartoons and she believed in it.

She said to Aunt Abbie, "Mom said we shouldn't come here by the river and sit. She said we shouldn't do this."

Aunt Abbie sighed. "This river is the closest thing to a grave. You need a grave, and if they find that body, you need to know about it. Otherwise you are going to spend the rest of your life believing that he will come back to you—thinking he's alive somewhere." Aunt Abbie paused and picked a piece of lint off Mia's sweater. "Like when you're seventeen you might be in some teenage hangout place, the Burger King on Parker maybe,

and you'll see a guy behind a newspaper who keeps looking at
you and you'll think, Is that him?"

Mia shook her head. "I'm not stupid."

"It's not that you're stupid. It's that . . . it's that sometimes
people want things so much, so desperately, that they dream and
dream and those daydreams can leak into reality. They can hurt
them." Aunt Abbie looked away from Mia at the grass beneath
them. "Like me," she said. "I saw your Uncle Patrick, I saw him
go right into the ground, but still, even now, I think he's . . .
around." Aunt Abbie's eyes were huge, magnified under her
Coke-bottle glasses. "One time I was at the beauty parlor, waiting in the front, near the window. I was reading some foolish
magazine and felt someone looking in, and before I looked up
to see, I already felt like I knew who it was. It was Patrick. I
hadn't looked up yet, but I could easily see, or I guess, picture
how he was looking at me. He had his hands at the sides of his
eyes, blocking out the sun, so he could see better, and he was
wearing this ugly jogging suit that he used to wear around the
house. It was black and yellow, a goddamn bumblebee suit he
had on." She laughed. "But anyway, I felt so sure before I
looked up from the page that it was him, that he was checking
on me, making sure I was OK." She squinted a minute. "But
then I looked up and it was just some guy, a young guy, looking at himself in the reflection of the glass."

Mia nodded—she understood. She wanted to tell Aunt
Abbie that maybe he was there, and when she looked up, he
changed and took on the shape of that young guy—it could've
still been him, maybe? But she didn't say this—she didn't want
her aunt to think she was weird.

"When I first met Patrick . . . " Aunt Abbie started to say and
then Mia knew; she was going to get lost in him now, talking
about him again and again. "I was only sixteen and let me tell ya,
I was built." She smiled and leaned back in the bench. "I was

walking with my sister, your grandmother. We were down on Oak Street and some boys started beeping and howling from their car. They were at a light, we were crossing. So, my sister waved at them, smiling, acting dumb. And I said, what the hell are you waving for? They were calling out to me, clearly. I knew it back then. I did, I did." She paused and smiled like she was watching all of this happen right in front of her, all over again. "When I got close enough, when I saw Patrick up close, it was like something hit me between the eyes. I knew it then, boy did I ever." She looked at Mia and then back out at the river. "There's power in what you know." Aunt Abbie smacked her lips, paused, and then started reading again.

Mia watched loose leaves scatter across the grass and tried to think of what she knew. But there was nothing really. So her mind drifted like the leaves, away from this bench, away from her aunt, to her father. She could still remember his voice—and she knew, she had been told, that it would leave her. But for now, she clearly remembered his voice, the pitch of it, even when he was whispering. When they used to go to the museum together, he used to whisper to her, his face close to hers. In those rooms full of skeletons and rocks, he used to speak so softly, as if he was afraid his voice might shake something, break something.

Mia used to spend countless hours, maybe even days, in the dinosaur hall of the Springfield Science Museum with her father, and sometimes her mother too. They went there mainly because her father loved it there, in that one large room with the murky green walls and the shadowy dim lighting. In the center of the room there was a life-size brontosaurus made from real bones. The roof had to be expanded to fit its tiny head on top of its long green giraffe neck. From the entrance of the exhibit only his legs could be seen.

They would get lost standing in front of it. They nicknamed the brontosaurus Borris and dared each other to climb over the railing and touch him. Once her father had reached over and taken one of the fake ferns near Borris's hind legs. He put it in his lapel. Mia's mother shouted, "Francis!" but when he began chewing playfully on some of the leaves, she laughed and leaned in against him, her arm around his waist, gazing up at Borris's vast brown stomach.

But Mia hadn't been to the museum in a while. Her father hadn't wanted to go—he just wanted be in the house. He still went to work, but at night he didn't sleep. He sat in the living room after everyone had gone to bed. The television would be on, the volume off, and the stereo would be playing. But the music would be soft, very soft. When Mia woke up in the morning, she would still find him there, but he was never looking at the TV. His eyes were always on the wall, the ceiling, or his hands in front of him.

"What are you thinking about?" Aunt Abbie asked Mia.

"Dinosaurs."

Aunt Abbie raised one eyebrow. "Why, have you seen one lately?"

Mia looked at her aunt, from her small veiny hands, past her green cardigan, to the deep wrinkles of her neck and face.

"Don't even say it," Aunt Abbie said, smiling. "Or I'll beat the shit out of you."

Mia covered her mouth and laughed.

The Johnston & Murphy's were the shoes Marilyn chose. The label was still visible in curly silver lettering. The shoes were a deep mahogany with silky thin laces. The soles were a bit worn, and on the inside of the shoe there was the light trace, an imprint, of his foot.

She had bought them last April—his birthday present. But when she looked at them, she didn't imagine him opening the box or the tear of wrapping paper or the sweet smell of leftover chocolate cake. She simply thought of the party that afternoon in their backyard and Francis dancing barefoot in the grass.

At first, everything had seemed normal. All of his friends from the restaurant he worked in were there, and they were drinking a lot. Dixie cups full of wine. Aunt Abbie was in charge of the grill. She had on a giant straw hat and Francis kept calling her—for some connected but indiscernible reason—Suzie Lou. On the edge of the yard, one of the busboys was trying to show Mia how to do a cartwheel. The two of them kept running and cartwheeling across the lawn.

Aunt Abbie said, "Don't you think she should be wearing pants, doing that?"

But before Marilyn could answer, there was the sudden sound of loud blaring music. Francis came out of the house holding a giant boom box to his chest. He had on green sunglasses. He put the radio down, unbuttoned the cuffs of his shirt, and began to dance.

He was playing the Commodores: "Brick House," a ridiculous discotheque-type song which he strangely knew all the words to: "She's got everything a woman needs to get a man. How can she lose with the stuff she use. 36-24-36. Oww . . . she's a brick . . . house." He kept singing along, although no one could hear him; the song was so loud that no one could even hear one another talking—they had to just sit there and watch him. He danced between the lawn chairs swinging his arms, snapping his fingers, his mouth moving to the words.

At first, everyone clapped, thinking he was just being funny. But then the dancing became too fast, faster than the music. Mia was watching a few feet away—the smile on her face fading.

Aunt Abbie was the one who stopped him. She went into the house and a moment later came out. She walked over to the boom box and turned the power off. "Francis," she said, "the phone is for you." She pointed behind her at the house.

"Who is it?"

Aunt Abbie paused, fingering the beads around her neck. "It's someone for you." She stared at him, her eyes serious.

"OK," he said, shrugging his shoulders. As he walked into the house, everyone slowly began talking again. Aunt Abbie mouthed to Marilyn, "Follow him."

In the kitchen, Marilyn found him standing in front of the refrigerator with his hands on his hips. "There's no one on the phone, is there?" He was panting a little bit and his forehead was sweaty.

Marilyn handed him a paper towel—he looked down at it and then wiped his face. She turned away from him toward the sink. "You're not taking your medicine again."

"And I'm not going to," he said, and sat down at the kitchen table. He had his back to her, arms folded.

Through the open window, Marilyn could hear voices. Aunt Abbie was saying, "I just told the lady, she was such an asshole, I just told her . . ."

Francis turned around, facing her again. "You know the busboy, Ricardo?"

She didn't answer him. She was looking at his hands. They were trembling.

"Ricardo's mother is from Guatemala and she's here and he was telling me that it's really hard for her to be here and not speak the language that everyone else speaks."

"What are you talking about?" she asked in a meek tone, looking down at the floor. Sometimes his ideas came too fast; she couldn't follow where he was going.

"What I am saying is, imagine what it is like to not feel the same emotions that everyone else feels. Do you see what I'm saying? At least if you react the same as everyone else, even if you can't say what you feel, you feel the same. I'd rather be from Guatemala."

"Then take the lithium."

"Then I'll feel nothing at all. I'm not me. I'm lost in this fogged-up feeling. Even my body, it feels like shit. All I want to do is . . . is . . . nothing. Because my mind, it's not mine anymore." He got up and began pacing. "Now, the way I feel now is better. Even when I feel horrible it doesn't matter because I know I'll come back up and it'll . . . it'll be OK." He shrugged his shoulders. "Marilyn, I feel good, really good."

"But it isn't OK, Francis. Don't you know you can't do this?!" She was angrily pointing out the window. There was the sound of distant laughter. "It's crazy," she said, trying to lower her voice. Tears fell down her cheeks.

He stood closer to her, his face inches from hers. "Do you remember the first time you met me, twenty-two years old, walking on the other side of the sidewalk? Hair up high on your head like a ballerina, lips chapped, eyes tearing from the wind. I was going straight somewhere else. I don't remember where, but I felt that surge in my chest to turn and be with you. Do you remember how fast I spoke to you, like I had to say everything I ever thought within a thirty-second period?"

Marilyn nodded yes. Because she remembered how wet his eyes were and those cheeks just as reddened as now. He had said, "Hi, um . . . I just passed you and I had to come back. Don't know why, but I had no choice. But I'm still standing here talking to you . . . wish I said something when I first saw you. But I came back, and now I'm saying nothing." How nervous he had seemed. She had seen him before in her apartment building. He lived on the fifth floor and she on the first. His eyes were almost always wet with excitement. Once she had seen him talking to the man from 108 and she had noticed how rapidly his hands moved as he spoke.

"Can we just go sit somewhere?" He had said to her on that sidewalk, pleading almost, his hand rubbing at the back of his head.

And sitting there, looking up at him twelve years later in their kitchen, Marilyn could see that this was all the same. He leaned over and hugged her—she could feel the heat of his face against hers. "Yes," she said out loud as if answering a question, but there was no question. Just the sound of his breathing as she leaned into him.

Remembering all of this, Marilyn stared down at the Johnston & Murphys that were sitting in her lap. Out in the living room, the television had been left on, and she could hear music and animated voices. With the shoes still in her hands, she got up and went into the living room to turn the TV off. She sat on the couch. In front of her on the coffee table, she noticed a set of Aunt Abbie's beads and thought again of how Aunt Abbie had taken over that day in the backyard. If Marilyn were to have a memory in the form of still pictures, there would be a picture of Aunt Abbie in her straw hat and beads, looking at Francis with her finger pointed at their maroon house with its half-open screen door.

Marilyn looked down at the beads in her hand. They were a light brown coffee color, almost wooden in appearance. She placed them around her neck and leaned back into the couch. "Yes," she mumbled, thinking as she turned to her left, to the empty space on the couch next to her, "the reason that I loved you was the very thing that destroyed you."

Mia and Aunt Abbie were still at the river. It had been an hour since they left the house and the September air felt noticeably cooler. A light wind blew, making ripples in the water.

"What are we going to do tonight?" Mia asked.

"I don't know." Aunt Abbie twirled her beads. "Your mother is going to be upset."

Mia didn't say anything. There was a part of her that was so sick of talking about her father. She wanted to watch a movie or eat ice cream or just laugh. She wanted these things so badly that sometimes when she looked at her mother's face, the pale cheeks and her eyes so dark, she felt guilty.

Thinking about this, staring out at the water, she hadn't noticed until now the little girl, about five, who was with her father, or maybe it was just an uncle, in the park. She was climbing up the stairs to the slide and he was down below waiting. Mia could tell from the way he was standing that when she got down to the bottom he was going to tickle her. His arms weren't stretched out, he wasn't standing strangely, but Mia could just tell. And then the girl did go down the slide and he did tickle her and she was giggling—loud, high-pitched.

This was when Mia felt it—the feeling that spread across her chest, hard and heavy. She felt her throat tighten and she had to look away from the two of them. But gazing out at the river, she could still hear the shrill laughing.

It was so strange the way that she could sit there with her aunt and talk about that foot they had found and be so certain it wasn't her father, that it didn't matter, that she would never be so stupid as to grow up and wish him in places. But the truth was you could sit around and make sense of things all you wanted, talking and talking, but at some point, from out of nowhere, you would still get hurt by the same thing again and again.

Mia looked over at Aunt Abbie. She was still reading. Her mouth was moving but no words were coming out. The girl on the slide continued to giggle, but Mia kept her eyes on her aunt, on the giant sweeping blue collar of her shirt, the shiny beads, and her little fuchsia lips reading away. After a moment, when the giggling seemed to end, or perhaps just get more distant, Mia looked down at the faded green space between where she sat and her aunt sat, and then without wanting to, she started to remember. She remembered the time that she and her father were sitting on the floor watching television, and Aunt Abbie was sitting in her own chair, her mouth going the way it was now, reading the Bible. Mia's father had heard the low mumble of Aunt Abbie's voice and he had smiled at Mia. He whispered, "She's trying to get into heaven." He looked over at Aunt Abbie again and then continued, "But it's not going to work."

"Fuck off, Francis," Aunt Abbie said, her eyes not even lifting from the page.

He shook his head and smiled. "She's not going to make it in. She's not even on the wait list." Aunt Abbie pursed her lips together—she looked like she was trying to ignore him. "But the question is," he said to Mia, holding up his index finger, "who really wants to go to heaven?" He looked over at Aunt Abbie. "You can't eat, you can't smile, because you don't have a face." Mia laughed. "And you're stuck up there behind some gate with a bunch of dullards."

"All right, you can shut up." Aunt Abbie sighed and looked at Mia. "You shouldn't be saying that to a child."

"I'm just saying that I'd rather go somewhere else," Mia's father said defensively. "Somewhere more exciting."

Aunt Abbie made a face. "Where do you want to go? A dance hall."

Mia's father didn't say anything. He just raised his eyebrows up and down. Aunt Abbie had looked at Mia, a small smile creeping up on her face; her smiles seemed to always maintain this quality around Mia's father: slow and resistant, yet inevitable.

"Do you want to go home now?" Aunt Abbie was asking. She was shivering a little—it had gotten colder by the river and the wind kept blowing, rippling the water. Aunt Abbie closed her book on her lap and said, "We can go, if you want."

Mia looked away from her aunt at the park around her. The giggling girl was gone now and it was quiet. Mia stood up.

"Yeah, let's go." She gave Aunt Abbie her hand so that it would be easier for her to get up out of the bench. But when Aunt Abbie got to her feet, Mia didn't let go, and so they walked like this, hand in hand, through the park and away from the river.

Marilyn was waiting at the front desk of the police station. There was a man in front of her filling out an incident report. She stood behind him, holding the shoes under her arms like a set of books. It smelled weird in the station, musty almost, like the smell of hot coppery pennies in a sweaty hand. She kept looking around the room, reading signs on the walls, waiting. There were a few people behind her sitting on chairs against the wall and a kid was on a pay phone saying between his teeth, "I already told you what happened, I already told you." She looked away, nervously pulling on the laces of the shoes.

When the guy behind the counter finally made eye contact with her, she said, "I'm here to give you my husband's shoes." He just stared at her. "They . . . they found a foot in the river, a bone, I mean." She blushed. She suddenly felt so foolish. This whole thing was foolish.

The man pulled a piece of paper out from under the counter. "I know what you're talking about. A number of people have come by today." He reached his hand out as if he was about to take the shoes from her. She didn't move.

"What do you mean, a number of people?" Her voice was louder than she wanted it to be.

He paused for a minute. There was the sound of distant voices and footsteps and papers being shuffled. He began, "The Connecticut River is very long, Miss. It runs through Vermont and New Hampshire and then cuts down Massachusetts into Connecticut." He rubbed his forehead. "Thirty-six other families were contacted. There were ten other suicides over the summer. There are other bodies, other people, missing."

Marilyn stared at him. She pictured a shelf somewhere in the police station full of shoes: sandals and flips-flops, high heels and sneakers, all of them lined up, waiting. "Why didn't you tell me this," Marilyn swallowed, "on the phone?"

"Miss, if it's your husband's foot, we might not even know from the shoes. It'll just rule him out if it doesn't match. But you never know," he said. "We might find other . . . parts."

Marilyn shook her head. She wasn't like the rest of them, those families. She didn't need to find out if he was alive or not. She knew he wasn't. But no one seemed to be able to understand that. What they didn't know, what they didn't get, was that for Marilyn, the very idea of that foot being his made her feel like there was nothing special about the world; it was a solid, scientific place with fossils and charts and rocks. But she wanted to believe in something, in something else.

Slowly Marilyn backed away from the counter. The shoes were still under her arm. The man just stood there, a pen in his hand, looking at her. She could see from the way his eyes traveled up and down her face that he felt sorry for her.

"I'm not doing this," Marilyn said, her voice angry and soft. "I'm not." She turned quickly, bumping into someone, and headed for the door.

Once she got in the car, Marilyn drove out of the parking lot onto State Street. She stopped at a light in front of the Civic Center. The windows were down and she smelled the scent of burned leaves in the autumn air. From where she was stopped she could see the city library and behind it the brick building that was the Springfield Science Museum. She decided to pull over and park.

Walking down the sidewalk in front of the museum, she still had the shoes—she held them tightly under her left arm. Her brown trench coat was bulky enough so that no one noticed what she was carrying as she headed through the main entrance of the museum. She passed the sign for the planetarium and went through the mammal hall, a narrow corridor filled with animals: American wolves, short-tailed weasels, grizzly bears, and Plains bison—stuffed and encased in glass. When she reached the Dinosaur Hall it was already 5:20, near closing and no one was there. At first she pretended to be looking at the various exhibits. There was a new one, the humerus, the upper foreleg, of a morosaurus. The bone had been replaced by minerals over time and turned to stone. There was a tiny window where a small child could reach his hand in and touch its grainy surface.

The lights where very dim and there was a strange humming noise which vibrated against the walls. It felt cold and a bit damp in that room full of fake ferns and painted palm trees. On the wall was the eerie shadow of the brontosaurus's neck and head shaped like a giant letter S.

When she finally turned to look at the brontosaurus directly, she began to tremble a bit. She patted her chest lightly, feeling for the beads around her neck. "Borris," she said, and smiled. Behind Borris there was a large painted wall full of leafy palm trees and dark cascading mountains. A single pterodactyl floated in the sky.

In that room with all those skeletons and bones, she suddenly felt a bit at ease. It was like things were coming together—or maybe just a justifiable argument was forming in her mind. She was thinking that the purpose of these bones was to prove that these dinosaurs once existed. But for Marilyn, it did not matter if that foot was Francis's; she already knew that he once existed and, indeed, he still did, inside of her, inside of Mia, laughing and talking. And it seemed that if such a man could be taken away from her then indeed she could easily believe—even without those skeletons in front of her—that giant green monsters had at one time or another roamed this earth.

Thinking all of this, Marilyn climbed over the low embankment that was only about three feet high, just tall enough to keep out a curious child. She placed the shoes behind Borris's long sweeping tail. It seemed like being so close would make you want to touch it—its body—but she didn't. She made sure to place the shoes straight, left on the left, right on the right, laces perfectly tied. She was on her knees and the fake sand felt eerily like that supersoft sand in Bermuda, her honeymoon land.

At that moment, it seemed to Marilyn that leaving those shoes with those dinosaurs—the ones no one could forget—was like letting Francis stay with them, but in some other unworldly way. She imagined that those shoes would stay there forever and ever. Although realistically, she could envision a guard or janitor seeing them later and searching the museum for some barefoot deviant. But in her mind, they would stay there untouched like the bones of the tyrannosaurus rex.

Hours later, Aunt Abbie, Mia, and Marilyn were in the living room eating fudge swirl. Marilyn and Mia were on the floor with their backs against the couch. The television was on, the volume off, but they weren't even facing the television screen. They were just looking into their bowls, eating.

Aunt Abbie was sitting in her chair above them. She was thinking about this day, how it started and how it ended— Marilyn had told her everything. Mia and Marilyn were being quiet, just the occasional sound of one of their spoons clinking against a bowl. In the midst of all this silence, Aunt Abbie wanted to say something important, something that would make things all right. But that was a hard thing to do.

So instead she was rewinding a tape in the stereo so that they could listen to a song, that Francis song, the "Brick House" one. She wanted Marilyn and Mia to hear that song so that they would remember that afternoon when Francis went a little weird—how painful it was, but now in retrospect, it was funny, and even a bit wonderful. She wanted them to recognize that things moved and changed through time, becoming something even brighter, larger, than they could ever have been originally. She wanted them to see that.

Even this moment, she thought they should know, would someday become something else.

The song came on. First it was just a drumbeat. Marilyn and Mia looked up from their bowls of ice cream. The words came: "Oww . . . she's a brick . . . house, she's mighty mighty . . . just letting it all hang out." Aunt Abbie was tapping her foot. Marilyn and Mia looked at the stereo, at Aunt Abbie, at one another. Mia was the one who smiled first, and then Marilyn. Seeing this, Aunt Abbie turned the volume up.

Mia

SOME MORE CRAZINESS

EMMA AND I WERE SUNBATHING on a blanket in the backyard. We were lying on our backs, arms out, legs slightly parted. The radio which sat at our bare, pointed feet was blaring a bit of boring news about the Persian Gulf, about war. An orange extension cord ran from the radio through the grass, up the cement steps, to an outlet inside of the house. Tanya, the eleven-year-old my mother and I baby-sat, was sitting on the steps pulling on the cord. The radio kept shaking.

I sat up, lifted my hair off my sweaty neck, and squinted at Tanya. "Do you want to lay down with us?"

She just shrugged her shoulders. Tanya was a shy little girl with blondish brown hair and eyes that always looked a watery blue. Whenever Emma came over Tanya always stayed apart from us; it was as if she felt unnecessary with this extra person being there. "No," she said. "I don't want to be on the blanket, there's no—" She stopped mid-sentence and stared at something that was in the far corner of the yard behind me. Her face was expressionless and stiff. Then she pointed and I turned.

There was a woman standing there—she was tall and thin, her skin white and ghostlike. She had cigarette in one hand, a coffee mug in the other. It was our neighbor, Silver Scott. She lived on the street behind mine; our yards were back-to-back, divided by a tall wooden fence.

Silver Scott had an in-ground pool and, late at night in the summer, light emanated through the cracks of her fence and a soft lulling music drifted from her yard into our back porch. The neighborhood paperboy had said that one morning during his rounds he poked his head over the fence and Silver Scott was curled up on her diving board, asleep from the night before, an empty liquor bottle at her feet.

"Can you hear me?" Silver Scott asked. Her voice was deep, scratchy. It was not the voice I expected her to have. I had never actually spoken to her in the sixteen years we lived side by side, I had only seen her from a distance—getting into a car, getting out of one. She was about forty-five, but she wore her hair long, curled up on the ends, girlish.

As I watched her move from one point of the yard, the farthest point, then closer, I turned and reached for the radio. Tanya was still on the steps—she had the orange extension cord wrapped around her wrist. After I turned the music off, Tanya began pulling the radio toward her by the cord and I wondered if that was her way of telling me: Let's go back inside.

Silver Scott continued to walk toward me, very slowly, as if she were purposely dragging the moment out. There was something in the way she moved, in the angle she held her cigarette, which suggested that she was once rather elegant. But now there was something so clearly off-kilter about her. Perhaps it was in the way that the left-hand side of her mouth turned up uncontrollably, or even just the fact that she kept adjusting her sunglasses, as if she was afraid they might slide off her face.

Once Silver Scott was only a few feet away, Emma, who had been napping the whole time, suddenly sat up with a jerk as if she had sensed something, as if somehow Silver Scott's presence had reached down and touched her pink sunburned face. I looked at Emma sideways, felt her arm brush against mine, but I didn't say anything.

"Your mother around?" Silver Scott asked. With those sunglasses covering her eyes, she could have been directing the question at any one of us, but I answered. "My mother's at work."

"Oh," Silver Scott said blandly. She took her left foot out of her sandal. Her toenails were painted purple. "She was in my pool last night. I saw her."

I curled my lip up. "Who?"

"Your mother." She took a drag of her cigarette. "I don't swim naked in my pool, you know. I don't know why she thinks she can."

Emma looked at me, her forehead wrinkled. She whispered, "Mia, what is she talking about?"

"Swimming with your father," Silver Scott continued.

I felt the heat rise in my face. I stood up and said sharply, "My father is dead."

Silver Scott shrugged her shoulders. "Oh, yeah. I forgot."

I glared at her—she hadn't forgotten. Everyone in that town knew my father had died. Six years before, when I was ten, he jumped off a bridge and killed himself. The story had been on every channel, in every newspaper, the details of what he wore, of what color and make his car was, swept through Springfield so that every Laundromat, every dinner table, every boisterous barroom knew about him and the mystery of his body, which no search party could ever find.

There was no way Silver Scott had forgotten, I was certain

of that. She was simply taunting me, trying to hurt me, and it made me so angry that I was on the verge of tears.

Emma stood up alongside of me and screamed, "What the fuck do you want, lady?" She had her hand on my shoulder. Then Tanya ran across the small stretch of grass and stood on the other side of me. The three of us were in a straight line standing on the pink blanket, and Silver Scott was about three feet away from us, the cigarette burning in her hand.

"Your mother was with someone," Silver Scott continued as if she had not heard Emma. "Some boyfriend, some sort of lover she has."

"Listen, my mother doesn't have a boyfriend—" I started to say and then she interrupted me.

"They weren't even quiet. Splashing around, laughing." She paused. "Embracing," she said in a low, sad voice.

"Come on, let's go," Emma said to me. She had the tanning oil in her hand and Tanya was holding the radio. I picked up my shorts, which were in a corner of the blanket.

"He had short, black hair," Silver Scott started saying, talking louder as if a distracting noise had suddenly come into the yard. "His hair was wavy almost, well, if it were longer. Big arms, hairy chest." She spoke slowly, as if she were putting him together piece by piece. "A dime-sized mole on the side of his neck." She placed her finger to her neck to show where it was.

I screamed at her, "You're describing my father! Why are you doing that? He's dead!" I felt a surge of heat go right through me, I felt like I could take the radio right out of Tanya's hands and smash Silver Scott in the face with it. I was trembling. It was like this uncontrollable energy going through me—electricity mixed with hate. "Get the fuck out my yard!" I screamed.

Emma started pulling me by the arm. Slowly we walked backward, the three of us, Tanya on one side of me, Emma on the other. The sun seemed brighter than usual all of sudden—it was hard to see clearly. There was just sky and heat and grass.

Silver Scott stood there and watched us back away with her hands on her hips. When we got to the white aluminum door of my back porch, she threw her cigarette in the grass and said, "I don't want them in my pool anymore. You tell them that."

The rest of the day Emma, Tanya, and I spent in my living room in front of the television. Emma kept looking over at me—she was on the love seat and I was on the longer couch. She said, "Are you going to call your mother?"

My mother was at work. She was an RN at the same hospital that Tanya's mother worked in.

"I think you should call her." Emma said, and Tanya, who was sitting on the floor Indian-style, nodded at me.

"There's no point in calling her," I said. I knew if I called my mother and told her what happened it would have just upset her; it would've made her feel locked in those white hospital corridors unable to leave until her shift was over at eleven.

I said, "I'll tell her when she gets home." And really, that's all I thought about while I watched the television shows flash past me hour after hour. I couldn't wait to sit down with my mother, alone in our house, and tell her not so much about what Silver Scott had said, but more how it made me feel: I had felt angry and violent and strangely disconnected, as if the blanket I was standing on was floating on water and the green space between Silver Scott and me was a distance I could never cross.

When my mother finally came home hours later, I was alone in the house. First Tanya left. Her mother came to get her around nine o'clock. When Tanya's mother first came in the house, she stood as she usually did, only a few feet in front of the door, as if she felt she was intruding somehow. I was still on the couch and I didn't get up when she came in. I just said, "Hi."

She kept looking at me and then at her watch while she waited for Tanya to get her things together upstairs. I thought she was annoyed at how long it was taking Tanya, but then she said to me, "What time were you guys laying out in the sun?" Emma was still on the love seat across from me. Tanya's mother was looking pointedly at me with her head cocked to the side. She said, "You still have your bikini on."

I looked down at myself, at my tanned stomach, at the blue butterflied fabric of my bikini top. I looked over at Emma—she still had hers on too. Apparently we had been so busy trying to pretend that nothing weird had happened that we forgot to change. We sat around the whole day smelling like coconut and melon, our heads resting lazily on couch pillows.

"I guess we forgot to change," I said to Tanya's mother, shrugging my shoulders.

She kept staring at me like she was waiting for a better answer. I couldn't tell if she was being perceptive or paranoid. Her eyes went from me, to the floor, to her hands. "Was everything OK today?" she asked, but she spoke as if it was some question she was directing at Tanya, who had just come down the stairs, and not at me or Emma.

Tanya said, "Yeah," and smiled. Tanya was a good kid; she knew when to lie.

A few minutes later, the two of them left, and I noticed as they walked out the door that Tanya's mother reached for Tanya's hand, and it seemed strange to me. It was as if she were pulling Tanya away from something, some sort of danger, that she believed lurked within my house.

Emma didn't want to leave. She said she would stay, sleep over. But I didn't want her there. I was looking forward, nervously anticipating my mother coming home, and the vision I had of us talking involved no one else there. Just me and her. So I told

Emma, who was my best friend, in the sweetest way I could, to leave me alone.

I said, "Besides, I don't know how upset my mother's going to get."

Then Emma said, her eyes examining me intently, "You don't, you don't think it's true, do you? That he was in the pool?"

"No, I'm not dumb," I said defensively.

She looked down. She was patting the arm of the chair, her long straight hair fell in her face.

I said, "It's not what she said. It's why. It's, it's, why people think they can just come in my yard and say shit like that. What they don't seem to get is that they have no business, no fuckin' business, talking to me about my father or anything else. I don't know them." I was getting away from Silver Scott. I was talking about other things that bothered me. But Emma listened, she nodded, and she seemed to understand somehow that the conversation I wanted to have with my mother could not involve her.

She swallowed and said, "OK, I'll go, but I think we should lock all the windows and doors before I leave." She did not say why—she did not have to. It was in case Silver Scott came back.

Together we went from room to room of my house checking the windows, making sure they were closed. In my mother's room, one of the windows was open and the curtain felt a little damp, which scared me somehow. I almost told Emma to stay.

When Emma left, she said, "Call me if you want," and then I stood on the front steps, still in my bikini, watching her walk down my dark street toward her house a block away.

When my mother came home, I was sitting in my Aunt Abbie's room. My great aunt had once lived with us, but she had died two years before. We kept her room the same way it had been when she lived there—the cameo pins in her jewelry box, the small silver cross above her headboard, and the Victorian curtains over the long windows. Even her bedspread was the same, so silky and beige. My mother and I left her room this way because it was a room that felt older than the other rooms, it had a presence. You could sit there and not feel sad, but calm, as if all the uneasiness you ever felt was temporary, a small step toward something else.

I was in Aunt Abbie's rocking chair when I heard my mother's car pull into the driveway. I got up and went downstairs to unlock the front door. We never locked our door and my mother didn't have a key.

Once she came through the door, dressed in jeans and a tank top, her uniform on her arm, the phone began ringing. And I knew who it was with such certainty—it was as if I had been waiting around all day for the next round, the next collision with Silver Scott.

My mother said, "Who is calling at this hour?" She had come home a little late; it was a few minutes before midnight. Silver Scott must have been watching our house from a high window, waiting for my mother's car to pull up.

"It's Silver Scott," I said flatly with my arms crossed.

"Who?" My mother put her car keys down on the coffee table and started to walk toward the cordless phone which was lying haphazardly on the floor next to the Sunday newspapers.

I said again, "It's Silver Scott," as my mother put the phone to her ear and clicked the receiver on.

Then I went to the kitchen. I couldn't stay in the living room with her. I knew she would begin by being exasperated, only slightly angry, and then it would build to a scream which would shake me up if I stood too close.

As I sat down in the kitchen chair, I heard my mother say, "What are you talking about?" A pause. "I've never been in your goddamn pool!" Another pause. "My husband is dead. You know that my husband's dead!" My mother's voice got louder until it was high-pitched and squeaky. "Everyone knows he's dead! It's like a goddamn sign hanging above my house!" Then there was a "What?!" and then, "Oh, fuck you!"

My mother hung up the phone. But the phone kept ringing in four-minute intervals: 12:08, 12:12, 12:16, 12:20.

Ring, ring, ring.

Finally she took the phone off the hook.

My mother looked at me. "Has she been doing this all night to you?!" Then she said quickly, before I could answer, "Why didn't you call me?!"

I made sure my voice was calm, as if that might calm her down. I said, "She came into the yard and started bothering us earlier. She didn't call, though."

My mother said, "Us? You and Tanya?"

"And Emma."

My mother frowned, as if she was picturing this: Tanya, Emma, and me—all of our little faces—and Silver Scott somewhere nearby. She said, "You know she's a drunk, right?" Before I could nod, my mother started picking up the newspapers that were on the floor. She put them in a neat pile and then adjusted the pillows on the couch. It was like she was expecting someone, which I suppose she was. Her movements were rushed and sudden—she was making me nervous. I picked up one of Tanya's Barbies off the couch and perched it on the bookshelf behind me. Then I fixed a pillow my mother hadn't gotten to yet. I still had my bikini on, but she didn't say anything. She just stared at me with her hands on her hips. Neither one of us could sit.

My mother said abruptly, "I've heard about her. I've heard bits here and there about Silver Scott. She called the police and said she was going to kill herself, set herself on fire or some craziness. But they stopped her. Obviously." My mother put her hand on her forehead, "Who told me that? I think it was

Diane?" I didn't know who Diane was. "Or maybe it was Jean." Jean was Emma's mother. My mother shook her head agitated. "I can't remember who said it."

I shrugged my shoulders. "I never heard that."

We both were quiet.

Then it came: a knock. In the front window of the living room, a shape appeared. Tall and thin in a long dress, Silver Scott was standing there, her arm on the back of one of our wicker chairs on the front porch.

"Jesus fuckin' Christ!" my mother screamed, and I was suddenly frightened. Not of Silver Scott, but of my mother. I saw it in her eyes, in her face—she was on fire. In the same way I had been earlier that day when Silver Scott spoke to me. In my backyard, I had felt this sudden hateful need to hurt that woman. For hurting me. And this anger had nothing to do with my father, a man I used to sit next to and draw baby hearts with my fingertip on his chest and face. This anger had to do with something else.

It had to do with a woman in the children's section of Sears, saying to me once, "So did your father leave a note?" It had to do with a drunk man at a pizza parlor telling my mother, "Your husband's not dead. I saw him yesterday. On a moped." It had to do with a letter we got in the mail that said, "If you're willing to pay a penny or two, I can find that body."

Silver Scott, it is important to understand, was simply one of many.

So when that knock came, it was no surprise to me that my mother—without one second of hesitation—threw open the front door and stomped out onto the porch. She screamed, "What the fuck are you doing here?! Is there something I can help you with?!"

Silver Scott didn't say anything, and I stayed in the living room, looking at my mother through the open door. I was too afraid to be on the porch with them. I was too afraid that my mother's rage coupled with my own might set that room on fire.

"What the fuck are you just standing there for?" my mother said, and put her hand on the back of her neck. There were red splotch marks all over her chest. "Why won't you answer me? Why are you here?! Is there something you think you are going to find?"

Through the window, I saw the shape of Silver Scott sit down on the wicker chair.

My mother said, "Hmm?" which came out like a deep tight growl—one that must have hurt her throat.

There was a pause and then Silver Scott spoke. I heard her through the open door and I could see her shadow through the curtains. She was in the chair, her hand on her forehead. She said, "I have been watching you for years. The two of you, and I'd like to know how you can do it."

My mother stood stiffly in the open doorway—her eyes looked as if she was waiting for Silver Scott to finish. Then she said, her voice a bit more calm, "Do what? What are you talking about?"

Silver Scott wiped her hands over her face. In her voice, there was an unsteadiness, as if she didn't know whether to shout or speak softly. She said, "So much has happened to you, the two of you. Him dying on you and all, leaving you a spectacle for everyone to stare at. But you continue to live. I've seen you in the morning, sitting out in the yard having coffee. Talking. And I've seen her year after year in that yard sunbathing with the other one . . . not caring, not feeling the difference."

My mother paused and said bitterly, "What difference?"

Silver Scott didn't answer, and my mother said, "What? You expect her to live like she's broken. Like her life has ended because her father died. Because my husband died."

And Mrs. Scott said loudly, passionately, "Yes!"

I moved from where I was to the doorway so that I was standing near my mother. Silver Scott was sitting only a few feet away. She was tracing the lines on her palm with her fingertip. Her face, now more clear without the wincing afternoon sunlight, was worn: Her lips were thin and pale, her skin deeply lined around her eyes and mouth.

She said, not looking at us, but at her palm, "I have never had anything horrible like that happen to me . . . but day-in day-out, I feel, I feel awful." She shook her head. "And I peep my head over the fence and I see you people living like the world is yours, like nothing has hurt you. Resilient you are, right?" She smiled mockingly, and then her face fell. She whispered, looking down at her lap, "I wish I could fix myself."

If I had been my mother, I would have told her to get out. Maybe I would have slapped her. But my mother, my mother just stared at her, her eyes watery, and then she left the open doorway and sat down next to Silver Scott. What my mother had, which I did not, was a vulnerability, a feeling of sympathy, for people with mental illness—it stemmed from my father, from her work, from the tricks her own mind played. She said sternly, "Have you ever seen someone for this?"

And Silver Scott began pulling on the fabric of her dress, bunching it up in her hands. She said, without looking up at my mother, keeping her gaze down, "I can fix it. I can do it on my own. I know I can." Her voice was desperate, as if she wanted my mother to pat her hand and say, "Yes, well, of course." But my mother said nothing. I said nothing. There was just the sound of insects and the occasional whoosh of a car passing.

The three of us stayed on that porch for a long time, or so it felt. When Silver Scott finally left she stood up and swallowed. She looked at my mother, at me, and then she left. She did not say she was sorry, she did not say she would leave us alone. But both my mother and I knew with an unspoken certainty that she would not be back.

As Silver Scott left our porch, I remember looking down at her feet, she was barefoot, and that was the one moment I felt badly for her, my anger erased by the sight of a dirty brown heel. My mother obviously felt something for her too; for years after that night, my mother gave Silver Scott vegetables from our garden and even small neighborly gifts on holidays. She left these things on the doorstep, though—she never rang the bell, never knocked.

My mother and I didn't ever talk about her either. Even that night when she finally left. It was as if that small experience on the porch had encapsulated everything we needed to know about Silver Scott. The mystery was solved.

I guess we did think about her, though. In our own way. We sat on the porch that night side by side in a thoughtful silence. Then together we got up from our wicker chairs and went into the house.

While I was changing for bed, taking my bikini off, my mother came into my bedroom. She was wearing her summer nightgown—short and blue.

She said to me, "It's not always going to be like this."

I had my bikini top off and I was looking in my drawer for a T-shirt. "What do you mean?" I asked.

"They aren't always going to know."

I paused for a minute like I was trying to guess what she was talking about. Then I said, "You mean about Dad?"

"Yes," she said.

I put my shirt on and then sat down on my bed. She was near the doorway. She swallowed, and then said slowly, as if she had been preparing what she was going to say, "Someday you'll move. You'll meet new people. And you'll get to decide who knows about your dad. You'll get to pick."

I nodded.

She brushed her hand along my wooden bed frame. "And whoever you tell, if they have any sense, will adore you for it."

I nodded again. And then I thought about that, what she was saying. But I didn't think of it in terms of the new places, the new people, I would someday meet. I thought about Silver Scott and what made my mother and me different from her.

The answer was grief. The sadness my mother and I lived through had forced us to look deeper within ourselves, it made us see what we were capable of, and as a consequence we came to adore ourselves with the same intensity that we adored one another. Perhaps that was why all those people, the many Silver Scotts of our town, were so fascinated by us: We had something inside of ourselves which they did not.

"Will you sleep OK?" my mother asked me.

I sat on the edge of my bed, rubbing my feet together. "Yeah."

She came over and kissed me on my cheek. "Good night, then."

I looked at her sideways. "Good night."

She walked toward the door and paused. I had not crawled under the sheets yet, and I had my pillow on my lap. My bikini top was on the floor between us. She picked it up and folded it. Then she gave me a faint smile and said, "But if . . . by chance, you can't sleep," she pointed in the direction of her bedroom, "you know where to find me."

Claire

HOME

THE PHONE WAS RINGING, but my sister, Tessa, and I ignored it. We were on the couch watching a late-night rerun of *The Dating Game*. An empty pizza box sat between us—our cat was sleeping in it. Bachelor number two was saying something about his tongue, but I couldn't hear him—the phone, it wouldn't stop.

I looked at Tessa. She was the decision maker—she was seventeen, three years older than me, and whatever she told me to do, I did. I said, "Ugh . . . should we answer it?"

Tessa shrugged her shoulders and kept her eyes on the television screen. "The telephone lady will get it." The telephone lady was my mother—she was an operator for New England Telephone. Usually she worked doubles back-to-back; she'd come home late at night, moving through the front door slowly, her face strained, shoulders slumped. That night, though, my mother was actually home.

She appeared in the doorway of her bedroom a minute or

two after the phone stopped ringing. She was wearing her lilac nightgown. "Your brother's on the phone," she said; her eyes were squinting from the bright light of the television.

I sat up quickly, upsetting the cat and the pizza box. "Steven's on the phone?"

Tessa didn't move—she was looking at her fingernail. "That loser hasn't called us in weeks." She was half kidding, half serious.

My brother, Steven, was in the navy. He had left six months before—one August morning—with a black gym bag over his shoulder, a toothpick in his mouth. Tessa and I had waved good-bye to him without moving from the couch. We didn't hug him or anything. We just said, "Bye, guy," our eyes half on him, half on the television.

And it seemed that ever since Steven left, Tessa and I barely moved out of those same hunch-shouldered positions on our couch. It was as if we were coming to realize, after watching our brother walk out that front door, that we too would soon have to leave—and that thought terrified us so much that we turned off the world and turned on our television set.

"Off the couch," my mother said to us that night my brother called. "Come on, it's Steven."

We talked to him together: My mother was on the phone from her bedroom, Tessa was on the phone from her room, and I was on the phone from the kitchen. We stood in the doorway of each room, the spiraling telephone cords pulled straight. From across the living room, I could clearly see my mother and Tessa, but I did not make eye contact with either of them as Steven said to us, "I'm calling you guys because they're sending me to Saudi Arabia." He was referring to the Gulf War. He paused as if waiting for us to respond, and then he said with an awkward laugh, "They're sending me, but not just me. Everyone on the ship is going. We're gonna . . . gonna help out."

On the television, the studio audience was clapping. But in

my ear, Steven kept talking. His voice was speedy, wavering; it was as if in having told us, in hearing our silence, he was getting more and more nervous. Tessa, my mother, and I glanced at one another occasionally, the phones pressed against our faces, but mostly we looked at the circular rope rug in the center of the living room floor. Steven was telling us how he would be leaving his base in Holy Loch, Scotland, and he would get to Saudi Arabia in ten days.

Listening to him, I tried to imagine what Saudi Arabia was like, what even war was like. The only thing that came to mind was the show *M*A*S*H* and its opening song, the one with those screeching flutes that always made me feel so sick inside.

My mother finally started to say something, but her voice shook.

Steven said, "Don't, Ma." He swallowed. "Just don't, OK?"

After we hung up, the television was turned off. Tessa went into her room, closing the door. I stood for a while in the doorway of the kitchen and living room. My mother came over and gently rubbed my back. I pulled away, embarrassed.

We stood there for a while, and then she said, "You're scared, aren't you, Claire?"

I thought: What a dumb question. Of course, I'm scared. What was she, stupid? It was strange how in my family sadness could so easily turn into anger.

My mother stood there in front of me, one hand on her wrist and the other on her throat. The house was quiet. It was late February and snow was coming down, down, down. Usually there was this light creaking sound from the weight of the snow piling on our flat rooftop, but that night I heard nothing.

"I'm terrified," my mother finally said, and I nodded distantly. I was thinking about what Tessa and I had seen on the news that same day—they were making more body bags at some company somewhere. We watched those body bags go around and around on a conveyer belt—they were gray and long. The anchorman had said that they were being made in "anticipation" of those soldiers who would die in the Gulf War.

Standing next to my mother, I tried to concentrate on swallowing so that I wouldn't cry. I wanted to be tough. The way my sister was tough, sitting on her bed, thinking of those same body bags. My mother, too, still standing tall, holding herself tightly, was being tough.

My father who left us when I was two made us tough. He never left us a note or an explanation. He simply walked out our front door one early morning at the same time that he usually left for work. He worked for New England Telephone just like my mother; he was a lineman—he climbed up telephone poles, fixed things. On the first night that he didn't come back, my mother said she knew he hadn't gotten electrocuted (as was often the worry) or fallen into a hideous accident in the company van. She knew he had left us. "I felt it somehow," my mother had said. "It was as if he had been threatening to do so all along—whispering it over and over in my ear."

For years, my mother tried to make up for this, for the fact that we had a father who clearly loved us so little that he would leave and never come back—not even a phone call. And that was the strange thing about the phone: When it rang, we didn't pick it up, not because we thought it was going to be our father, but more because we knew it wouldn't be him, and there was a continuous disappointment in hearing someone else say "Hello."

My mother said to me that night, "I'm not going to go away with Jack this weekend." Jack was her boyfriend and she took trips with him once a month. I hated Jack, Tessa hated Jack, we all hated Jack. He was a very clean man who had perfectly parted hair and wore corduroy sports jackets. He was always sneezing—the dusty air of our house made him sick.

I said, "If you want to go, then go. Tessa and me will be fine."

The words came out so simple, so easy, even though I didn't mean them, and I guess I expected my mother to somehow know that, to feel that, in the very way that I couldn't look at her.

If there was anything I really wanted, it was for her to stay, for us to sit in the kitchen and do something as simple as play a game of cards. Because when we did this, I always got this strange sense that whatever was upsetting me could be reversed, could come undone. With my mother in that yellow kitchen playing a simple game of gin rummy, the world suddenly appeared controllable and even safe.

I ended up telling my mother, who was still standing there as if she were waiting for me to say something else, "I'm tired. I'm going to bed."

She sighed. "Yes, we both should."

Together we walked out of the kitchen, into our separate rooms.

The following day at school during homeroom, I traced the path that Steven would take from Scotland to Saudi Arabia with my pinky along the smooth paper surface of our classroom globe. He'd go through the Irish Sea, moving farther south along the Atlantic Ocean until he got to the Mediterranean Sea; he'd pass the Italian boot, move through the Suez Canal into the Red Sea, then the Arabian Sea; he'd pass the Gulf of Oman, go through the Strait of Hormuz, and then he'd be there, the Persian Gulf. Ten days, it took only ten days.

At the time that I was doing this, standing over the globe in front of the window in the Tuesday morning grayness, there was this kid in my class who was bragging how his brother was in the army and he was going to Saudi Arabia too. But to me, people who were in the army were people who wanted to get in fights. Steven was in the navy. He belonged in the water with the sun all around him, a beer in his hand.

Since the day Steven had left, it had seemed so unfair to me that he was going to go somewhere so far away, so distant from my house. Steven was special to me, to all of us. He looked just like my father. He had the same eyes, big and froglike. The shape of his face was the same, the set of his eyebrows, and even the slight gap between his two front teeth. And it seemed that we, the three of us, Tessa, my mother, and I, were always nicer to him than we were to one another. As strange as it may sound, I think that we thought—because our father left us—that Steven was our last chance to have a man love us for who we were and not for what we looked like or pretended to be.

On the Friday night that my mother left—she went away with Jack—my sister told me, "I'm having a party tonight."

I said, "What do you mean?"

We had never had one in our house before. True, there was always opportunity. My mother was always at work, but still we just didn't. Perhaps because our house was so small. We lived on a street called Scarsdale, which was known for its weird-shaped houses—they were all shoe box–shaped with long skinny bodies and low flat roofs. There was no basement, no attic. Even the rooms were small, and the walls, on the inside and outside, were a pale yellow. It was the kind of house that someone we didn't know well might walk into and suddenly know too much about us—too much about how little we had, and how much we were forced to share.

I said to Tessa, "We can't have a party here." We had just finished our takeout and I had my plastic fork pointed at her. "Tessa, it's wrong."

She put took a cigarette out of a blue Parliaments box. She lit it. "What are you talking about?"

"Because . . . " I looked down at my sleeve. "Because of

Steven." She didn't say anything. She was smoking. I said softly, "He might die."

"Shut up!" she screamed. "God, Claire, you're so fuckin' dramatic!"

Then we were quiet. In the stillness of the house, I could still hear her shouting. I was standing a few feet away from her—she was at the table. The smoke from her cigarette floated between us.

She rubbed her eyebrow. "Go in your room and don't come out. I don't even want to even see you all night long."

I stared at her for a minute, waiting for her to change her mind, to say she was sorry. But nothing happened, so I went into my room, slamming the door shut. I was used to it, though, her moodiness, her anger. She was so hateful sometimes. And we let her be like that. We were always trying to give her what she wanted.

Tessa was my father's favorite. She knew because he told her one day sitting at a picnic table while they crushed ants with their thumbs. How did I know this? Tessa told me. She told me and Steven one night when we were up late watching *Brady Bunch* reruns. Perhaps silently we were all marveling at the idea of an even-numbered group of children having an even number of parents who could sing and dance together. When Tessa told us, Steven and I were sitting on the floor. She said, "Daddy told me once that he loved me best, better than you guys and Momma." She was not bragging. Her voice was soft, almost a whisper, and I thought of turning the television down. I remember Steven turned and looked at me. He hadn't said anything to Tessa, but his eyes were saying to me: Is this hurting you?

Tessa repeated, "He loved me." There was such an urgency in her voice that it seemed clear that she believed no one would ever pick her out like that again. No one would love her the way he did. And as we got older, I came to see that she blamed us—the lesser ones, particularly my mother—for letting him leave. Tessa never believed he left; she believed we made him leave.

Perhaps this was why I tried so hard to please her. Alone with her in that house, I wanted to be so much like her that I watched her every movement and copied it. The way she held a glass. The laugh she made. The way she twirled her hair between her fingers while she talked. Even the conversations she had with her boyfriend, Bill, I listened to, although I pretended to be watching the television.

Every morning, Tessa got up early, three hours before she had to leave for school, to do her hair and makeup. I would hear as early as five in the morning the hiss of the blow-dryer, and sometimes underneath it all I could hear her voice—she was talking to herself. I often wondered what a person could think about standing in front of a mirror for three whole hours. Among all the mascara and lipstick and blush, in that blue room of a bathroom, I wondered, Could anyone be happy?

But back in my bedroom, feeling sorry for myself, I couldn't feel sorry for Tessa. I wanted her to get in trouble, and I knew inevitably she would. My mother would find out about all of this. She was already mad at us. That's why she went away with Jack (Jack Jack with the super plaque, I had said as they walked out the door). She was mad at us because the night before Tessa and I had ordered an extra large pizza with a coupon, but then we couldn't finish it all. So we left that veggie supreme on the kitchen table. Our four cats had a festival. They crawled all in it, eating bits here and there. There were tomato sauce stains shaped like paws all over the blue-and-white striped tile. My mother became angry. She called us lazy fuckers. She put her face in her hands and said, "Why can't you two ever help me? Why?" Her face was red, her voice pleading. Then she said, "I'm your mother," as if we had forgotten.

I knew she was acting like this because of Steven—she was taking things too far. If Steven had been there he would have gotten up quietly and cleaned the floor. He would've waited for her to go lie down in her room and brought her a cup of tea; thinking of this as she yelled at us, I could picture the pink mug, his fingers around the handle. I almost got up off the couch, to go to her. But Tessa looked at me and shook her head as if to say, Don't you dare, Claire, and I listened. I put my hand on my forehead and I looked at my mother sideways, through the spaces of my fingers. She was standing there in the kitchen, her hands at her hips. She was a very pretty, small woman, only five foot two, and sometimes I pictured her when she and my father first looked at our little yellow house. I imagined that she picked our house not because it was probably all they could afford, but more because it fit her—it was a small house, a manageable house, one where you could know where everything was at all times—nothing could be lost.

But my mother was losing it a little—she got so angry with us. Sometimes she even smashed plates. Tessa and I would be in the living room, and with the crashing sound of each plate, we would jump a little, straightening our shoulders, tensing our necks like little baby birds. And my mother somewhere in the kitchen knew we were doing this and I believe that made her feel better to know that somehow she was having an effect on us—we knew she was there.

Yet lying there on my stomach in my bed, I wasn't afraid of my mother. I'd tell her tomorrow about the party. I'd tell her when she arrived holding a dozen doughnuts from Dunkin' Donuts—she always did this when she slept over Jack's house. My brother and I used to have contests, who could eat more. I used to eat and eat until my stomach hurt. But Steven always won, a ring of white powdered sugar all around his mouth.

Just thinking of those doughnuts, of my mother coming

back home, somehow soothed me. I realized it would be over in the morning. I turned over on my back, I fell asleep.

But later, around eleven o'clock, I woke up. There were two people kissing and giggling in my room. They turned on the light, saw me, and then turned the light off. They kept laughing.

With my face against my pillow I imagined my sister's boyfriend, Bill, on the couch with his legs spread apart. He was always wearing black shirts that were unbottoned to the middle of his white hairless chicken chest, revealing various moon-shaped medallions. Bill was a rocker. All of his friends were too. All of his rocker friends were in my house, and I could hear their voices under some Cinderella song that was blaring.

Without saying anything to the giggling kissing people, I got up off my bed and went into the living room. I couldn't find Tessa. There were seven or eight people sitting on each couch. Some sat on each other or on the floor, but most of them were standing. Through the window, I could see the tips of lit cigarettes and occasional movements on the front porch. It was so smoky that the fire alarm kept going off, a loud screechy noise that cut right through the music into my ears. Finally, a kid with a pink fluorescent bandanna took the batteries out. I noticed that he put the batteries in his pocket.

What upset me most was that they had moved the furniture: The coffee table was against the wall instead of between the couches, the kitchen table was in the living room, and the old ugly desk that was supposedly my father's had been moved only inches, but still, it wasn't where it belonged. It seemed at that moment like the room had been tilted to the left like the deck of a sinking boat.

"Where's Tessa?" I asked, directing the question at the room, instead of at one specific person.

Someone said, "She went to Denny's with Bill."

The guy that stole the fire alarm batteries said, "She went to get some eggs," as if I didn't know the types of dishes served at Denny's.

I sat down on the couch, not sure what to do. This guy, Tony, started talking to me, and he gave me a beer. At some point—perhaps after my second beer—I started calling him Tone. I thought it was really funny to call him Tone. I snorted every time I said it. I guess I was thinking of Tone Loc.

Tone was really touchy. At first I thought it was just because we were wedged in between everyone else on the couch. He kept putting his hand on my leg when he spoke. Tone was not that attractive. He had long curly brown hair, mangy. And his nose, it was big and pink.

He told me, "I'm a friend of Bill's. I'm in Richter Scale." That was Bill's band. He started telling me about being a drummer, about the many problems he faced: the heavy equipment, the sweating, the obsessive weird girl fans. I kept nodding my head and smiling every once in a while as Tone spoke, even though the words weren't registering.

After two beers, I was starting to feel bigger than that room, like I could go anywhere. It was like I could just float up into the ceiling, out the window, into the sky, where I might see my brother in his white uniform on the deck of his ship, the USS *Yosemite*. Wind and water all around him. I pictured him with hair even though he didn't have any anymore, his long curly bangs blowing in the breeze. I could feel the cold railing that I imagined he was holding on to. All around him there were thick brown ropes like a net, and his ship kept moving forward past Abu Dhabi, Qatar, Manama, Jubail, and Abu Hadriyu.

While Tone was moving his lips and talking, while the lights on the ceiling seemed to get brighter and brighter, I kept thinking, Steven isn't going to die, he isn't going to die, because I will it not to happen, I will it, I really really do. As I thought this, I felt my whole body tense up like I was pushing all of the force I had, the mental and physical force, out onto that ship a thousand miles away.

Tone must have noticed that I was somewhere else. Perhaps I was clenching my beer too tightly or even squeezing my eyes shut, I can't remember. But he just stopped talking and stared at me.

Awkwardly, I smiled, not knowing what to say, how to explain myself.

He said, "You're really cute."

I laughed, putting the beer can up to my face as if it might hide me. He was smiling back. He had such big, square teeth. I said, "How old are you?"

He said nineteen.

I nodded—I was so drunk.

Tone kept touching my leg. He was doing this rubby rubby thing which I wasn't sure how to react to. If I pushed his hand away, I would look like an uptight sort of person. But it was reaching this point at which his fingertips used more pressure and a reaction of some kind was needed.

"Think your sister will be home soon?"

I shrugged. But Tone wasn't really waiting for me to answer. He was leading me by the hand through the crowd of people into my sister's bedroom. I stopped him at the doorway. He smiled and squeezed my hand. "Hey, are you a virgin?"

I hated, hated, hated that question more than anything. I turned my head, looking past him at my sister's bed, at the dark flannel sheets. I had to say something, but I didn't know what. I got so nervous, dizzy actually. That room, that whole entire house, felt like it was as round as that globe back in my home-room and someone was standing over it, spinning it around and around with their index finger.

But then it sort of slowed down and I was able to think of what I could say. I could say to Tone, "Well, technically I am a virgin; however, in the summer, during the second week of July, July twelfth to be exact, I let a person by the name of Aaron King take off my daisy print bikini bottoms and stick his finger you know where." I could have said that to Tone, but my mind ended up drifting, way far back to that summer night when I had told Tessa all about it, all about Aaron. We were whispering in the dark kitchen and I could only see her smiling face from the light of the open refrigerator. And she had said approvingly, "Sometimes letting him do that is better than undergoing the whole shebang." I was thinking all of this, almost smiling, in the doorway of my sister's bedroom, when a girl in a fuzzy sweater came over to us and said, "Are you Claire, Tessa's little sister?"

I said, "Yeah."

She looked down at Tone's hand clasped around mine. "And who are you?"

"Tone, Tone Loc," I said and snorted. He didn't say anything, he just shrugged his shoulders.

The girl led me away into the kitchen and gave me a glass of water and two aspirin. She told me to go to bed by myself.

I must have nodded. Then I said, "Tell my sister when she gets back . . . tell her . . . tell her she's a bitch. Tell her that I . . . " I stopped talking, unable to finish. The girl with the sweater was just staring at me, her head cocked to the left. I looked down at the muddied footprints on our kitchen floor. "In the Still of the Night" by Whitesnake was playing. That's when I started to cry, standing there alone in the kitchen, holding an empty glass shaped like Ronald McDonald's head.

When I woke up, there were three bodies on my bedroom floor. They were sleeping bodies, male bodies. One was not wearing a shirt and there were cat hairs and dust bunnies stuck to his splotchy white back. When I sat up, I could see another one lying facedown with his arm wrapped around the leg of my desk.

The third guy noticed I was awake and said, sitting up, "I have a Caucasian, I think I have a Caucasian."

I said, "It's a concussion and you don't have one."

"Yes I do." He rubbed his head. "I have a Caucasian."

One of my cats was sitting near him, his black tail swinging. He reached over to pet him and my cat hissed.

"Leave him alone!" I screamed and laid back down and stared up at the ceiling, at the cobwebs in the left-hand corner of my room. I felt sick to my stomach, but not from the alcohol. It was that I knew that somewhere within the walls of the house there was a sleeping Tessa lurking. I knew that they must have told her that I came out of my room, that I got drunk, and that I called her a bitch. I felt so embarrassed that it hurt—it was like a lead plate had adhered to my chest.

And so . . . at 8:56 according to my clock radio, I squeezed my eyes shut and made a deal with God that that was OK. I agreed that Tessa could hate me, no zebra-striped sweaters would be borrowed, no foot wars during commercials, not a single bangle bracelet would be within my reach. In return my brother, Steven, would come back to us.

As I laid on my bed, my palms pressed together, I imagined that door, the one that led outside my house, and I pictured myself pushing it open. What I was doing, or what I thought I was doing, was mentally showing God what I'd do if he'd just let Steven live: I'd leave this house myself someday. I was promising God that yes, I would live in that apartment which I later lived in, the one eighty miles from my hometown, the one in Boston. The apartment that I'd move into with a boyfriend that my mother would sometimes playfully, other times bitterly, call Johnny Rock-n-Roll. And when that Johnny Rock-n-Roll would be gone late at night working at some foolish nightclub, I'd sit in our living room, which consisted of a chair and a box. Alone in that awkward silence, sitting on the wooden floor, I'd miss the hum of the old furnace that used to heat my house. I'd miss the cat hair, the purr of the blow-dryer early in the morning, and even the sound of a car rolling into the driveway late at night.

But in my deal, in my arrangement with God, I agreed to miss all of this, to grow up. If only Steven could come back.

Two hours later, I got the nerve to get out of my bed and go into the living room to find Tessa. I sat rigidly at the kitchen table chewing stale Cheetos out of a salad bowl. Tessa had apparently opened all the windows to air the house out. It was freezing. I tucked my knees under my oversized T-shirt, trying to keep warm. When she came into the room, I was sucking the orange cheese off my fingers.

She started yelling immediately. She said that I shouldn't have come out of my room, that I'd made a fool out of myself. She said that I was throwing myself at Tony. And Tony was her friend. She pulled her hair behind her ears and said, "You need to learn how to act." She picked beer caps and loose chips off the table and said, with her head down, "You are well on your way to becoming a whore if you don't watch it." She walked out of the room into the kitchen. I followed her.

I stood there with my arms wrapped around myself. I was shivering. I said, "You are the one who left me alone with a bunch of people you don't know. I'm your sister, your little sister. That guy was on me. That guy was trying to fuck me, in your bedroom. He asked me if I was a virgin. Do you hear me? He wasn't just asking." I wanted to hit her, I wanted to punch her right in the face, I wanted to feel my knuckles graze her Barbie doll lips and see blood trickle down her chin. Why didn't she feel the way I did, why? What was wrong with her?

But what I didn't know—what I wouldn't know until much later—was that she did feel the way I did. When she had gone to Denny's, she had only made it to the Denny's parking lot, where she cried into Bill's silky blue shirt and drunk off two beers and three swigs of Jack Daniel's. There she sat on the curb among all the gray snow. She kept pulling on Bill's collar, fingering one of those pearly buttons of his. With the yellow and black Denny's sign looming over them and the streetlight making this strange electrical humming sound, she cried and cried, saying once and only once, "Steven."

But I knew none of this standing over her in the kitchen, my hands shaking. I said, "How could you have left me?"

In those words she must have heard something—something which struck her. She said, "Don't you dare say that. Don't you fuckin' dare." Her eyes started to tear. "You were in your room. You were supposed to stay there."

There was silence for a minute, and then I said softly, "*I* would never leave *you*, Tessa." Which was a lie—we both knew that. In that smoky kitchen staring at one another, we both knew we'd get older and I would leave her and she would leave me. Maybe that's what we were always fighting about, fighting against. I said again to Tessa, my voice weak, "You fuckin' left me."

She stopped cleaning the muddied footprint she was working on. She got to her feet, the Windex bottle was in her hand. It was then that I thought she might for once be my big sister, that she might just come over and hug me, or even put her hand on my shoulder. But she didn't. She walked past me to the sink and turned the faucet on. I waited with my back to her. There was no rattle of plates or any sponges being squeezed. It was just me and her, our backs to one another, and the sound of rushing water.

Three hours later, my mother came home. She was holding a box of Dunkin' Donuts in her hand when she came through the door. I was sitting on the couch, the TV on low.

My mother knew immediately about the party; even without seeing it quite yet, she could sense it: the smoke in the cushions of the couch, a crack in her favorite picture, bottle caps under the rug. She set the box of doughnuts down on the table. "Did we have a . . . party?" She smiled strangely.

Tessa didn't say anything. Neither did I. My mother pulled back the curtain in the kitchen. There were two cans of Bud Light and a paper cup filled with brown water and cigarette butts. I glared at Tessa. She wasn't a very good cleaner.

"Well," my mother said, walking toward the kitchen sink. "Thank you, thank you very much." She picked up a plate off the wooden dish rack and smashed it to the floor. "How dare you? It's . . . it's such an . . . invasion, letting strangers in my house. Who do you think you are? Tessa?" She screamed, hissing the *S* in Tessa's name.

She flung plates one after the other on the floor. The red plates broke the cleanest, in three or four triangular chunks. Soon she ran out of plates so she randomly picked knickknacks off the shelf over the counter and smashed them. Until, by accident, she broke one of her favorites, three blue birds perched on a tree branch. My brother had bought it for her. When she realized what she had broken, she started to tremble. She got down on her hands and knees and carefully picked up the pieces. She smoothed her hand over the tile, checking for more. I think I even saw her kiss a chunk of bird head, but I'm not sure, because I kept my eyes averted, staring down at the tarnished buttons of my jeans.

I finally looked up when I felt my mother had been quiet for too long; she was sitting Indian-style on the sticky floor, pieces of birds in her hand. I got up off the couch and crouched next to her. I put my hand on her arm, but I didn't squeeze too tight, didn't lean in. My mother pulled me toward her anyway—with my face near hers, I could smell the sweetness of her makeup. I rubbed her back, loving the feel of her ivory sweater, such softness. Still holding my mother, I looked up at the ceiling, at the cigarette smoke that still hovered, and then back down at Tessa, who was sitting on the couch. She was crying, maybe because my mother had yelled at her so loudly or because of Steven or because of everything. With my chin on my mother's shoulder, I stared at her, watched her get up and look over at us. Then she turned, headed for her bedroom, and there was something about that moment, about seeing the backside of Tessa: the square pockets of her brown corduroys, the linty sweatshirt, her black hair falling in one straight line across her shoulders—it hurt so much to see her walk away.

But I had told God hours earlier, at 8:56 according to my clock radio, that I could deal with this. That I would endure. That's the word I used in my head, "endure." In return my brother would come back to us, all body parts intact. A thumb or toe could be lost out of absolute necessity, but otherwise, he would be as before. I even explained exactly where Steven could be found: somewhere above the Tropic of Cancer, between longitude '26 and '28, between latitude '50 and '52, in that perfect square of blue water. To seal my agreement with God I had licked the tip of my index finger and extended my arm into the air. I let out a "tsst" sound much similar to the sound of sizzling bacon. Two out of the three rockers on my bedroom floor had seen this action and broken into the giggles. They thought I was a big freak.

That was fine. It was all part of it.

Yet I had not known that Steven would be calling us so soon. Ten days later he called, and we assumed our usual positions in the doorways of our living room. He said that his ship had been sent back to Scotland. There was apparently some sort of problem with the ship's engine, or maybe it was the boiler. I can't remember. My mind was sizzling.

That night we ordered food from my brother's favorite restaurant, Joy of the Wok. We ordered a pu pu platter for four.

We ate off red plates that had cracks in them which we pretended not to notice. We sat on the couch in a row: Tessa, my mother, and me. The television was off, the radio on. When my mother went into the kitchen to bring us seconds, she walked about the clean tile floor on the balls of her feet.

After biting into a spring roll, Tessa actually spoke to me. She hadn't spoken to me for ten days. It was like she had associated the party, the pain, the trouble she was in, all of it, with me. But now she was saying to me, "I saw Tony at the Richter Scale concert last Saturday."

"Yeah." I took a sip of Coke, trying to be casual.

After chewing for a while she swallowed and said, "I accidentally scorched him in the arm with the tip of my cigarette."

"Did you say you were sorry?" my mother asked, pushing the hair out of Tessa's eyes.

"No," she said, and looked dead at me, "I didn't think I had to."

And right there it was so simple, so easy, to like her again. I felt all warm inside like the thick red sauce I dunked my wontons into. I had missed her for those ten days, the same way that I missed my brother an Atlantic Ocean away.

But I told Steven that I missed him. On the phone when he was telling us about the boiler or whatever it was, I just blurted it out: "I miss you sometimes." Immediately after I could feel my cheeks redden. My sister and my mother had heard what I said through the receiver of the telephone as well as from across the living room. Normally we never spoke to one another that way—it was too expressive, too meaningful, too much.

But when I said that—"I miss you sometimes"—when I exposed a piece of how I felt, we were united under those doorways, Tessa, my mother, and I, along with Steven, wherever he was. I pictured him in his white navy uniform, hatless though, with his arm resting heavily on someone else's desk, the phone in his right hand. Didn't he too feel a pinch in that beer belly of his?

"I miss you sometimes." The words that I would never be able to say years and years later to the man I had once. A boyfriend of sorts, but the big one, the one you always love. In the middle of some party, after three Sapphire and tonics and a Surfer on Acid shot, I wouldn't be able to say to him, to that Johnny Rock-n-Roll sitting on a maroon velvet couch—the music going thump, thump, thump—I wouldn't be able to say, I miss you sometimes. Even though I was standing so close, so close that I could see his eyelashes and even the baby freckle on his chin. Even with those urgent lights flashing and my mind going, *Say it, say it.*

I just couldn't.

But to Steven, I did. I miss you sometimes, I really really do. Because he belongs to me, like Tessa and my mother and even that house with its yellow aluminum and flat roof—that little place I still miss: home.

Claire

SUMMER

THE LAST SUMMER Claire spent in Springfield was the worst. It was the summer before she moved to Boston. The summer she fell in love. It was the summer that a neighborhood girl was found murdered. It was the summer that another neighbor of Claire's, Silver Scott, succeeded in setting herself on fire—the woman's house remained intact, only her bedroom, the front corner of her big white house was missing, a gray haze across the aluminum siding. The fire happened in June, the murder in August—their deaths were like bookends to a long hot season.

When Silver Scott set herself on fire, Claire found out about it in the morning newspaper. She was sitting on the front steps of her house, the June sun hot on her face, the Springfield *Tribune* unfolded in her lap. The front page read: WOMAN ON FIRE. They had a photo of Silver Scott's house, too, but it was taken at night—in black-and-white it looked like nothing, just a square of smudged ink.

After reading the entire article, Claire sat there stiffly, the cement stairs hot on the backs of her legs. She watched a little ladybug crawl across her knees, but way far back in her mind, she kept picturing Silver Scott right before she struck that match, before the whoosh of flames came. She could clearly imagine it all: Silver Scott sitting on the edge of her bed, legs apart, one foot on the ground, the other settled underneath her. Her hair pulled back with childish pink kitty cat barrettes. An unlit cigarette hanging out of her mouth.

The actual image of Silver Scott's face, however, how the eyes, the nose, the lips came together, was blurry to Claire, which seemed strange. How could she imagine all this and not the face?

Perhaps this was because Claire had only met her once—Claire had lived in this neighborhood, Wilbraham, for only nine months. When she and her mother first moved in, Silver Scott had come into their yard. Claire was holding a big box marked "FRAGILE" and her mother was trying to pull the box out of Claire's hands. Her mother kept saying, "Gimme it. Gimme it, you little shit!" She was half joking, half serious, and Claire was laughing at her.

Then a voice from behind them said, "Are you my new neighbors?" A tall, gaunt woman stood in the corner of their yard. It was Silver Scott. She had a coffee mug in one hand, a cigarette in the other.

"Yes, we are," Claire's mother said cordially, her voice sweeter than usual.

Silver Scott smiled at them; she was wearing a long blue dress. She looked around as if she were observing the yard and said, "You won't be happy here. This isn't the place for happiness."

Claire and her mother didn't say anything—they just stared.

Silver Scott started walking out of our yard as if she already expected them to tell her to leave. She said over her shoulder, "Ask around. You'll see." Then she had walked down the street barefoot, a cigarette in her mouth.

That had been the only time Claire actually had seen Silver Scott face-to-face. They were not friendly neighbors; they did not exchange morning hellos, or casual waves, or even silent smiles. Yet Claire couldn't help reading and rereading that newspaper article about Silver Scott, her eyes glassy and wet.

What exactly Claire was so upset about, she could not decide. It actually embarrassed her a little to feel the emotion, that heat on her face and the sting to her eyes. It seemed pathetic somehow, as if she was reaching for something to feel sad about.

A few hours later Claire sat in the middle of a party; a guy named Mattie Malone was throwing it. He lived in Claire's old neighborhood, a neighborhood full of small houses, shoe box–shaped, all lined up on a street called Scarsdale. The Malone house was a particularly unkempt house. It was painted black with pink trim and there was the hood of car, green and spotted, on their front lawn. Inside there were overflowing garbage bags in the kitchen, bowls of brown water in the sink, pots with hardened macaroni sitting on the stove. Above the living room couch they had a cracked picture of the Eiffel Tower and pieces of chewed-up gum were stuck all over its brass frame.

Most of the kids at the party were in the living room, which was the size of a bedroom in a normal-sized house. Everyone stood in tight clusters, beer cans in their hand. Claire was sitting on the couch. Her boyfriend, Louis, was next to her.

Louis kept asking Claire if there was something wrong with her. "Are you OK? Are you sure?"

Claire shook her head no and he sat there staring at her. His eyes looking into hers. Louis had a pretty face, heart-shaped and girlish, and he was tall, six foot three, with long limbs and bony wrists. Often he touched Claire's face, whether she was talking or just staring off, and it embarrassed her, made her fidget. She was not accustomed to being in love.

"Hey Larson, you hear about the fire lady?" This guy, Tom, asked Louis. Tom was a tall, big-shouldered guy with long hair that he consistently had to pull out of his face. He was the type, older and jobless, who just liked to drive around in his rusted gold Camaro and taunt the younger kids in the neighborhood. Normally he wore this intimidating leather trench coat, which he buttoned all the way to his neck. Right now, though, he didn't have the coat; he was just standing in front of Louis and Claire, smoking a cigarette. He said, "Some crazy bitch over in Wilbraham set herself on fire, did you hear?"

Louis nodded. "Claire lives right near her."

Tom moved closer to Claire. He said, "155 Bernette, right? Did you see the fire?"

She shook her head no. Claire couldn't stand Tom and she didn't want him so interested, so close.

"How did she do it anyway, gasoline?" Louis asked, touching Claire's arm.

"Yes, with gasoline," Claire said matter-of-factly, as if she had been a witness, as if she had been standing right there with her hands on her hips, watching Silver Scott splash gasoline out of a quart-sized orange can all over her satin nightgown, her sheets, her rug.

"Must have seen it in some goddamn show," Tom said, and put the can of beer to his lips. Claire could hear the sound of his throat gulping and gulping. He wiped his mouth with the back of his hand. "You know, like when they go all around some house with a gallon of gasoline trying to smoke someone out."

"She lit herself on fire, not the house," Claire said flatly.

Tom didn't say anything; he seemed to be thinking about this. He smiled. Claire looked away from him and shook her head; whether he was the epitome of evil or stupidity, she could not decide. He seemed always amused by misfortune and suffering.

Mattie Malone, the guy whose party it was, had a little sister, Misty, who had mysteriously disappeared in mid-February. She was only fourteen and she had taken nothing with her except her coat. During parties at the Malone's house, Tom often went into Misty's bedroom and took out a pair of underwear, a strapless bra, a one-eyed teddy bear, and said, "Do you think Misty will need this now? Do you think?" Then he laughed, high-pitched and repugnant, as if he already knew she was frozen in some woods.

"Why the fuck is he like that?" Claire had asked Louis one night outside of the Malones' house.

Louis answered matter-of-factly, as if it was something everyone knew: "Because no one cares about him." He shrugged his shoulders. "No one does. He could die and no one would notice." Then Louis moved closer to her, traced the outline of her chin with his fingertip, and said, "Why do you let him bother you?"

Claire didn't answer at first. She frowned. "Because he hurts people and likes it," she had said, glaring back at the Malones' small black-and-pink house.

But now, listening to Tom talk about Silver Scott, it seemed to Claire that he liked any kind of hurt, whether he himself inflicted it or someone else did. It thrilled him somehow.

Tom was currently in the middle of saying something else about how flesh melts when Claire abruptly got up from the couch, pushing the coffee table away from her. She went into the dark kitchen and stood in front of the dish-filled sink, her arms wrapped around herself.

Shortly afterward, she left the party with Louis. As they walked across the Malones' dandelion-filled lawn, Louis kept saying, "Why do you let him bother you? He's just a jerk. Why do you care?"

*   *   *

When they arrived at Claire's house, they sat in Louis's blue Monte Carlo with the windows open. They could've gone inside, Claire's mother was still at work, but they didn't. Louis kept asking Claire questions about Boston. Did she find out yet what room number she had at the dorm? What kind of roommate? What was the telephone number going to be? It was like he couldn't bear sitting next to her without having a firm visual image of where she would be in three months. He kept asking and asking until finally she said angrily, "I don't know yet, OK?"

He stared at her a moment, and then he moved closer to her so that he wasn't behind the wheel anymore. He had his face on her shoulder. He said, "What?"

But she couldn't possibly decide what it was. Was it Boston, or Louis, or Silver Scott, or the simple fact that her house didn't have any lights on—it was empty and dark.

Louis kissed her and then put his chin back on her shoulder. He said, "I would go with you if you wanted. I would go with you anywhere." There were crickets all around the car. They sounded like little muffled alarms going off.

"Yeah?" She said, and then staring out the windshield, not looking at him, she pictured that. Him moving with her. She imagined them carrying boxes up some brownstone stairs, through a red door, down a green hallway, and then into an empty apartment where their voices would echo. That thought sent something right through her: It turned everything she dreaded into something perfect. It turned a wide-open place full of brick buildings and concrete into a small room where she would get up in the morning and feel Louis's arm across her waist.

But that sudden shift, the sudden lift of hope, bothered Claire, made her nervous. It made her feel like she was desperate, like someone out of a nineteenth-century novel, some pathetic girl pining and pining for a man who in actuality may or may not come.

"Maybe you should come," Claire said to Louis. Her voice

was purposely casual, as if she did not take him seriously, as if she thought he had only made the offer because it was nighttime and they were sitting very close.

Louis slid back over to the driver's side. He traced the circle in the center of the steering wheel, his index finger going around and around. A few minutes later, when Claire got out of the car, he didn't kiss her, didn't squeeze her hand. He just turned the key in the ignition, and said, glassy-eyed, "Bye."

After Louis left, Claire stayed in her house for about five minutes. She had difficulty being in that house alone. It was too big. There were two floors and seven rooms. Four of those rooms were unfurnished: Those rooms had a box or two, a lamp without a shade, a bare hanger on the doorknob. Claire's mother had no time for decoration—she had gotten promotion after promotion in the past two years. She had a beeper and a cellular phone and a briefcase. She wore wool suits, pearl earrings, and a scarf around her neck. She was all business. She was in the business of sending her children to college.

Tessa, Claire's older sister, went to Uconn, and her brother, Steven, was not in college yet—he was in the navy. Steven was five years older, Tessa three.

From school Tessa wrote letters full of crooked sentences across unlined paper. Steven sent pictures of himself in front of European churches and crowded cafés. Steven did not write, and neither one of them called often. Their voices were voices which were clear and identifiable when Claire heard them, but some time afterward, she wouldn't be able to remember the sound of their voices; it was like forgetting the words to an old familiar song.

In Claire's kitchen there was a basket on the table that had Tessa's letters and Steven's pictures. When she first came in she shuffled through them as if she were looking for something in particular. Then she put them back in the basket and stood there, her arms wrapped around herself, thinking about Louis. She did not want him to be angry with her—it often seemed as though he was the only person she had now. In between the moments that Claire's mother's car moved mechanically in and out of their star-lit driveway, Claire was alone without Louis, alone without anyone to ask: What did you do today? How do you feel?

If she wanted, Claire knew, she could sleep for days without getting up, and her mother would have no idea. Only Louis would notice. Only Louis would call her or touch her cheek or say: Honey come on, you've got to get up.

Her mother only saw her at night, standing distantly in the doorway of Claire's bedroom. Often Claire woke up and stared at her mother in the dark shadowy light, but in the morning she could never be sure if she had actually seen her mother watching her or dreamed it. Her mother's image became shadowy, ghostly.

Strangely it seemed to be this new house that brought all of this on, all of this loneliness, which made Claire hate the house, hate its gray walls, its enormous rooms, its big peak roof. Standing there in her kitchen, thinking of all of this, thinking of Louis, Claire walked out of the house and wandered into her big backyard.

Silver Scott's fenced-in backyard was diagonal from hers. Claire dragged a lawn chair from her yard into the yard of her next-door neighbor, Marilyn O'Connnor. From her yard Claire could see, even in the night, how Silver Scott's house had been damaged: The roof's peak was almost completely gone, but the frames of the second-floor windows were still there. Claire propped the lawn chair against the fence and stood on it. With her hands on top of the fence's pointed boards, she could see into Silver Scott's yard. She had a rectangular in-ground pool and it was still there—the white pool light was glowing beneath the blue water. Claire had thought that the light would be off, that there would be burned wood and jagged shingles floating in the water, but there wasn't. It looked as peaceful as a dream, the water perfectly still except for the occasional ripple made by the warm breeze.

Claire stood there for a few minutes looking at the pool, at the shape of the dark house. Then, carefully, she lifted herself over the fence barefoot, leaving her sandals on the lawn chair.

Once she was in Silver Scott's yard, she went over to the edge of the pool and dipped her foot in the water. It felt like lukewarm bathwater. Pulling her foot out of the water, she looked behind her for a moment, paranoid that someone was watching, but there was no one. Just crickets and the pool and the occasional zap of a bug light somewhere nearby.

Claire took her shorts and T-shirt off. In her underwear, she slowly lowered herself into the water at the shallow end of the pool. Then she walked farther in, toward the deep end, the water coming to her belly button. She stood there for a moment looking down at her hands in the water—they looked whiter than usual, deathly.

She leaned back and floated on her back, her arms out at her sides. Above her the dark sky looked so big and starry that it made her dizzy. She closed her eyes.

For some time she floated like that. The warm water beneath her, the faint smell of chlorine and burned wood in the air. There was an easiness that came over her, a calm. She felt the heat of the day, the heat of her heart, leave her and move somewhere else.

But then she heard a sound. Something moving in the water. She looked up quickly: Tom was at the end of the pool. He was on his knees, hair in his face, one hand splashing in the water. He said, "Hey, little girl."

Immediately Claire pulled herself upright, treading water. "What are you doing here?!" she shouted.

He got to his feet and smiled down at her, his hands in his jean pockets. He did not at any point try to be polite and keep

his eyes cast down at the ground or at the fence which surrounded them. He was looking dead at her. He could see it all:
her hair wet, pulled straight by the weight of the water, falling
just barely at her shoulders, tan lines visible, nipples erect
through her cotton bra, her long legs dangling beneath her.

"How long have you been here?" she asked, trying to keep
her voice steady.

He shrugged his shoulders. "Not long." His dark brown
hair, which was short on the sides but long on the top, was mat-
ted from putting his hands through his hair too many times.

"Why are you here? Why did you follow me?" she asked, one
question running into the other.

He frowned. "Please, I didn't follow you." He stood up. "I
came to go in there." He pointed at the house. "I want to check
it out." He sank back down, rocking on his heels. "I was on my
way in and I saw you."

She nodded, looking away from him, her eyes fixed on the
fence. How hard would it be to jump back over? Without a
chair? But of course she didn't want to get out of the pool,
somehow the water protected her, kept her separate from him.

He said, "You look so pretty in your underwear, Claire. Does
Louis ever tell you that?" He was taking off his boots and socks.

Claire said, "Don't be an ass."

Tom smiled. "Are you scared? You shouldn't be scared. I
would never hurt you." Barefoot, he walked around the edge of
the pool. "Your pretty-boy boyfriend would be so mad, so mad,
at me."

"Then leave," she said, her teeth clenched.

He kept walking around the rectangular pool and Claire
walked farther into the deep end so that she was standing in the
center. As he walked around, she turned with him, facing him.
"Aren't you hot, Claire?" he asked. "I think you should take off
your underwear, don't you?"

"Fuck you."

He laughed. "I tell ya what, you take your underwear off and I won't get in the pool." He put his toe in the water and lightly splashed her. "Or I can get in and help you take your underwear off?" He put his hands through his hair and looked over at Silver Scott's house. "Which do you want?"

Claire didn't answer; she had her arms across her chest. He started walking around the pool again and she kept turning in place. She was getting dizzy.

When he got to the deep end, he walked onto the diving board. With his hands on his hips, he said, "Do you think Silver Scott will come, Claire?" He was smiling, amused at himself. "Maybe Silver Scott's ghost will come and save you?" He looked around him in an exaggerated way and shrugged his shoulders. "Or maybe not." Then he put his hands above his head as if he was about to dive in, about to dive right into Claire.

But before he could jump, a girl appeared on the other side of the fence. A cordless phone at her ear. She said, "Yes, at 155 Bernett. Where the fire was. There's a boy, Tom Bailey, about to attack a girl in her underwear. I can see them. Through my window."

She was obviously talking to the police.

Tom glared at the girl and said, "Where the fuck did you come from?" He backed off the diving board. Claire didn't look at the girl and the girl didn't seem to be looking at Claire. The two of them just stared at Tom. At first he started to run toward the fence's gate, but then he turned and scrambled to find his shoes and socks. He ended up only taking his boots—his socks were under the patio table. At the gate he had trouble getting out; the latch was stuck. He was pushing and frantic. Finally, the gate swung open and he ran through, the door clanking shut behind him.

For a moment, Claire just stared at the gate as if she was still trying to come to terms with the fact that he was gone. She was safe. The whole time that he had been taunting her, scaring her, she had been thinking how much she wished she hadn't come into Silver Scott's yard, she wished she hadn't climbed over that fence. In her dizziness as Tom encircled her, she strangely felt that if she just concentrated, if she wished hard enough, she might get out of it—she might not be in that pool, she might end up back in her own yard staring up at the missing peak of Silver Scott's roof.

Claire looked up at the girl behind the fence and said, "Where did you come from anyway?"

The girl motioned behind her at the O'Connor's house. Then she said, "Do you think he's really gone?" Her voice got lower. "I didn't really call the police. I just heard him and I saw you two through the crack in the fence. I had the phone in my hand already. I just pretended to call, it was like . . . I just did it automatically." She looked down at the phone. "I didn't have time to press the numbers."

Claire stared at her for a minute. Then she said, "Thank you."

The girl shrugged her shoulders as if she didn't want to admit she had done anything. She said, "I saw everything by accident. I was on the back porch talking to my mother on the phone and I noticed the lawn chair against the fence."

Claire nodded distantly—she was only half listening. She was still calming down; it still felt so unreal that Tom was not there. That she was OK.

The girl behind the fence was looking down at the phone in her hand. Claire stared at the girl for a minute and then realized something that she probably would have realized sooner if it weren't for the fact that only the girl's face and hair were visible over the fence. Claire said, "You look familiar," and the girl said, "My name's Tanya. You used to live near me."

Tanya lived on Scarsdale Street in between Claire's old house and the Malones'. She was probably fifteen, already in high school, but she looked like she was only twelve. Her hair made her look young—it was in two braided ponytails. There was also something childish yet angelic about her face.

"I stay here in Wilbraham," Tanya said. "Marilyn O'Connor watches me while my mother works." She paused. "But she's not here tonight."

Claire nodded as if all of this was something she understood. She had her arms wrapped around herself. She was shivering a little.

"Do you want a towel?" Tanya asked. Before Claire could answer, she said, "I'll go get one. There's one on the clothesline."

When Tanya came back, she didn't just throw the towel to Claire, she crawled over the fence, almost falling, and handed Claire the towel from the edge of the pool. She brought the cordless phone along too—it was as if she planned to use it as defense in case Tom came back.

Tanya stood with her hands at her side, looking up at the burned house. She said, "I saw it, you know, the fire."

Claire had gotten out of the pool—she was drying off. She said, "Yeah?"

"Me and my friend, Gwen, were out walking around late at night, no reason, just bored, and then we heard the sirens. We were near here, a block over. We decided to see what it was." She paused. "It was one of the worst things I've ever seen." She turned to Claire. "Have you ever heard what a fire sounds like?"

"In a fireplace, yeah."

"But it was bigger than that," she said. "There was that crackle of wood or aluminum or whatever, but then it also sounded like wind, like it could just take off, through that house, into your yard, into Marilyn's. It could go everywhere. It could burn and burn."

Claire nodded as if she knew what Tanya was talking about. In a sense she had seen the fire too—in her imagination.

Claire sat down in a chair at the white patio table behind her. With Tanya's pink towel wrapped around her, she looked up at the house, at the way it looked against the starry sky. Tanya stood alone, awkward for a moment, and then she sat down across from Claire. There was a glass ashtray on the table in between them. Tanya picked it up and stared down at it. She said, "I started crying, you know. While I watched it burn down. I just started crying. I don't know why. I didn't even like that lady, Silver Scott." She shook her head and Claire noticed in Tanya's side profile that her eyes were, even now, a bit wet.

It was then, looking at Tanya, the small delicate shape of her face, that Claire remembered seeing Tanya's older brother hit her in the face once—they were in their front yard and Claire was walking past. He hit Tanya with a loud smack, but she did not cry; she just stood there in front of a giant lilac bush, her face reddened and splotchy.

Remembering this, Claire stared at Tanya from across the table. Tanya had put down the ashtray, and now she was looking up at the flowered umbrella which hung above the patio table. She touched the white dangling fringe of the umbrella lightly, hesitantly, and in that one moment it seemed to Claire that anyone who looked at Tanya long enough could see what her brother had done to her. It was in the set of her eyes, in the way she pressed her lips together before she spoke. That nervousness loomed all around her.

Tanya caught Claire looking at her. She said, "Gwen and I watched the fire from across the street. No one said anything to us. There were people in their bathrobes, a few cars that stopped. But I was the only one who was crying. The only one. I didn't even know I was crying, though—my face just felt hot and wet." She swallowed. "Gwen laughed at me. She said, 'You act like your own mother was in there or something.' "

Tanya's lip curled up. "She's kind of a bitch, my friend Gwen."

"Some people develop a sensitivity later, not now," Claire said, and then hearing herself, she almost laughed. She was trying to sound like the older girl, the wise one, the one who saw hope. She said, "You're just different. You learned it faster." But even as she said this, she knew it wasn't true. She knew that there were people in their town who were older, in their fifties and sixties, and they seemed to feel nothing. They could read newspaper after newspaper. They could see people lying facedown in the street, and it was like nothing to them, like walking over a piece of wood. And it seemed strange to Claire, could these people actually fall in love, could they actually care about anyone? Was it possible? Or did they just walk around and do things. Sit in chairs. Talk.

"Do you think it's because . . . " Tanya paused like she wasn't sure she should say what she was going to say. Then she said, "Do you think it's because we grew up . . . poor? Do you think that's why we care about stuff that other people don't?" She made a doubtful face as she said this, as if she were afraid Claire might get angry, might get up and leave.

But Claire didn't. She looked around the yard. Bugs were in the lamplight. She said hesitantly, "Maybe. But I don't think you have to be poor. I think you have to be . . . something else." Claire made a face—she couldn't quite figure out how to say what that something else was. And she wanted to be able to tell Tanya. Sitting in that patio next to the fluorescent blue pool it seemed that she owed Tanya that. For saving her.

She said, "We care because, because, we know what it's like to be in danger. To be at risk." This was perhaps an answer she would not have come up with if Tom had not been encircling her only half an hour before. But it seemed at that moment to be the right answer. What propelled Claire throughout her entire life was not just wanting to do well, wanting to be happy, but also wanting to avoid danger. It seemed to be all over the place, lurking and waiting.

Even in the car that night with Louis, when he had said he would go with her to Boston, Claire had considered almost immediately the danger of it. What if he said he would come and then he didn't? Or worse, what if he came and then, at some point later, he left? She pictured the hardwood floor of the apartment they might move into, a yellow note on the floor that said "I'm going." That thought, that simple image, set her heart pounding in the same way that Tom had as he leered at her, an evil smile on his lips.

This fearfulness Claire had never considered before, and now, sitting in Silver Scott's yard, the summer night all around her, it seemed to be something she should have always been aware of, something obvious and large.

Claire looked at Tanya, who was staring at her, and realized she had not completed her original thought. She said, "If you're used to danger, then you know that those people who actually get hurt aren't that different from anyone else. From us. But some people don't think like that. They don't know."

Tanya nodded. She looked over at the pool and then, swinging her leg, she kicked one of Tom's socks out from under the patio table. They both looked at the sock, and then Tanya said, "And me and you—we know danger."

Claire smiled as if it were something to laugh about. She said, "Yes. Yes we do."

Shortly afterward, Claire put on her T-shirt and shorts and they both crawled back over the fence. They walked through the O'Connors' backyard silently. A neighbor's dog was barking in the distance.

Tanya said shyly, "Well, maybe I'll see you. Over the summer."

The dog in the other yard was still barking, and even though they still couldn't see him, it sounded louder, nagging. They stood there for a moment listening. Awkward.

Then Claire said, "Yeah, I'll see you later."

But Claire didn't actually end up seeing Tanya that whole summer. Not in the O'Connors' yard, not in a passing car. They had met that night and that was it. Yet Claire found herself thinking of Tanya, of where she might be, of what she might be doing, one afternoon at the end of August. At the time, Claire was in a Burger King parking lot at a rest stop on her way to Boston. Louis was inside getting them milk shakes and French fries. Behind Claire in the backseat of his car, there were boxes of his CDs and Claire's books.

The Springfield *Tribune* was spread out on Claire's lap. The headline read: AREA WOMAN SLAIN. Claire read the article, which was about a girl from Wilbraham who had been murdered. Claire stared at the girl's photograph: her white teeth, her black hair falling across her shoulders, the silver cross at her neck. Claire read about the knife, about the number of wounds, about the mother who would not comment. She turned page after page, her moist fingertips sticking to the paper.

She had seen this girl before, but she had never spoken to her, never known her. Yet still she couldn't help feeling it. The tightness across her chest, the stiffness in her throat. It was the feeling that only certain girls knew. Ones like Claire. Ones like Tanya. Ones that understood: It could happen to any of us. It really could.

Gwen

THE SECRET

WHAT HAPPENED TO GWEN the night before she left for Madrid was a secret. As she flew through the air in a DC-10, warm clouds all around her, her hands still shook as she reached for the plastic cup on the tray in front of her, Coca-Cola spilling down her arm. She couldn't eat anything—not even the Saltines her mother had packed in her bag. The woman next to her was praying softly, and that somehow put Gwen further on edge. She pulled the shade down over the window next to her and pressed her head into the chair, an American Airlines blanket covering her.

With her eyes shut she kept going over and over what had happened only twenty-four hours ago. She had gone out with a group of girls who all lived on the same floor as she did in Charlesgate, her college dormitory. They were celebrating the fact that she was leaving. Escaping was the word they actually used. She was going to spend her whole summer in Madrid, taking an intensive language course at the Universidad Complutense.

"The men, imagine the men," her roommate, Leslie, had said as they stumbled through Kenmore Square, already drunk off a cheap bottle of pink champagne. Gwen just shrugged her shoulders, smiling. She was so nervous, couldn't they tell?

They walked to The Red Room, one of the bigger nightclubs in Boston, where they got in with their matching fake IDs. Once inside, they went directly to the second-floor bar and ordered round after round of shots: Killer Kool-Aids, B-52s, Sour Apples, and even a little bit of bourbon, Jack Daniel's, straight up.

It was not clear—Gwen couldn't quite remember—when exactly she had met Dennis, if that was his real name. It must have been after she went to the bathroom, after she stared at herself critically in the mirror: her thin blonde hair pulled behind her ears, her blue eyes gone gray against the black wallpaper, and her pouty lips, a flashy zinc pink. Funny that she could remember all that and not the moment she first met Dennis.

Dennis was the guy who asked her to dance.

Any other night she would have said "No," not even smiling. But that night everything had felt sort of electric, which is a stupid thing to say, but that was the way she felt: electric. It was as if all that nervous energy that had made her stand in front of Leslie's dresser parting and reparting her hair worrying about airplanes and passports and taxicabs had suddenly evaporated, leaving her with a giddiness which kept her palms damp and her head bobbing up and down to the beat of the music.

Besides, Dennis was cute. He had his hair in a short ponytail, a nice, soft, unshaven face, his eyes were brown or so, she guessed, maybe they were blue or green or even violet, she would never know. When she first spoke to him she had been standing by herself in her mini-dress and high-heel sandals—looking almost twenty-one. She had been trying to find Leslie's red hair and purple tank top among the crowd, but the lights just kept flashing. The music was loud, restless. She couldn't stand still.

Perhaps she had even asked Dennis to dance instead of him asking her. She couldn't quite remember. In any case, they ended up dancing together. She had felt so good, her hand over her head, laughing. And when she closed her eyes, she could feel the patterns of the changing lights without actually seeing them. She danced well—her hips swaying loosely and her arms arching out.

He rubbed closer against her, his eyes looking into hers. That's when she started to feel as though there was more than just a dance going on. Gwen had not had a boyfriend since she left her hometown, Springfield, Massachusetts, two years ago. She had dated, but it was never anything great, never that pull in the pit of her stomach to put her hands up under his shirt, scratch his sweaty back, his nose against her cheek, breath coming in and out, in and out. But here with Dennis, it was there, finally. She let her hips rub up against him. He smiled at her, such pretty pink lips.

In her mind she zoomed forward to July 31, when she was scheduled to come home from Madrid. He'd be at the airport: black shirt, green eyes, flowers. Postcards would be sent to Dennis with charging bulls and fuchsia dancers on them. She would write, "I miss you, I really really do."

At some point—it was in the middle of a good song—Dennis stopped dancing and led her through the crowd. They went all the way to the back of the club. He stroked her hair with one hand and pulled her toward him with the other.

They kissed and kissed, the music and smoke unimportant.

After a few minutes, Dennis gently pulled away from her and

took her hand; Gwen followed. He led her to a black door that blended into the black walls, making it seem as though he had merely tapped on the wall and an exit appeared. She had followed without hesitation, as if he were bringing her into a hallway or adjoining room.

The door led outside. Although it was late May, the night air felt cold and damp. She wrapped her arms around her waist as she looked around the alley. There was a huge Dumpster on the right. Loose plastic cups, crumpled cocktail napkins, and chewed-up straws were scattered around the Dumpster. He was standing in front of her, his hands on the sides of her arms.

He moved closer and pressed his forehead against hers. She felt the tickle of his eyelashes against her skin when he blinked. He whispered, "I want you to suck my dick."

At first, she didn't move. She wasn't sure if she had heard him right. The music from inside was still audible and there was a nagging ringing in her ears.

"Will you?" he asked.

She tried to back away, but her heel sank deeper into the mud. He tightened his grip on her arms. "I . . . I . . . I chang' my mind," she stammered, trying not to slur her words. "Jus' forget it."

He didn't say anything.

Gwen laughed nervously. She pulled her heels out of the mud awkwardly and turned to the door. She put her hand on the flat metal surface, feeling the vibration of the music inside. That's when she felt a sudden jerk at the back of her head. He was holding on to her by her hair and pulling her by the arm toward him. Once he had her against him again, he let go of her hair and touched her cheek lightly with his fingertips. His fingers traced across her nose, to her forehead, and then with the force of his entire palm, he began to push her head down.

Gwen quickly pulled her arm loose and pushed with both

hands against his chest. Once she felt his hand give against her forehead, she started to turn away and run. He lunged forward, though, grabbing her by the shoulder. The force of his hands pushed her down on the ground. She felt the mud on her bare knees.

With both hands free, he unbuttoned his pants and pulled them down. He tilted her face up by her chin and pressed her against him. She felt his fingers sinking into her chin. She let out a whimper, realizing that he might break her jaw. Gasping for air, Gwen opened her mouth. With his free hand, he began stroking the back of his penis. He continued holding her face up toward him. She felt him sink into her mouth in short quick movements.

"There you go," he said, half moaning. He pulled the hair away that was falling over her face. "I like to be able to see."

She could feel his skin rubbing against her tongue. Drool came out of the side of her mouth as she tried to turn away, but she was still held there by his hands.

Her knees were pressed into the dirt and she thought she could feel something scurrying against her legs. She squinted her eyes shut, imagining a hoard of rats crawling along her legs. She envisioned the soft flesh in her mouth to be the smooth body of a rat. She pictured the middle and upper torso in her mouth while the second half hung out. The pink cordlike tail flipping side to side, slapping against her lips. She could almost feel the whiskers twitching against her tongue. She started to gag.

Then someone came out. A doorman, emptying garbage. Dennis, in one blurred moment, pushed her down on the ground, pulled up his pants, and ran. The doorman paused as if he didn't quite understand what had just happened and then chased Dennis half-heartedly, knowing he wouldn't catch up. When he came back to Gwen, he tried to help her up, but she pushed him away, screaming. She pushed all of her weight against the wall behind her and stood up slowly. When her legs finally stopped shaking, she followed the doorman around the front and got in a cab. She was hysterical, unable to stop crying, gasping for breath in the back of the cab with its torn red seats. The whole ride she kept looking down at the floor of the car, fearing irrationally that rats with long thick tails would come out from under the driver's seat and nibble on her feet.

Back on the plane, remembering all of this, Gwen instinctively tried to tuck her feet up underneath her but the seat was too small. She shifted abruptly. The woman next to her glanced over at her. "Do you want to get up?" she asked in Spanish.

Gwen just stared at the woman. She was slowly remembering that she was actually going somewhere, that this airplane was not just a way station for thought.

Even as she stood in Logan Airport waiting at the boarding gate, she had not been thinking about Madrid, she had not been thinking about anything. It was like she had lost control of her own face, her gestures even, everything was on automatic. Her mother, who was standing next to her, said, "You look as white as a ghost." She rubbed Gwen's arm for a moment, and then said, "You don't have to go if you don't want to." Perhaps her mother had noticed something in the glossiness of Gwen's eyes. She kept staring at Gwen, and then she said again, "You don't have to go. You can still spend the summer at home."

Perhaps a week before Gwen would have entertained the idea. After all, going somewhere far away all by yourself was scary, even at nineteen. But now, after everything, after Dennis, the world had shifted—she didn't want to be around people she knew. She wanted to be far far away, where no one could say, "Gwen, sweetie, what's wrong?"

But Gwen's mother knew none of this and never would. "You're afraid and that's OK," she said, her voice sounded more hopeful than concerned. "I mean, a lot could happen alone, in Madrid." She paused and then sighed. "This was all your father's idea, anyway." She shook her head. "Making your brother spend a year in Germany and now you in Spain.

"See the world," she added, mimicking Gwen's father's voice. She frowned. "You don't have to go, Gwen, if you don't want to." There was something in the rapid way her mother was speaking—her words so quick and jumpy—that made it clear that it was she who did not want Gwen to go. Her mother just wanted her to stay in their woodsy town, in their log cabin of a house. She wanted Gwen to sit with her in the backyard, with only the picnic table between them. She wanted Gwen to eat ice pops and get blue sugar all over her face. She wanted Gwen to stay young.

When Gwen was a teenager, her mother had maintained this same sense of wariness. Once Gwen had won a modeling contest in a mall and her mother had not talked to her the whole car ride home—she pretended to be absorbed in traffic, in the signs that passed over their heads. It was only years later that her mother finally told Gwen that she had behaved that way because she felt suddenly frightened. Being beautiful, she explained, put Gwen at risk.

"You don't have to go to Madrid if you don't want to," her mother repeated, and Gwen shifted away from her a little, feeling suddenly sick of her mother's voice. Or perhaps it was her mother's voice in combination with another voice inside of her that kept saying: Last night happened, it really did.

Her mother was still talking. "You'll come back to Springfield with me and work." They were at the front of the line now. "You'll work at the Olive Garden, you like it there, don't you?"

Gwen tried to ignore her mother, looking straight ahead, but the sick, tired feeling was going away and something larger was taking over: anger. "Will you stop, Ma? Will you shut up?"

Gwen whispered, her cheeks hot. They were the next in line and the stewardess stared at the two of them for a moment before taking Gwen's ticket.

Gwen's mother stood next to her stiffly, her face red. Gwen knew that her mother was only upset because the stewardess had heard them. She wasn't angry; she never was. "Honey," her mother started to say, but Gwen interrupted her with a kiss on the cheek. "Good-bye."

"Be careful," her mother shouted, and then said even louder, "I love you." But Gwen acted like she didn't hear, walking through the carpeted corridor, both hands on her leather carryall, her chin trembling.

In Madrid Gwen lived in a giant five-bedroom apartment with glossy wooden floors and yellow-curtained windows. She had gotten the apartment through the university—it was a sublet. The girl Gwen lived with was named Carlota. She was a year older, twenty, but she appeared younger. She had a sweet, round face and her hair was long, almost to her waist. From the minute that Gwen arrived, Carlota treated her with such warmth— unpacking her bags for her and making her a cup of chamomile tea—that it almost made Gwen a little uneasy. Almost as uneasy as the giant metal cross that hung over her bed in her new bedroom. It looked so heavy that Gwen pictured it falling on top of her in the night.

That first night she slept in her new bedroom, she awoke abruptly, sweat at her temples. Deep in her dream she had felt the pressure in her chest of someone lying on top of her. She felt a tongue, his tongue, moving in her mouth. She could feel the bumps of his taste buds and then there was the bitter taste of champagne. But she broke away from it, waking up to those stiff red numbers on her alarm clock. Sitting up in her bed she could see through her window a *farmacia* sign across the street.

Somehow the sight of that blinking green sign made her feel OK. That along with the sweet scent of her new apartment—vanilla mixed with baby powder. It was a smell that said firmly, loudly: You are not home.

But, of course, there were a lot of things which made that clear.

The following morning, when Gwen and Carlota walked together through the narrow hot streets of their neighborhood, Moncloa, there were all these voices calling out to them. Ones that went: *Tsst, Tsst, mamacita, rubia, estás buena.* These catcalls came from all sorts: a postman smoking a cigarette, a police officer standing in the middle of traffic, and even a white-haired man who was wobbling against his cane. The Spanish word for this was *piropo* and, according to Carlota, these catcalls were a normal part of Spanish culture. "They all do it," she said casually. "You shouldn't be scared."

"I know," Gwen said, a little too quickly—defensive. "But regular men, they just don't do that where I'm coming from."

Carlota smiled patiently. "Where I *come* from," she said, correcting Gwen's Spanish.

Gwen nodded. She was always making mistakes. At school, they rated her advanced. But she found it so hard to convey everything she wanted in Spanish. It just wasn't easy, even if you knew the words. In the first week that she arrived she often took long walks just to be by herself and think in English. That's how she stumbled upon the cathedral, Santa Cecilia. Normally she would have been intimidated by the gray gates, the looming size of the actual church. But now, being so far away from home, it felt as though she had to see everything, not out of choice but obligation. She walked up the cobble walkway in front of the cathedral and opened the heavy wooden door. Inside it was dark, just the flickering of candles. The air was damp, the kind of place where you might expect to hear water dripping. Gwen walked toward the pews in the middle of the cathedral, her clogs making a loud awkward clatter against the cement floor.

In the very front, where the light was the strongest, a wooden figure, a woman, presumably Saint Cecilia, stood behind wrought-iron bars. She had long black hair, pop eyes, and thin, delicate wrists. But what Gwen noticed most were the slash marks on the woman's neck. The sign above her read VIRGIN AND MARTYR.

Gwen would have read on, but she suddenly felt so uncomfortable, like she didn't belong there and never would. Perhaps it was those few people standing next to her, not close, but just enough to see her out of the corner of their eyes. She had that same sense, only worse, that she often had walking on the streets with Carlota. It was the way they eyed her, knowing she was foreign, seeing it in the shape of her face, the freckles on her pale arms, in the way she stood apart, arms wrapped tightly around herself.

But these people in the cathedral weren't staring right at Gwen, they were murmuring under their breath, heads bowed. Their Spanish words—full of *s*'s—sounded like hissing, like they were hissing at Gwen, who had never spent a day in church, who didn't understand the relationship between the Father, the Son, and the Holy Spirit; she wasn't even sure if the Holy Spirit and the Holy Ghost were the same thing or separate, cavorting friends. Gwen in the presence of religion felt a bit sick to her stomach, like she had been predetermined as ugly or sickly, unable to know the sweet secrets they knew, the Spanish knew, those secrets which propelled them, gave them meaning, that said: This is why.

All of this, the people standing in that cathedral seemed to know about Gwen, just by glimpsing in her direction. Gwen backed away from the statue and walked out quickly, her eyes cast on the dark cement floor.

That same afternoon, when she got home, there was a man waiting for her in the stairwell of her apartment building. The hallway was dark, poorly lit, a place where the sun couldn't get in, and she was instantly afraid when she heard the man say in perfect American English, "I'm a friend of Carlota's. I've been waiting for you."

It seemed strange, unworldly, to hear at that moment alone in the stairway an English voice, and then see a figure, a man's figure, only a few feet away. He pressed the button for the hall light to go on and said, "I'm your neighbor, Marco." He must've seen the shock in her face, because he went on to explain hurriedly, "I live upstairs with my mother on the fifth floor. I'm half American."

In the light, Gwen realized he was nothing to be afraid of. He was tall, but he looked delicate somehow; there was something in the hunch of his shoulders, in the thinness of his arms.

He said quickly, nervously, "I wanted to say hi."

Gwen smiled, letting the uneasiness go away, and said, "Hi."

They talked for a few minutes in the stairwell, their voices echoing. Marco was a student at Complutense too. He studied *derechos*, rights, meaning law. His father lived in Florida and his mother was Spanish. He told Gwen, "When my mother likes my father, I visit for the whole summer. When she thinks he's an ass—this summer she thinks he's an ass," he smiled, "I only see him for a week."

There was something sort of genuine about him. His face was soft, boyish, and sometimes when he was talking to her, even when he was being funny, he looked away from her—so shy.

Every Thursday from that point on, Marco came over for dinner. Carlota said they had been doing this for months now, but she insisted that she and Marco were just friends.

One night when Marco was over, the three of them were sitting together at the table when the phone rang. Instantly Gwen knew who it was. It was her mother—she could feel it in the ring of the phone somehow. Usually her mother called every Wednesday during siesta, which meant that she got up at six o'clock in the morning eastern time, probably setting her alarm, just to talk to Gwen. If Gwen was alone in the apartment, she wouldn't answer. Sometimes the ringing seemed to keep going and going like a shrill plea from her mother. *Pick up the phone, honey. Pick it up. I know you're there.*

But this time Carlota was there to pick up the phone by its third ring. She said awkwardly into the receiver, "Yes, yes," and then looked up at Gwen. *"Es tu madre."* She handed Gwen the phone and went into the kitchen.

Gwen held the phone in her hand, hesitant. "Hello," she said, and in that moment she heard herself: the fear. She was afraid of her mother, afraid of the sound of her voice. Her mother was waiting, it seemed, just waiting to hear Gwen tell her something that she was wasn't ready to tell. She could almost hear her mother's voice saying: Did he hurt you, did he?

Of course, this was paranoia. How could her mother know anything was wrong? She just missed Gwen, just wanted to hear her voice, say hi.

Gwen's mother asked, "Is everything OK?" Gwen answered yes, and her mother said, "Are you sure?"

"Yes, I'm sure," she said defensively, her voice louder than it needed to be. Marco was sitting across from her, flipping through a magazine on his lap. But he had to be listening—how couldn't he?

For the rest of the conversation, Gwen tried to soften her voice, but she felt so unnerved. Each of her mother's phone calls seemed to mark the fact that days and nights were passing, weeks going by, and Gwen was feeling no better, no worse. The same.

Later that same evening, Marco and Gwen sat on the balcony together drinking a watery *rioja*. Carlota was doing the dishes in the kitchen. It was very dark—no stars in the sky. There was music coming from one of the bars down the street. They sat there in an awkward silence. Marco finally said, "It sounded like you weren't getting along with your mother. On the phone."

Gwen made a face and touched the rim of her glass. "I'm awful," she said. "And the worst thing is, I can't control it. I get so upset with her for no reason." Gwen shrugged her shoulders. "It's wrong."

Marco nodded. "I know what you mean. I do that sometimes." He propped his feet up on the balcony. "It's because you love her."

Gwen didn't say anything—she stared at his feet. They were small, strangely clean, and each toenail was shaped in a perfect rectangle. She was about to make some comment, some joke, about how girly his feet were, when he said, "I'm twenty-two years old and I still live with my mother." He let his empty glass of wine rest between his legs. "Do you think that's weird?"

"No," she said, shrugging her shoulders. They were quiet for a minute; there was the sound of men laughing in the street down below. "Can you cook?" she asked.

Carlota came onto the balcony. She filled their glasses with more wine. Marco looked up at her and said in Spanish, "Can I cook?"

"*Tortilla Española*." Carlota looked at Gwen. "*Muy rico*."

"My tortilla isn't just great. It's fabulous." He looked Gwen straight in the eye and said in English, "It's like a little bit of heaven."

Carlota must have understood the English word, "heaven," because she smiled as she took a sip of wine.

Marco took a pack of cigarettes out of his pocket. He handed Carlota one and then put the other in his mouth. He looked over at Gwen and said, "But it's normal here to live with your parents." He was talking in Spanish—they had to now that Carlota was there. "Even after you graduate from college and you're working, you live with your parents."

Gwen nodded, knowing that Carlota planned to return to her hometown, Gijon, once she finished school. Even Carlota's friends who were in their late twenties still lived with their parents. She looked up at Marco. "But when do you finally leave?"

"When you get married," Carlota said, leaning over the balcony.

Gwen frowned. It seemed so terrifying, the idea of staying with your parents, going back to where you came from and staying there until someone came and got you. "What if you don't get married?" she asked.

Marco shrugged his shoulders. "You have to. Otherwise, how would you ever have sex?"

He was kidding, of course, but Gwen was beginning to put something together that she had noticed throughout the past month that she had spent with Carlota and her friends. They never talked about sex. They talked about guys, *tíos*, but they never really went there, to the sex: to the kissing, the sweat, the heat. That was separate. And it seemed to Gwen that that could only be because they lived with their mothers. Still sleeping in their childhood bedrooms—the dollies and pink butterflies still intact—there was no room for it.

"Everyone waits to have sex . . . until they get married?" Gwen asked, her eyebrows raised skeptically.

"I'm still a virgin," Marco announced. His lips were quivering into a smile.

Gwen laughed. "You lie."

Carlota turned around so that she was facing the two of them. "It's not that we don't have sex, but we do think it's more special than you do. Than Americans do. Well, not all of us, but most." She took a sip of her wine, and then held the glass near her lips for a while as if in deep thought. "I don't know how to explain it. It's just . . . it's intimate, it's personal."

Gwen stared at Carlota for a moment, and then she looked out the doorway of the patio into the living room. She could see the cross that hung on the wall over the television. There were not just crosses in her bedroom and living room, but there was one in every room. They were silver, shiny, righteous. There was also a card that had a picture of the Virgin Mary—a bubble around her head—on the coffee table, mixed in with the coupons and phone bills. A few times Gwen had held that card in her hand, thinking it might make her feel something, but it never did.

Sitting on the balcony with Carlota and Marco, Gwen looked down at herself and thought: I don't belong here. I could never stay.

Two weeks later—it was already mid July—Carlota had a party for La fiesta de San Fermin. She invited all of her friends over; most of them were girls. They all had names which Gwen had difficulty remembering: Marimar, Marisa, Alancha, Daniela, and more. Marco was there, but he was in the kitchen making tortilla Española. The girls all sat in a circle in the living room drinking cans of Cruz Campo beer and telling stories in high-pitched voices. But Gwen was unable to keep up, tired from the hot sun, eyes lazily following the mouths of each speaker. Her mind drifted.

As the days passed, that night back in Boston having more distance from her, she started thinking more about Dennis and not so much about what physically had happened to her. She found herself wondering if he had thought she was going to go along with it. If she would let him put his tongue in her mouth, why not anything else? What was coming to her slowly, piece by piece, sharp and jagged, was the question: Did I bring it on myself?

Thinking this, she remembered her first kiss with Mattie Malone, an older boy she had not known that well. He had kissed her hard, bruising almost—he was trying to be passionate, though, not rough. Yet she hadn't pushed him away. Even at the tender age of fourteen, she had thought that she had asked for it. She shouldn't have followed him into his empty bedroom. She shouldn't have sat on his bed with the mismatched sheets. She shouldn't have done any of that. She knew better.

All of this reeled around in the back of her mind as she sat there listening to the Spanish voices, watching the cigarette smoke float in the air. Then, she realized Marco was talking to her. He was standing in the doorway, wearing an apron. He said, "The tortilla is almost ready." His forehead was shiny from being in the hot kitchen, and his wavy black hair looked messy, like he had just come out of bed.

She nodded at him and smiled.

Carlota turned to Gwen. "You've been so quiet? Are you OK?"

"I'm tired, that's all."

"But you're coming with us to La Pachá tonight, *sí?*"

Gwen didn't answer. La Pachá was a nightclub that Carlota had been trying to get her to go to for weeks. Gwen always said, "No, I can't." Nothing more. Which seemed strange, severe almost, but what could she do?

She was so afraid that just being around the music, the sweat, and the smell of yeasty beer would bring it all back: the nausea, his hands on the back of her head pulling on her hair, drool.

Besides, what if she freaked out? What would Carlota think?

It was bad enough that Gwen felt weird, out of place, but what if she started screaming, envisioning rats all around her like she had in that cab, the driver talking to her through the plastic panel, saying, "Honey, you all right? You all right? Want me to call someone for you?"

Carlota said, "Come on, you have to come out with us."

Gwen scratched her head and tried to think of an excuse. Even though she was considered by her Spanish professors as "almost fluent," she still had difficulty sometimes. It was easy to say yes, and no, and "the milk is over there on the counter," but to say something complicated, or even to lie, was hard.

But then Marco saved her. He said, "She can't go tonight. We're supposed to go to Plaza Mayor." He looked at Gwen. "Remember?"

She nodded eagerly, realizing that somehow he had sensed her discomfort.

Carlota said, "Oh, OK." Her voice was soft.

Gwen looked across the room at Marco. The apron he was wearing had lace around the edges and it was tied too tight. He was looking back at her, his face serious. At that moment it seemed as though there was an invisible string between the two of them, and if Gwen just pulled on it, he would come to her.

Plaza Mayor was the center of old Madrid; it was a giant square full of old town shops and bars, all in the same condition as they had been long ago. That night they sat in a café sipping whiskey and Coke. The air was cool and the moon was out. They weren't really saying anything to each other, just looking around at the people at the other tables, the waiters in their ornate suits.

After a while, Gwen caught Marco looking at her, deeply, steadily. To break the awkward moment, she said, "You know, I was all freaked out when I first met you."

"Why?" he asked and took a sip of his drink.

She shrugged her shoulders. "I don't know. Because I came from that cathedral, Santa Cecilia's." She looked around the plaza. A man was walking a poodle. "The Spanish are so religious," she said slowly, not sure how he might react.

"Does that bother you?"

"I guess. It makes me feel weird. Out of place. That's the way I felt, out of place, in that cathedral in front of that statue. Have you been in there?"

He nodded.

"It just bothered me, that place, and then I came home and you were talking to me in perfect English, which made me feel like it wasn't just in Spain that I was out of place, but somehow, everywhere."

He shook his head. "Why would you feel like that?"

"I don't know. I don't really feel like that. It was just then."

They were quiet again. The music was low, a Spanish lullaby.

"Do you want to know her story? Santa Cecilia's? It's a good one." Marco was leaning forward, closer to her.

She made a face as if she didn't really want to hear it, and said, "OK."

Marco waited a moment, as if he was trying to get the story straight, and then he said, "Santa Cecilia was devoted to God, but her father had other . . . ideas. He tried to marry her off to this guy, but she told the guy—his name is something with a V, I can't remember—but she told the guy, 'I have a secret to tell you. I have an angel of God watching over me, and if you touch me, he will be angry and you will suffer.'"

Gwen said, "That must be a nice thing to have."

Marco smiled and lit a cigarette. "So the guy said, 'Show me this angel,' and she did. So then she ended up converting him and his brother. But the Romans found out much later and killed the three of them." He leaned forward. "Cecilia was sentenced to be suffocated to death in the bathroom of her own house. They fed the furnace seven times the amount of fuel, but she didn't die, so finally they sent a soldier in to behead her. He struck her three times in the neck." Marco put his hand up to his neck for added emphasis. Gwen made a face. "For three days she stayed alive, but then she died."

Gwen took another sip of her drink. She could clearly envision this woman soaked with sweat, a man standing behind her, holding her by the chin. But she couldn't really imagine the soldier's sword or even the cut marks—that was too much.

As if noticing the expression on her face, Marco said, "Hey, are you all right?" He laughed. "I brought you to a bullfight last week and that didn't bother you, but a story about some saint does." He was just trying to tease, but she wasn't really responding.

Just thinking about something like that happening so far back in time made her feel like everything she had ever feared, the violence of torn skin and blood, had always existed, and it always would. It was an eternal presence, like the stars, the sun, the moon.

Later, they walked along the cobble square. They were holding hands; it just sort of happened naturally. He was looking at her. She could tell the way his eyes were scanning her face that he thought she was pretty. It was a wonderful feeling to have, better than the feel of the light breeze against her cheeks.

At some point, he leaned over to kiss her. His lips were almost against hers when she pushed him away and turned her face. "No," she said.

He squeezed her hand. "Why?"

"Because," she said. Her eyes went glassy. She couldn't explain it. Standing there in front of him, it was like she could see herself and all the things she was feeling like solid colors of blue and red and purple. She knew if she let him touch her, she wouldn't know how to let go.

"Is there something wrong?" he asked.

She didn't say anything—she didn't know how. The way she felt was so strange—it was like having a heavy bag on her back and knowing that she couldn't fit anything else inside, no matter how special or pretty. She just couldn't.

They stood there for a while. Her hand was in his, against his chest, in between them.

She said, "I'm sorry, I just can't," and then they walked alongside of one another—separate and silent.

When Gwen got back to the apartment, she went directly into her room. She sat on her bed. She thought of that night when she met Dennis and all the things she wanted him to be—those were the things that Marco was. The pain of knowing that was like a weight on her shoulders, on her chest really, bearing down on her.

At that moment she wanted to tell someone, finally, what had happened to her, to let someone know about that night, about Dennis, because it felt as though it was caught deep inside of her, pushing everything else out.

Carlota was in the living room. Gwen could hear the buzz of the television. She got up and went to find Carlota—she was lying on the couch. The lights were off, there was just the blue light of the television screen. Immediately Carlota asked, "*Qué paso?*" Her eyes looked soft, caring. She said in Spanish, "What's wrong? Did something happen? With Marco?"

Gwen shook her head. "But I want to tell you something." She paused, feeling the heat rise in her face. She felt so nervous, and at the same time, relieved. Someone would finally tell her that it was OK, that that night wasn't her fault, it was a horrible accident. That's what it was: an accident.

She tried to get her Spanish right in her head, align everything with the verbs. She said, "Before in Boston, I went out with my friends."

Carlota looked confused.

Gwen said, "This is why I'm so upset. It's about something from before."

"OK. OK," Carlota said, her only English words.

Gwen swallowed. "I was in an alley. Well, I was dancing with this man I met and he brought me into an alley." She stopped, not knowing how to say the word rape in Spanish, or even penis. She didn't know how to say that. "He took off his pants," she started to say. "And he he put his," she pointed between her legs. "His thing, in my mouth." She clenched her fists, frustrated with how slow she had to talk to get the right words out. She wasn't sure how to phrase that he had held her by her face, that she was paralyzed with fear—she couldn't move. She said, "I couldn't move and then a man," she wanted to say doorman, but instead she said porter. "A porter came and the other man ran away."

What Carlota said in response, Gwen would only come to understand years later when time created a livable space between Gwen and these painful moments. She would realize that her story, the one she told Carlota, had lost meaning in her trembling translation. The force, the violence, was missing. It sounded to Carlota like Gwen was having sex with a man in an alley and someone interrupted it all. Carlota did not have the right impression of that alley: the Dumpster, the smashed beer bottle glass all over the ground, or the chain-link fence hovering in the distance near some train tracks. Instead Carlota saw: a small smooth space made between two brick walls, a man with his pants down, his hand stroking Gwen's hair, Gwen's face—an eager face—between his legs, her hands massaging his buttocks and thighs, her nails even slightly scratching him and then there was some moaning. Carlota heard moaning.

But Gwen knew none of this standing in the doorway with her arms around herself. She was waiting for Carlota to say, "Oh, how awful." *¡Qué horror!* To reach out and hug Gwen, rock her back and forth, smoothing the back of her hair, Carlota's cheek against hers.

But instead Carlota said, shaking her head slightly, "Why are you telling me this?" Her eyes were narrowed a bit, disgusted. She put her hands up in front of her and said, "*¡Por que . . . ?*" The word hung in the air between them: Why?

After a minute or two, Carlota got up off the couch and walked into her bedroom. She left the television on. Gwen stood in the living room, leaning stiffly against the wall, her cheeks sweaty and hot.

For the next two weeks, Gwen and Carlota did not really speak. In the morning, they drank coffee in separate rooms. There was a steady distance between the two of them, whether they were sitting at the kitchen table, or in front of the television, or even passing each other on the street. Their interactions became silent, wordless, just their heads nodding.

Gwen spent those last few days alone, and it seemed to mark the end of her trip, that time alone. By July 31, her departure date, she felt ready to be home, to find out what would happen. It was time.

Gwen came home on Flight 848, landing at about midnight. Her mother picked her up and drove her back to Springfield, where she had to stay until her dorm in Boston opened up for the fall semester. Her mother kept asking her questions about her trip. Gwen felt tired, annoyed; her ears were still blocked. "Come on, Ma. Stop it. Let me just sit here."

Her mother didn't say anything for a minute. There was just the darkness outside, the yellow lines in the road. Then her mother spoke again, her voice shaky, "Why are you so nasty, Gwen? Why do you have to be so mean? I'm your mother and . . . and . . . I've missed you. That's all."

Gwen heard the quiver in her mother's voice. Sitting there stiffly she looked out the window. She knew she was mean to her mother. It seemed uncontrollable, automatic. It was as if her mother was the personification of home, of a place that could no longer save her, and she felt angry, cheated.

When they got home, Gwen said to her mother in a soft voice before she stepped into her bedroom, "I'm sorry about earlier. It's not you, it's me." She was standing in the doorway of her bedroom peeling the edges of a crocodile sticker which was stuck to the doorknob. She said, "I've missed you too, Mom. I have."

Her mother, who was only a few feet away, walked over to Gwen. With a slight smile, she rubbed Gwen's back, slowly, methodically—her fingertips saying: That's all you had to say, sweetie, did it hurt that much to say?

Later that night, Gwen was able to sleep, but only for a few hours. It was so hot in her tiny bedroom—the door had been closed for months. The air conditioner in the living room was not reaching her and the oscillating fan on her nightstand did nothing but whirl hot air against her face.

In her dreams she had thought of St. Cecilia suffocating, but not in just some ancient Roman bathroom—in Gwen's bathroom, the daisy wallpaper clearly visible. Perhaps that is what the heat made her feel like, like she was indeed suffocating, her hair moist at the back of her neck and her skin so soft, tender.

When she first awoke, her clock radio read 7:10 and it was beginning to get light out. It was 1:10 already in Madrid. She thought of Marco coming down the stairs of their apartment building, a backpack on his shoulders, his forehead shiny. She would never see him again. Oh sure, they had said they would write and he could even visit, but she knew better. She would never see Carlota either, never see those bright orange walls of their kitchen. It was done, over.

Her mother had said in the car on the way home, "Now you know so much more about the world. I can't even imagine. . . . "

But sitting there in her own bed now, it seemed to Gwen that she had learned nothing more about the world except for its size. It was big, enormous, crushing.

She got out of bed and walked down the stairs, the wooden boards creaking. She stood in the kitchen, arms wrapped around herself. Still dazed from the plane ride, she didn't know what to do with herself, where to go. She didn't want to wake anyone.

She went out the back door through the kitchen into the wet grass. She was barefoot, wearing a black lace tank top with matching underwear. She stood in front of the clothesline. The sheets on the line were still damp; it was too humid for them to dry. She thought of how when she was little she used to hide in between the rows of sheets, giggling, the smell of Downy softener and that cottony whiteness against her face. Gwen winced. Thinking of herself as a child upset her. It made her realize somehow that the life ahead of her might be a very long, difficult one.

She leaned up against the metal poles of the clothesline— they were rusted from age. She thought about how she would be going to Boston in a month; the dorms opened at the end of August. She took a clothespin off the line and played with it, pinching her finger and then letting go, over and over.

What if she saw Dennis again in Boston? What if she saw him in Star Market, a box of cereal in his hand? What would she do?

Or even that doorman back at The Red Room, what if she saw him? He'd recognize her, wouldn't he? Although she could barely remember him. He was more like a giant rectangular shape coming toward her. He had been wearing a long black trench coat. He had a mustache, too, but what color she couldn't remember. She wondered if he would ever think about her years from now. If someday he had his own daughter, would he think of that night? When his daughter asked for money to go to a dance in the basement of some church, would he lean back in his brown corduroy chair, rubbing the hair above his lip, and say, red-faced, "Absolutely not"? Or did he think that Gwen had brought it on herself? Just another dumb slut in an extra-tight dress?

Her eyes teared. Fuck him, she thought. Fuck him. She could have pushed him away, that's what he thought. He thought she brought it on herself, liked it even. Didn't he see, didn't he know that it happened so fast, so fast, that in her memory there were no voices, just a steady roaring noise like that of a speeding car passing. She was left paralyzed, unable to think or feel. Why hadn't she pushed him away? Why? Because she had become limbless. No legs. No arms. Just a stump.

Gwen gritted her teeth, her arms wrapped tightly around herself.

"Everything all right?" she heard a voice say.

It was her neighbor, Mr. Roberts. He was standing in front of her on the outskirts of where her yard met his. He was holding a hoe in one hand. He put his free hand through his gray hair, waiting for a reply.

She said, "Everything's fine."

He nodded, his eyes averted. Mr. Roberts was a good, pious man; he wouldn't look at a young girl in a pair of see-through underwear, legs and arms exposed, skin so translucent and white. He wouldn't do that. Or so she thought.

She turned on the balls of her feet and walked back toward her house slowly, not wanting him to think he had chased her away. But he was just standing there. A tall skinny figure out of the corner of her eye in gray pants and a blue T-shirt. He made no effort to go away. The thought of those people in St. Cecilia's cathedral returned to her—the way that they had been looking at her and she at them, so judging.

She had done nothing wrong. She turned back to face him. His eyes moved across her lace tank top, from her nipples to the slight curve of her belly, and then between her legs. It was so obvious, so outright—as bad as if he had pulled one of his sweaty hands out of those yard gloves and pulled ever so lightly on the curls of her pubic hair.

Gwen narrowed her eyes and said as clearly as she could, "This is my yard."

"But are you OK?" His voice sounded concerned, but his eyes were still yo-yoing up and down, up and down, never looking directly into her eyes.

It was at that moment that something became clear to Gwen: Her head could just roll right off her shoulders onto the ground and he would still be standing there looking, all eyes and bony elbows. It had nothing to do with her, or how good she was.

It was him, them.

She said, "What the fuck are you looking at?"

He opened his mouth, exasperated. "Sweetie, you shouldn't swear like that. You're a lady, a pretty thing. Don't swear." He took another step forward and said, "Now tell me, are you all right?"

It was like he was on film. Like someone hidden in the pine trees had a camera and they were filming him and he had to pretend to be good. Gwen thought of how he and his wife every Sunday morning got into their sky blue Chevy, the rustle of the car pulling out of the gravel driveway heading for Sacred Heart Church. The church bells would ring and ring while Gwen and her family had year after year, Sunday after Sunday, slept soundly with their heads on their goose-feather pillows, dreaming.

She walked back toward the clothesline, toward where he

was standing. Gwen took a T-shirt off the line and put it on. She walked closer to him, practically in his yard. "This is my yard." She licked her lips. "My yard."

Seeing her face so close to his seemed to click something inside of him: She knew. She knew that when he prayed in church with his wife sitting next to him with her fuchsia lipstick and ivory pumps that he really didn't want to be there. He could just as well be home rubbing himself, listening to the soft drip of the leaking faucet in the other room. None of it mattered, really it didn't. She knew it and so did he. Defensively, he said, "You're the one half dressed like that. You . . . " He didn't continue. He didn't have to. *You asked for it.*

Mr. Roberts pushed his hand through his wavy hair and pulled his sleeves down. He was trying to put himself back together. She smiled at him, smugly.

She watched as he turned and headed back toward his house, the unused hoe swinging in his hand. Standing in the doorway with the aluminum door against his back, he called out to her, speaking formally, as if he was reading lines off a page, "I hope whatever is bothering you will pass."

The corner of Gwen's lip turned up and she nodded. She watched him go into his house before walking back into the middle of her yard. She stood there in her white T-shirt. The sun above her was bright. One of the neighborhood cats came from out of a bush and grazed against her legs. He was purring. She bent down and petted his head, his neck, and even the soft white fur of his back.

Claire

MAINTENANCE

I WAS CRYING with my back against the couch, the phone against my ear. Across from me in the wide-open white kitchen, there were broken pink plates and pieces of shattered glass all over the checkered tile. One of the cabinet doors was sitting upright in the kitchen sink, the other door hung on one hinge looking like it was about to come down with a crash at any second.

I screamed into the phone, "He smashed everything, Ma. He fuckin' smashed everything!" Then I paused for a second—I didn't want to be screaming. I wanted to be calm, collected—a person who knew that things could be swept up, put back together, moved. I began again, my voice more level, "I came home from work and he, he, had broken everything in here. Everything that's mine."

My mother said, "Does Louis have a key to get back in?" Her voice no longer sounded groggy. It was three o'clock in the morning and originally, when she picked up the phone, she had sounded as though she was lost in a dream, a dream of dazzling blue light and lulling hair-blowing music.

"He smashed the mirror in the hallway," I said, wiping my nose, which had started to drip. "Then he must've come in the living room. There's, there's a hole, a fuckin' hole in the wall."

My mother said loudly. "Claire, I'm asking you a question. Does *he* have a key?"

"I don't know! I don't know if he still has a key." I shrugged my shoulders and said, "Yeah, I guess he does." Then I crawled on my hands and knees over to the window and looked out into the alley below. I half expected to see him standing in between the green Dumpsters, looking up at me, his soft boyish face looking darker, meaner, unshaven. But there was no one. Just the nearby streetlight which flickered and buzzed as it illuminated the junk in the alleyway: white torn-open trash bags, loose cans, sheets of newspapers, an old bladeless fan.

Kneeling in front of the window, I said, "I don't know where he went. He said he was going to move, to move." I was still crying and I was having trouble talking and breathing. I sat back down, my back to the sill. "He told me he was going to move tonight, but I don't know where."

My mother made a noise like she was clearing something from her throat. She said, "You can't stay there. . . . He could come back, he could come back and hurt you."

"He's not going to hurt me!" I screamed at her. She was always doing this, I thought, making things so dramatic, so do-or-die. I took off one of my shoes and slid it across the floor so that it hit the wall with a slam. I said, "Why are you saying that? Why are you always doing that? He's, he's just mad at me for breaking up with him, he's just mad."

I heard a light creaking sound on the other end, like the phone was being squeezed too hard. My mother said, "You listen to me, OK? He is not the man you have been living with for the past two years. He is someone else," my mother's voice started to shake. "You don't know him right now. You don't." She paused and said more calmly, "You need to leave."

"No," I said defiantly, as if I was twelve instead of twenty. I kicked my other shoe off and it landed near the trash can, which was lying on its side—some of its contents were spilled on the floor: a wax butter wrapper, two tea bags, a cardboard paper-towel roll, cracked eggshells.

"Don't do this!" my mother yelled, her voice had turned to a growl. "I can't leave this house right now and drive eighty miles to go get you. I just can't, OK!"

"I'm gonna stay up and clean," I said flatly.

"Goddamn it, Claire!" my mother screamed. "I can't come!"

I didn't say anything. I wiped my face with the back of my hand and then began fiddling with a shard of pink plate which was on the floor in front of me. I pressed the pointed edge against my fingertip.

I said, my voice bitter, "I never asked you to come. I know better than that." Which was, of course, a lie. I had not called my mother simply to have a late-night talk, a brief update of my crumbling situation. I had called my mother because I wanted, and expected, her to come.

I expected her to get up out of that bed of hers and search for her purse in her darkly lit house and then drive to Boston in her pajamas. From there it didn't matter what happened. We could drive back to her big stony gray house. We could stay in my apartment full of Louis, full of his cigarette smoke and garbage. Or we could go to the Copley Hotel and stare at one another in a bright pink room. It didn't matter. As long as she came.

My mother said, "You know, I have to work tomorrow. I already told you before this happened that I would come Friday." Friday was two days away.

I didn't say anything again. Across from me, behind the trash can, my books were scattered all over the floor—Louis had knocked over my bookshelf. Among the books, one of my journals was wide open, looking like it been read. A teacup full of cigarette butts was next to it.

"Your bedroom door has a lock on it, right?" my mother asked.

I had the phone hanging loosely at my neck. I was staring off at a loose photograph of my brother sitting in a wrought-iron chair, his white navy hat in his lap. The picture was upside down on the floor.

My mother was saying, "If you're gonna stay there, lock that door when you sleep." She paused. "Can you do that, Claire?" My mother's voice was a combination of being concerned and irritated.

"Yeah," I said distantly. I was half listening, half planning on hanging up.

She repeated, "I'll be there Friday." Which meant nothing to me; Friday was the same as next year. "I love you," she said, but it sounded weird, like a question, as if she was asking me: I love you, do you understand that?

I nodded. "Uh-huh."

After we hung up, I stayed on the floor. It was hot in the room, no air conditioning. All of the windows were open and a dull breeze came by occasionally. The air smelled like summer, but not suburban summer with its mix of sweet grass and lilacs; it was instead the smell of the city, of hot black tar, of gasoline, of cigarette smoke that would not drift.

All of the lights were on in the apartment, as they had been when I came home, and along with the heat, the bright bare bulbs on the ceiling made the disheveled room seem enormous and unmanageable. The stereo was gone, so was the TV. They were both his, but it seemed ruthless somehow, as if he had planned that I would come home, that I would be stuck in all of this mess, and there would be nothing to distract me. I was left with just myself and the apartment and his lingering anger.

Where the stereo had been, there was a stack of Louis's CDs, and to the left of the couch in the doorless closet, three of Louis's dress shirts were hanging in a row: white, black, blue. It was then, looking at the sleeves of those shirts, that I realized he might come back, and what that meant to me I could not distinguish. There was a strange part of me that wanted to find him already behind the closed bedroom door, a part of me that wanted to lie down next to him and not say anything, just be very quiet.

But of course, he was not in the bedroom. When I went in there, all I discovered were the things that were missing: his drawing table, his guitar, and a red bathrobe which he usually hung on the back of the door. I tried to imagine him somewhere else now in that bathrobe, but I couldn't really imagine whose apartment, whose couch he might be sitting on.

The day before, when I had told him that I thought we should be apart, I had paused momentarily, trying to phrase everything perfectly, accurately, in the way that I would've wanted someone to phrase such words to me. But before I could finish, he said abruptly, "I'll leave tomorrow night." Then he got up from the kitchen table in his red bathrobe, a small pink plate in his hand. He put the plate in the sink, and as he did so, I saw the way his hand was shaking. It was then that I had momentarily sensed whatever was going on inside of him, the sudden impulse to throw something.

Thinking of all this, I shut the bedroom door and tried to lock it, but it didn't actually work. I hadn't known that; I had never tried to use it before.

Out of duty to my mother, or perhaps out of my own uncertain fears, I ended up pushing, dragging, my bureau until it stood, heavy and barricading, in front of the closed door. Etched in the hardwood floor there were tracks, scrape marks, from the legs of the bureau. I grazed my bare foot over them and then crawled into bed.

At about noon, the buzzer kept ringing. At first I didn't hear it through my closed bedroom door, but then it woke me. I immediately thought it was maintenance coming to change the locks; I had not called them yet, but I had dreamed I had.

It took a while for me to push the bureau out of the way. Whoever was downstairs kept buzzing persistently. Stumbling through the living room barefoot, I almost slipped on a butter wrapper, but I caught myself. My balancing heel came down so hard I cracked a plastic CD case and knocked over Louis's ash-filled teacup.

When I got to the buzzer, I said, irritated, "What?"

"Claire?" a woman's voice said.

"Yeah?"

"Buzz me in. It's Mia. I'm Marilyn's daughter."

I looked at the wall, at the speaker, and made a face. "Who?"

"My mother, Marilyn O'Connor, is friends with your mother, and they asked me to come by."

I didn't say anything. I just stood there with the listen button pressed down. Marilyn was a woman who lived next door to my mother. She had a big maroon house with white shutters. Marilyn had a daughter named Mia, but I didn't know her; I hadn't grown up in the house my mother now lived in. I knew of Mia, had seen her in the hallways of our high school, but we had never spoken, and by the time my we moved next door, Mia had moved to Boston. She was two years older.

"Claire?" Mia said loudly again.

Without replying I buzzed her in and then stood there leaning against the wall wishing I hadn't.

A few minutes later, I heard the heavy clank of the elevator doors shut and then there was a knock. I didn't answer right away. I was standing only a few feet from the door, but I waited as if it might deter Mia, might make her go away.

"Are you there?" Mia said, in a soft voice, as if she knew I was close.

I still waited. I looked down at my hands, adjusted the opal ring on my finger, and then answered the door.

The first thing she said to me was, "Hi, how are you?" Her voice was not fake, it wasn't high-pitched or enthusiastic; it was flat and level. She did not smile at me, or frown for me, she simply stood there, waiting to be asked in.

I just stared at her. She didn't look the way she used to. In high school she had long wavy hair, almost down to her waist. But now her hair was shorter, darker, and it was pulled back in a low ponytail. She also used to wear a lot of jewelry, silver in particular, jewelry that jingled, but now there was nothing, not a bracelet, not a ring.

I stood with my arms on each side of the doorway so that the inside of the apartment wasn't visible. I said, "It's messy in here," which was my way of saying, "You don't have to come in, you can leave now."

She said, "I know," and took a step closer, which made me back away a little.

Once she was in the hallway, we stood there for a minute or two, awkward, staring at one another. Mia was probably twenty-two, but she could easily pass for twenty-eight. There was something about her eyes that made her look older; maybe it was just her serious expression, the burgundy lipstick she wore. Perhaps it was her dress; it was sleeveless, black cotton. A straw bag over her shoulder. She looked elegantly put together, as if she might have been on her way shopping when she decided to stop by.

"I think we went to high school together," Mia said to me.

I nodded. Then I stared down at my toenails—they were a pale pink. I said, "Who called you? My mother or your mother?"

Our mothers had become good friends over the past two years since I moved out. They went on daylong shopping excursions in neighboring towns, or they made elaborate four-course dinners for one another, or they just sat next to each other on a park bench, talking.

"They both called me this morning," Mia said. "They asked me to come help." She paused for a moment, and then said, correcting herself, "They asked me to come and visit."

I nodded and started to walk toward the living room—she followed. In the doorway of the living room there was a big potted fern on its side. Dirt and yellowed leaves were scattered around it. Mia bent down and leaned the plant against the wall and I watched, feeling stupid. It was something I should've had the sense to do myself.

In the living room she looked around, her eyes moving slowly from the plugged-in upside-down VCR to the trash, the knocked-over bookshelf, the hole in the wall, the broken kitchen cabinets.

She smiled wryly and said, "Very nice." As she took a few steps farther in, glass crunched under her shoes. She looked at my feet. "You need to put on some shoes. You're going to cut yourself."

I nodded, but didn't make any effort to put on shoes.

"We need to get your locks changed first," Mia said and I knew without asking that those were my mother's direct orders.

She put her bag down on the couch. "I'll call maintenance if you want." She looked around the room some more. "You can take a shower while I do that."

I looked down at myself—I had forgotten about what I looked like. I didn't need to gaze in any mirror to know that there was mascara smudged under my eyes and splotch marks of a revealing sort all over my face. I was also still wearing what I had worn to work: tight sexy-girl pants and a silver-and-black–striped tank top. I worked as bartender in a nightclub, but now, at twelve in the afternoon, I looked like some hungover disco queen who had woken up in the wrong place.

"What's the number for maintenance?" Mia asked.

I went into the living room and found my address book on the floor underneath two other books. I flipped through its tabbed, partially torn pages, looking under *S* for superintendent, but I found the number on the same page under the heading Superfreak—it was written in Louis's handwriting: small, neat, black letters. Next to the number there was a drawing of a giant roach sitting with its arms behind its head on a flowered couch.

"Here," I said, handing Mia the open book, and then I looked behind me, embarrassed that I was letting someone I didn't even know make phone calls for me.

I scratched my head for a minute. "OK, I'm going to go in there. To take a shower." I pointed behind me at the bedroom which connected to the bathroom. "It might take me a while though." I paused. "I think I just want to stand around in there."

Mia had the phone in her hand. "Then do that," she said, smiling faintly. "I can take care of this."

The maintenance man arrived about an hour and a half later. His name was Ernesto. He was a big guy, barrel-chested, with stiff hair that looked overly combed and hairsprayed. His mustache curled up on the ends, and occasionally when he spoke he touched his chin, as though he once had a beard.

"I'm just curious," Ernesto asked, loud enough so that either Mia or I could answer, "why do these locks need changin'?" He had not seen the rest of the apartment yet—he was on his knees, eye-level with the doorknob.

Mia was in front of him, arms folded, as if she was monitoring him, making sure he was doing everything right. I sat in the living room, near the entrance of the hallway, putting books back in the bookshelf.

"She lost her keys," Mia said, "and it's, it's just best that she gets new locks. Just in case."

Ernesto nodded. He was working on the lock, but occasionally he looked up. "You can never be too safe in this fuckin' city," he said. "Especially in this neighborhood." I lived in the section of Boston called Fenway on a street which was right behind Fenway Park. It was an area full of nightclubs and bars, as well as roaming, unpredictable drunks.

"Just the other day," Ernesto was saying to Mia, "I caught this piece of crap guy trying to crawl through a window on the first floor." He stopped for a moment—he locked the dead bolt and then unlocked it. "I had to stop him, the guy breaking in. So I took a board that was loose in the alley and hit him with it. Bam, bam! Right on the ass. And then you know what happened?"

"No," Mia said, and looked back at me.

"The guy started to cry." Ernesto shook his head. "Fuckin' guy, he was probably havin' flashbacks to his childhood. Right there stuck on the windowsill he was just flashing back, flashing and flashing."

Mia said, her voice flat, "Really?"

Ernesto stood up. He put his tools back in the green pail he kept them in. He said, "I'm done with this, but I need to use the phone and call the office for a sec. Where's your phone?"

I shook my head at Mia. I knew he was going to have to come into the apartment at some point, but we hadn't cleaned up all the way. The furniture was straight and most of the trash in the living room was bagged, but the kitchen was still a mess. The apartment also smelled bad—like cigarette smoke and curdled yogurt and cantaloupe rind. I had tried lighting a vanilla-scented candle in the living room, but now the room smelled sweetly rotten.

Mia led Ernesto down the hallway anyway; I stood up, one book in my hand, one under my armpit. All of my books were now wedged alongside one another, the authors in alphabetical order, and I stared at them, all of the different-colored spines.

Ernesto came and stood in the doorway next to me. His blue T-shirt had a porcupine on it that was drinking a beer. The caption read, "Needles are bad." I was about to ask him what his shirt meant when Ernesto shouted, "What the hell happened?" He pointed at the hole in the wall in the living room.

"Yeah," Mia said. She was standing beside him. "We need you to fix that."

He looked at Mia, eyebrows raised, and then he looked to the left in the direction of the kitchen: glass was still on the floor, the beige cabinet door still hung off one hinge. It hadn't fallen yet.

He said again, "What happened?" He looked at me. "Was there a tornado? A fuckin' kitchen tornado?"

"*I* didn't do it," I said, defensively.

"Well then who did?"

I swallowed. "My boyfriend."

Ernesto just stared at me, and I could sense in the way his eyes traveled across my face what he was thinking. I said, "He doesn't hit me, OK?" I stood there stiffly, a book still tight under my armpit. "I don't let people hit me."

"Hey," he touched his mustache, "I didn't say anything."

I said sharply, "Well, I'm just telling you." I looked at Mia, wondering if she thought that Louis hit me too. I said, "He's passionate, that's all."

Ernesto mumbled, "That's a real fancy way of putting it." He walked into the living room and stood in front of the hole, arms on his hips. There was a broom inside of the hole, its dusty yellow bristles were visible—the rest of it was somewhere inside of the hollow space. Louis had apparently made the hole by repeatedly hitting the wall with the broomstick.

Ernesto touched the broom, tried to pull it out. Pieces of plaster loosened and fell on the floor. He turned to me, "They're going to charge you for this. You can't just blow holes in the wall and expect them to be fixed for free."

"That's fine," Mia said, and I looked at her, shaking my head. I didn't want to pay for the hole. I said, "What if I just put a picture over it?"

Mia ignored me.

"Tacked a towel over it?"

Mia shook her head. "You've got to get that fixed."

Ernesto was still looking at the hole; he looked like he was going to put his entire head inside of it. He turned back toward us, wiping his forehead. It wasn't that hot in the apartment for an August afternoon, but it was humid and breezeless. He said, "Christ, I'm going to be here all goddamn day plugging this thing." He shook his head and went over to the phone, which he had apparently just spotted on the floor in front of him. He dialed some numbers and then, putting the phone to his ear, he said to me, "Do you guys have anything to drink? A Shasta or something?" He touched his sweaty forehead again. "It's too hot in here. I feel like I'm gonna die."

Mia gave Ernesto a beer. That was all there was to drink in the refrigerator, a six-pack of Coronas. Louis drank Corona.

Standing in front of the open refrigerator, Mia said to me, "Did you eat today?"

I shook my head. I was squatting on the floor picking up pink pieces of plate. I said, "Food is the enemy." I was trying to be funny.

She stared at me, shook her head. "You can't not eat, Claire."

I didn't answer her. I went over to the trash, threw the plate pieces away.

Soon afterward Mia decided to go to the convenience store up the street. She said, "I'll buy bagels." Then she left, her straw bag over her shoulder.

That left me alone with Ernesto. At first he was still downstairs in the basement getting supplies, but soon afterward he came back, humming. He had pieces of plasterboard in his hand. I nodded at him—I was sweeping the kitchen floor.

His Corona was sitting on a can of plaster mix. He picked it up and turned toward me. "You don't by any chance have lime?"

"Yeah, we do," I said, but didn't stop sweeping. All of the big pieces of smashed plates and glass I had already picked up with my fingers. Now there was just the smallest of shards leftover, along with dust bunnies, a broken Certs, loose pennies and dimes. I kept sweeping and sweeping.

Ernesto was staring at me. I looked at him, glaring a little, not sure if he was looking at me now because we were alone, because he thought he could.

He said, "Hey, you all right?"

"Yeah," I said, and realized he was still interested in the lime. I stopped sweeping and opened the refrigerator. On the rack, where the eggs were supposed to be, there were three limes. I put the limes on the bare counter and opened the silverware drawer. There was a piece of paper, notebook paper, torn and folded on top of the forks and spoons. I ignored it and took out a knife. I began cutting one of the limes into sections.

Ernesto was looking out the living room window. He said, "There's a game tonight."

I frowned and said, "Great." All summer long everyone in our neighborhood lived their lives around the times and dates of games; Louis and I kept a big red copy of the Red Sox schedule on the refrigerator. I looked up at the refrigerator to see if the schedule was still there. It was. But the picture next to it was gone. The picture had not been of me, it had been a Kodak ad with a five-year-old girl wearing red lipstick and a straw cowboy hat. Louis claimed the girl looked like me. He had said, "This is you."

"The game starts at 7:05," Ernesto remarked, as if he thought I was looking at the refrigerator for the game time.

I said absently, "Four more hours," and began cutting again. I didn't cut just one lime, but instead all three of the limes. I put the wedges in a heaping pile the way I did on the bar at work.

Ernesto said, "I fuckin' hate Red Sox fans." He took a sip of beer. "They're all a bunch of pukes."

I nodded, thinking of the week before. Louis and I had been in the Star Market when a cluster of gray-haired men in Red Sox hats came in; they were all sunburned and drunk. Fleetwood Mac was playing on the overhead speakers and they sang along as they moved through the front of the store, "Don't stop thinking about tomorrow, don't stop!" Between the five of them, they tossed a box of Cat Chow. They sang louder, "It'll soon be here, better than before, *better than before.*" They ended up hurling the Cat Chow box into the pyramid-shaped Cat Chow display—there were cardboard cat heads all over the floor. When the manager yelled at them, they laughed and meowed at him.

Louis and I had been watching from the check-out line. I was holding the basket and Louis was behind me, his finger in the back pocket of my jeans.

"How's that piece of lime coming along?" Ernesto asked and came into the kitchen.

I handed him his lime and watched him push the wedge into his beer bottle with his thumb. The beer fizzed. Ernesto said, "You look like maybe you should have one of these too."

I smiled half-heartedly.

The phone began ringing. I put the knife down and stared into the living room in the direction of the phone. I wanted it to be Louis, but I didn't want him to say anything. He should just hang up.

The machine went off. The announcement was Louis's voice, which was deep, older than his age. "Hey, we're not home. If you want, leave a message. If you don't want to, that's fine. We have caller ID." His voice became ominous: "We know who you are."

There was a beep.

"Hey, it's me, Tessa. The person who's your sister." My sister lived in Connecticut and I hadn't talked to her in almost a year. She said, "I'm coming to visit you with Ma. She called me. She told me about Johnny Rock-n-Roll." My mother called Louis Johnny Rock-n-Roll because he had long hair and he knew how to play the guitar. Tessa continued, "So I'll be there on Friday. OK?" She sounded like she was going to hang up, but then she added, "I'll bring some Cadbury eggs, remember how much you used to like them?"

Ernesto had returned to the wall now that the lime was in his beer bottle. He said, with his back to me, "I love Cadbury eggs. I could eat ten in one sitting." He turned toward me. "One time I ate so many that my hand couldn't stop shaking. It was awful, I had to lay down."

I nodded. I was looking at the blinking red light of the answering machine.

Ernesto kept talking. "I don't know where she's gonna get Cadbury eggs this time a year." He turned to me. "In August, it's impossible."

When Mia came back, she toasted the bagels she had bought. The apartment smelled like burned cinnamon bread from the bottom of the toaster mixed with Pine Sol and wet plaster. I sat at the kitchen table, which was small and rickety, the type of table that could only hold two plates.

Mia put a flowered paper plate down in front of me and then opened the silverware drawer. She looked at me. "There's a note in here."

Ernesto was humming again, but it had become softer, more melodic.

Mia said, "Do you want it?" She had left the drawer open— she was in front of the toaster, a butter knife in her hand.

I shrugged my shoulders. "Yeah."

I unfolded the note on my paper plate full of dangling daisies. The note had no punctuation and it was written in curly rushed penmanship:

Claire I didn't mean to break everything but you shouldn't have left that there The journal I'm talking about You should've known what it would do You shouldn't have written it You will never know what it felt like to read that

He was referring to the journal that I had seen wide open on the living room floor the night before. When I put all of the books back in their places, I left that one separate, and I put an envelope in the spot where it was opened to. But I hadn't read it. I knew not to—it might upset me, push me somewhere. For the time being I had allowed myself to believe it was nothing, it just somehow opened like that.

After reading Louis's note, I looked up at Mia, but she wasn't looking at me. She was giving me my privacy, looking into the toaster, at its orangy light.

I got up from the table and went over to my bookshelf in the living room. Ernesto looked at me, took the last sip of his beer. With my back to him, I opened the journal to the page marked with the envelope:

June 23.

I don't want to live with him anymore. I just don't. I want to come home and be alone. I don't want to see his robe on the doorknob or his shoes in front of the couch. I just want it to be my place with my things. I don't want to hear the television or his stupid guitar strumming or his breathing next to me. I just want: me.

I wish he would leave without me saying anything. I wish he would just feel it and go.

I put the journal down and went into the bedroom, the note from Louis still in my hand. I sat on the bed and stared at my bureau, which was in the middle of the room. It looked bigger away from the wall, harder to move.

Mia came in. "Are you all right?"

I was crying a little so I shifted my weight so that she couldn't see me. I hated when people saw me crying. It made me feel pathetic, like one of those girls I often saw crying in women's restrooms, mascara running, a wad of toilet paper in their hand.

"Is he coming back?" Mia asked.

"No," I said and started to cry harder—that was what I was so upset about. I had wanted Louis to leave, but I didn't ever consider for how long. A month? A few weeks? Days?

"What exactly happened between you and him?" Mia asked, making a face, one of caution, as if she were concerned about seeming nosy, or overbearing.

I didn't answer her at first. I stood there feeling hot, feeling the beam of sun come into my shadeless windows, onto the floor, a dull burn on my curled-up feet. After a minute or two, I said, "I don't know what happened." Which was the truth. All those words I had scribbled out in my journals or in margins of loose paper were difficult to explain—they didn't even make sense to me. The only thing I could clearly identify was this nagging tight feeling that often had been running through me as I walked down sidewalks, rode in subway cars, ascended stairs.

Sometimes late at night when I came home from work, I used to take the stairs instead of the elevator to our apartment. I'd count the stairs, and then go back down again, counting them backward. It was there in the echoing stairwell that I could be as quiet as I wanted, just the tap of my shoes and the rusty-sounding movement of the nearby elevator moving up and down.

But Louis—who seemed to always be home, to always be waiting for me—was against silence. He interpreted it as being cold, as being distant; he'd say, "What's wrong with you?"

In particular, he thought silence meant something about him; he thought it meant ill will toward his new shoes or his recent drawing or his latest haircut. He thought silence had some hidden, ulterior meaning. Which of course it did. It meant peace.

"I broke up with him for no reason, none at all," I said to Mia, looking down at the scratch marks on the floor.

She sat down on the bed, one leg underneath her. I rubbed my fingertip over a small ink spot which was on the beige bedspread between us. She said, "It's all right, you know, to want to be alone."

I didn't say anything. I leaned back on my elbows and looked at Mia from behind. She had a sunburn on the back of her arms and neck—it looked like it must've hurt. I almost said something about it, but then I didn't. I was too busy being caught up in myself. Sitting on that bed, with the musky scent of Louis, of what he smelled like when he slept, still lingering on the sheets, I already felt regretful, regretful at the idea that someday, lost in all that silence I had wanted, I'd come to miss Louis.

He had adored me with a certain intensity that I knew most men would not.

Mia stood up, her back was to me. I heard her swallow, and then she said, "There are people who can live by themselves and there are people who can't. And . . . and," she faced me, "it's important to know which one you are."

Without having to ask, I knew that Mia was the type that could live alone. It was clear in just the way she stood in the middle of the room without needing to lean or cross her arms or hold a meaningless object in her hands. Her long arms were plainly at her sides.

I shrugged my shoulders. "I don't know which one I am."

Mia said, "A lot of people don't." She touched the edge of my bureau with her finger. "Which is a shame."

I thought about that, about what Mia was saying. I thought about all the girls I knew and I saw how in all of us there was something similar: We had all come from somewhere else, had lived a whole life with our families, and then we moved. But most of us weren't lone travelers. We brought someone, or we picked someone up along the way, we attached ourselves. Because if we didn't, who would we be? We'd be empty. Without our mothers, without our families, we were just lost shapes moving around, feeling for things.

"Have you always known that you could be alone?" I asked Mia. "Did it always feel right?"

She tightened the elastic on her ponytail and then smoothed the brown curls of her hair. Shaking her head, she said, softly, as if it were some secret, "No. I had no idea."

While Mia and I were in the bedroom, Ernesto had fixed the broken kitchen cabinet doors. When we came out, he said, "I fixed the window too." He pointed at one of the living room windows. "It didn't open completely. The alignment was off."

I said, "That was always messed up."

"Yeah," he said, "but I fixed it." He stared at the window rubbing his chin, and then he picked up a terry-cloth rag from his tool pail. In methodical straight rows he wiped dust off the window. As he did this, he glanced at me. It was then that I knew the bill for the hole in the wall would never come.

Before he left, he told me he would have to come back when the plaster dried to sand everything down and paint. I nodded. He had already given me my new set of keys, and I was looking down at them in my open palm. Ernesto stood in the hallway with me for a minute or two, and then he said, "I still think you should have a beer."

Mia left shortly after Ernesto. She carried with her a full bag of garbage which seemed heavy and cumbersome. "You don't have to take that," I said, but Mia ignored me.

I walked with her down the hallway, leaving my apartment door open. We waited for the old elevator silently. When it arrived I said, awkward, my eyes cast on a red thumbtack that was loose on the floor's tile, "Thanks for helping me out."

Mia said, "No," softly, as if the thanks embarrassed her.

"No, but really," I said.

She rested the white garbage bag near her feet and shrugged her shoulders. "I came because my mother asked me to." She opened the elevator door with a shove. "Sometimes I do these things anyway. It makes you feel good if you help people." She looked past me. "Sometimes you need to feel good."

I nodded and held the elevator doors open while she dragged the garbage bag behind her. When the doors shut, I could still see her through the wrought-iron gate. She said, "See you," and I said, "Yeah."

In the living room, I sat by myself drinking a Corona. It was 4:30. Soon there would be the sound of a distant cheering crowd at Fenway, the announcer's muffled voice, the jumpy organ music which marked the beginning and ending of each inning, and then an occasional isolated scream: Red Sox!!!

For now, though, everything was quiet except for the kitchen sink—it was dripping. With each plink I imagined the droplets that formed and fell. Across from me on the windowsill, the vanilla candle I had lit earlier that morning was now half melted and flickering. In time with the leaky sink, yellow wax dripped off the sill onto the floor. I counted the drops—my beer was pressed against my chest. The bottle felt cold, uncomfortable. But I held it there.

Claire

TALK A LITTLE TALK

CLAIRE IS A BARTENDER in a nightclub called The Red Room. It's Friday night, eleven o'clock, and no one is there yet. Claire is wearing a pink top, black pants, and a necklace which is chokingly tight. She feels cold. There are lamps hanging on chains above her, and candles are lit on shelves behind her, but the room is dark.

The owner is standing as he usually does at the left-hand corner of her bar. He is a short man with ruddy cheeks who has a way of looking angry all the time even though he's not. He orders a Bacardi and Coke. His friend, Lee, who is tall and tan, stands next to him. Lee doesn't drink—he just looks about the room, his neck stiff and giraffelike.

The owner stays at Claire's bar all night—it's the VIP section of the club. There's nothing particularly special about Claire's bar except that there are velvet ropes that section it off and there's a guy named Rich who decides who gets in. The owner doesn't call him Rich, though, he calls him Dickie. Rich is only allowed to let pretty girls into the VIP section—no skanks, fat asses, or chicken faces (the owner likes to say chicken faces). But Rich is young, only eighteen. He is a big kid, broad-chested, and tall, with a round face and a nervous way of pressing his lips together. He has trouble, he says, deciding who's pretty and who's not. It's dark in the club, crowded; it's hard to see their entire bodies. So most nights, he takes no chances— only men get in.

"Where did Dickie go?" the owner asks Claire.

She acts like she doesn't hear him. She is lighting the candles on the bar.

"Hey, space girl," the owner says louder, "where's Dickie?"

"He's over there." Claire points. "Talking to the coat-check girl."

"He better get his ass back over here." The owner shakes his head and stirs his drink. "Is he talking to Terry?"

"Her name is Kerry."

"Right," the owner says, and takes a sip of his drink. He looks over at Lee, smiles, and then says to Claire, "She's dirty, ya know." He raises his eyebrows. "I'm talkin' real dirty."

Claire leans against the bar. She is eating an orange slice. "OK, why is *Terry* so dirty?"

The owner leans forward. "Me and Lee were fuckin' around with her in the back of my friend's van last week."

Claire says flatly, "Uh-huh?"

"First she gave me a blow job," he says, and pauses. He looks around the room like he doesn't want anyone else to hear. "When I came, she didn't swallow." He takes another sip of his drink. "Which I thought was OK because when I come, let me tell you, I come like a fuckin' fountain." He puts his hands up. "I'm talkin' everywhere. But anyway . . . she didn't just let it drip all over the place. She let it drip into this cup, which I thought was kinda nice. It showed she was neat—she didn't want to stain up the seat."

"Wait, wait," Claire says, "a cup?"

"She must've found it on the floor of the van. It was a fuckin' coffee cup, you know, like Dunkin' Donuts or something. I mean, I'm not sure. I was leaning back, I wasn't exactly examining the cup. But listen . . . when she was done with me, she started blowing him." He points at Lee and Lee nods. "And when he came, she did the same thing."

"The same thing?"

The owner gives Claire an irritated look. "OK, my cum went in the cup," he says in a slow exaggerated way, "and then . . . she did the same thing with Lee. His cum went in the cup. There was a whole lot of cum in that cup. Understand?" Claire stares at him, her lip curls up. He laughs. "But listen, get this, she put the lid on the cup—I don't know where the fuck the lid was, but it was there, somewhere. So she shook it up like it was a martini. And then, and then, *boom*, she drank it down." He slaps his hand on the bar and laughs. "How dirty is that?"

Claire stares at him and blinks. "That's . . . that's pretty dirty, I would have to say." She shifts her weight so that she is not leaning toward him anymore.

The owner says, "Yeah, well, if you ever want to try it yourself, me and Lee, we're here for you, we're here."

Claire smiles and then lets her face go blank again. She walks to the other end of the bar. She stands there with her arms wrapped around herself and stares at the empty dance floor in front of her. The music goes *boom, boom, boom* and the lights, fuchsia and blue, flash in the same dull pattern.

Claire is twenty-two. She has an English Lit degree from Boston University and she doesn't know what to do with it. She has worked in this nightclub since she was eighteen, since she first moved here to Boston with three hundred dollars and a boyfriend who she ended up living with for two years. The boyfriend is gone now, and Claire spends her nights off, Sundays and Tuesdays, with her friends. Although Claire sometimes wonders if her friends are really her friends, or just people who keep the same hours. Often they buy her things, makeup and tank tops, and they kiss her on the cheek. But Claire knows that when she is not around her friends say she is bitter and depressing, and they make fun of the way she walks.

Claire does walk funny though. She struts, particularly when she is at work, when the bass is so strong that the floor feels like it's thumping, and the talk all around her isn't talk anymore: It's yelling.

Right now, though, Claire is still. The owner and Lee stand at the left-hand corner and she at the right. Claire leans against the bar, warms her fingers over the lit candles. She stares off.

About a half hour later, Micah comes up to the bar. He's a regular and Claire kind of likes him. Well, he's bearable. He has clean brown hair, his teeth are straight, and he only has three drinks per night. He also has a beach house in Nahant and he goes to Paris for the weekend sometimes. He's probably lying about Paris, but people are always lying to Claire. It seems natural almost, and so she doesn't necessarily get mad about it. Besides, she believes the part about the beach house. She can even picture it: the big white shape of the house, the curtainless windows, the porch with its sliding glass doors, and the beach with its bright white sky.

Micah says to Claire, "How have you been? I've missed you terribly." He's being dramatic on purpose and she likes it.

The music is loud. Claire leans in so that he can hear her. "It's been two days," she says flatly, as if he's annoying her. "I was working on Wednesday night, remember?"

"Well, it's been too long. Just too long."

She smiles and says sarcastically, "Yes, it has. Hasn't it?"

There are a few guys at the bar now, but it isn't busy. Most of them have their backs to Claire and they are looking out toward the dance floor—only a few people are dancing.

Micah says, "You look like Kathy Ireland tonight."

Claire rolls her eyes. She does not look like some super-model. She is tall and white like Kathy Ireland, but her hair is cut above her shoulders and she has a round childish face.

"Give me a champagne," Micah says, "when you have a moment."

"When I have a moment," Claire says and starts making drinks for two other guys just to make him wait. Then she pours him a glass of champagne. He has his money out. Micah's good that way; he pays for his drinks. He doesn't turn his back or pretend he can't hear her when she tries to charge him.

When she hands him his change, he says, "Fill it up more," and points at his glass. "You didn't fill it up all the way."

"You're not supposed to."

"In France they do."

She gives him a dirty look. "No, they don't," she says, and fills his glass up to the point that the champagne overflows onto his hand.

He smiles, and somewhere in that smile, she thinks she can tell that he really likes her. He must. "Have you ever been to France?" he asks.

"No."

"I could take you there."

"How about you buy me the ticket and I go alone?"

"You couldn't go alone." He takes a sip of champagne. "I would get so worried about you. Frenchmen are such pigs."

"Worse than here?"

He shakes his head and says gravely, "Much worse."

"I can't imagine," Claire says, and takes a sip of his champagne.

At about 12:30, it is finally busy and there are people all around Claire's bar. Micah isn't there anymore—he went looking for friends. The owner is still around, though. He's with two girls that Lee found on the dance floor. Both girls are significantly taller than the owner and one has a feather boa around her neck. The girls want two shots of something "nice and sweet" and two Buds. The owner wants a Bacardi and Coke and he'll have a sissy shot too.

Everyone else wants something also. Lee wants a Pellegrino and Rich would like a Sprite. A guy in red wants two Tanqueray and tonics, a Makers Mark straight up, a margarita (rocks, no salt), three shots of Jager and a Coke. The one next to him wants two Absolut martinis extra dry and dirty, a cabernet, a Sex on the Beach, an Alabama Slammer, a Coke, a Bud, a Pearl Harbor, and six waters. Another guy, a jumpy guy, wants ten Budweisers. He's in front of the register. He keeps saying, ten Budweisers, hello, ten Budweisers, yes ten, I want ten, ten Budweisers. Someone else with an unlit cigarette in his mouth wants matches. "For Christ sake, can I get a match please?"

They're all shouting things, but the music is louder.

Claire's good though—she's fast and she can do this. Occasionally someone does get a Baybreeze instead of a Seabreeze, a lime instead of a lemon, or a drink doesn't taste right, it's too sweet, too much ice, *Hey, did you put any alcohol in here?* This is when the music seems to go faster, the speakers above her are louder, and the smoke burns her eyes. But Claire keeps going and going.

In the middle of all this, some guy who ordered a Sapphire martini is freaking out. *I said a twist, not olives, what the fuck, a twist, you can't fuckin' remember that?* He is drunk, so drunk that even when he stops talking his mouth stays open and his lips are wet with spit. When Claire gets close enough to him, he grabs her by the arm and says, "Make this over." Claire pulls her arm away and ignores him—she is picking money up with one hand, making a vodka tonic with the other. He keeps staring at her, though, so she looks up and reads his lips. He says to his friend, "I bet she's the one that Jimmy was talking about." Jimmy is the owner. The guy leans over so that his face is close to Claire's. He says, "Hey, are you the cocksucker?"

Claire picks up a drink, a red one, and splashes it in the guy's face. For a moment, he does nothing—there's just the music and the blur of people around them. Then his hands extend across the width of the bar, touching the wet bar mat, and he starts to climb over. Drinks spill, ashtrays slide. Claire does not back away. All that adrenaline running through her, along with the techno loud in her ears, makes her feel as though no one can hurt her, no one.

The guy reaches out, trying to grab Claire by the face, but two guys are pulling him back. His hand lands on her shoulder. Once Claire feels his touch, the moist heat of his hand, she scratches him, and at the same time, he is pulled back farther by the guys who have each of his legs in their hands. He is panting, his forehead sweaty, and one of the hanging lamps above the bar is swinging over his head. Once he is back on his feet, his shirt is no longer tucked in and his stomach is showing. The doormen escort him out.

Claire stands there for a minute and then she looks up at the owner. He is clapping, and he says, "Go, Claire, go!" One of the girls next to him puts three fingers up in the air—they want three more shots.

Claire tries to continue working, but she's shaky. She can't seem to get the ice into the glasses and she keeps dropping things. Her eyes are a little glassy and her face is flushed. She makes no eye contact. When people order drinks, she nods, makes the drink, and holds out her hand for the money. In between orders, she struts, back and forth, picking up crumpled napkins, chewed-up straws, and the wet one-dollar bills stuck to the bar. She is searching for anything to wipe, clean, or throw away, anything to keep her moving.

At two o'clock, the music stops. The doormen are shuffling people out the door. There is practically no one at Claire's bar now, and in that emptiness, Claire is starting to feel calm. Her hands do not shake.

Micah is standing at her bar again, but she acts like she doesn't see him. He has a full glass of champagne. He must have gotten it from another bartender. This bothers Claire—he should only be getting his drinks from her. Out of the corner of her eye, she sees him watching her clean.

"Claire?"

"Yes," she says and looks up at him. He has his jacket off and he is only wearing a T-shirt. His arms look nice—thin and long, without too much muscle.

"Do you want to do something ever?" he asks. He has one arm on the bar.

"With you?"

He looks around the room in an exaggerated way. "Yes, with me."

Claire says, "OK," and doesn't look up at him. She is cleaning bottles with a wet rag.

"When?" he asks.

Before Claire can answer, a woman comes up to the bar who is so drunk that only one eye is open. "Water," she says, "I need water."

Claire ignores her and looks over at Micah. He is smiling.

The woman says even louder, "Please, can I just have a water?"

Claire puts the bottle she is wiping down—it clanks against the other bottles in the rack. She pours a glass of water and puts it down in front of the woman, letting some of it spill. Claire says bitterly under her breath, "Here's your fuckin' water."

The woman doesn't say anything. She just stares at the glass like she's not sure how to pick it up. Micah asks, "Do you want a straw?" and hands the woman one.

Claire says to him, "I have Tuesdays off. We could do something then?"

Micah is still looking sideways at the drunk woman. Her head is bobbing around. He looks at Claire. "What about now?"

Claire frowns. Men who want to take her out after work are bad. They're always married, or they live in their cars, or they're so drunk that everything about them, even the palms of their hands, smell of sweat and whiskey.

"We could get something to eat," Micah says quickly, as if he senses her annoyance. "You must be hungry."

Claire shakes her head. "I can't eat this late," she says, and turns abruptly. She's embarrassed that she somehow revealed something about herself in using the word *can't* instead of *don't*. Claire wants to weigh 116 and she doesn't. It seems to Claire, particularly late at night when she looks at herself in the mirror behind the bar, that if she weighed 116 things might be better. She's five pounds away right now, but she can get there; she just has to concentrate.

Micah says, "We could share a fruit salad?"

Claire doesn't answer. She's watching the owner come toward them. He is kicking stray bottles across the dance floor and yelling. The girls who were with him left, so did Lee. The owner stands a few feet from Claire's bar and looks at the woman with the water. One of the pink feathers from the girl's boa is caught in his hair. He says to Rich, who is sitting at a near-by table rubbing his eyes, "Dickie, how many fuckin' times do I have to tell you? I don't want any chicken faces clucking around my club." He points at the drunk woman. "You see her?"

Rich gets up quickly and comes over to the bar. "Miss, it's time to go," he says politely, "we're closing."

"I'm sorry, I'm just tired," the woman tells him and doesn't get up. She stares distantly in front of her.

Rich gives her his hand. "Let me help you." The woman gets up and they walk arm in arm across the room to the exit. The woman wavers a little but Rich smiles and pats her arm. Claire watches. There is something about the way that Rich is holding the woman's arm, the way that she leans into him, that saddens Claire. No one has held her like that in a very long time. Claire rubs at the back of her neck and looks away from them.

Micah has come around the bar and he is standing beside her. His champagne glass is in front of them. He says, "Claire, you've got to learn to relax." He is rubbing her shoulders and his face is next to hers. She can't smell his breath, just aftershave. His hands feel warm on her bare shoulders—she leans in. They stay like this for a minute. The candles of the bar flicker around them.

"You could come to my place," he says into Claire's ear. "We could take a bubble bath."

Standing there with his hands now at her hips, Claire imagines Micah bare-chested in a bathtub, clumps of foam and bubbles all around his neck and shoulders—the champagne glass still in his hand. Her lip curls up, disgusted. It's as if she can clearly see within that imagined brightness of Micah's bathroom that this guy doesn't like her, he doesn't know her—he's simply someone who desperately wants to touch.

Claire pushes him away from her. "All right, enough."

He says, "What?"

"No, really," she says, and motions for him to get back on the other side of the bar. He grabs his glass and takes a sip. His pinky goes up. Claire starts going through the money in her tip bucket. He walks around to the other side of the bar, his glass still in his hand. Claire moves her lips like she's counting, but she isn't. She's waiting for him to leave.

He puts on his coat and fiddles with the collar for what seems like a very long time. He stands directly in front of Claire on the other side of the bar. He says, "You need someone, Claire."

She looks up at him. "Who doesn't?" she says, feeling angry, invaded. It's as if in letting him touch her for a moment, he now thinks he knows something extra about her. Claire repeats, "Who the fuck doesn't need someone?"

"I don't know," he says. His voice is soft. In the dark gloom of the candlelight, Claire notices the lines in his forehead, the redness to his cheeks, and the way the part in his hair has started to zigzag. He stands there for a moment, as if he expects her to say something, to do something, but she doesn't. He puts his glass down and turns. As she watches him cross the empty dance floor toward the exit, she picks up his dirty glass and puts it in the sink.

When Claire is done cleaning and counting her money, she leaves The Red Room without saying good-bye to anyone. Out front, she hails a cab.

When she gets in, she says to the driver, "131 Salem Street, please."

They drive for a minute or two. It is quiet. The taxicab driver asks, "How was your night?"

Claire sighs. In his tone, she can tell he knows she was working, and not just out. Sometimes it feels like even when she's out of that place the bottle caps, the wet one-dollar bills, the rotten limes and lemons are all still hanging around her. She says to him, "Tonight was long."

"For me too," he says, "I've been driving since three this afternoon."

Claire doesn't say anything.

"What are you," he asks, "a cocktail waitress or a bartender?"

"Bartender."

They pass a park called the Fens. There is a man sitting Indian-style eating a sandwich under a tree. It is very cold outside. "Bunch of idiots out tonight," the cabdriver says.

"Yeah," Claire says distantly. "But aren't there always."

They drive farther down Boylston Street. Out the window Claire can see two men yelling at each other on the corner. One is holding a teddy bear, the other is trying to take it from him. As they pass by, the cabdriver says, "What the hell was that all about?"

"Idiots." Claire shakes her head. "More and more of them."

The cabdriver laughs a little, but stops as if he realizes that Claire is being serious. He clears his throat. "Sometimes working this job I can't believe the things people do." The plastic panel which divides the cab rolls down and his voice seems to get louder. "Like tonight this girl, pretty little thing, eighteen maybe, she was throwing up in the cab." Claire stiffens and looks at the dark stains on the seat. "Out the window, she threw up out the window, I swear." Claire slowly leans back. "I stopped the car so she and her boyfriend—she was with her boyfriend—so they could get out. And he slapped her because she wiped her face on his jacket. The fuckin' prick slapped her, can you imagine?"

Claire looks at the back of the driver's head. His hair is brown with bits of gray. "Sounds like a real asshole," she says. The cabdriver seems to expect her to say more; his head is turned in such a way that if he were not driving, he would probably be turned all the way around.

Claire doesn't want to talk. She looks out the window and doesn't say anything more. They are in Copley Square now. No one is around, not even a passing car, just empty shops and clumps of muddied snow on the curb.

Claire closes her eyes and then opens them. She is tired, so tired that when she gets home she's not even going to take her coat off. She'll go directly to bed. Claire lives alone—no one will be waiting up for her. When her boyfriend used to be there, he stayed up, waiting. When she got home, he used to make her a cup of tea in the same blue mug. He even used to undress her, slow and careful, like he was tending to a child too exhausted to move. But that was a long time ago. That was back when she used to work only two nights a week, back when she had school, back when she used to spend most nights with him reading side by side in bed. In the soft beige light of their bedroom, every-thing used to feel so still, just the flick of a page turning and then the slight heat of his arm, his shoulder, next to hers. But lying there with him, she had thought that somehow she was ignoring something: An entire world seemed to be rumbling around inside of her, a world that was mighty and bold, a world that did not include him. So one morning she actually told him, she asked him to leave; it was half past nine, the windows were open, they were sitting in wooden chairs.

All of this, what she once had, Claire thinks about often, particularly when she is at work or out with her friends, or when she is alone as she is now in the back of this cab.

They have stopped at a light and Claire can feel the driver looking at her in the rearview mirror. Claire looks up at him.

"What's your name?" he asks.

"Claire," she says. She doesn't ask him his name, but he doesn't seem to notice.

"I haven't eaten all day, Claire," he says, "and we're right near Chinatown." Chinatown is one of the few places where restaurants stay open after 3:00 AM. "Do you care if I stop to pick something up?"

Claire wants to tell him no. It's not like he can't drop her off and then pick something up. But she doesn't want to get into it; without even saying anything, she already imagines an argument. He'll say, it won't take that long, I promise. She'll say, no, I want to go home. He'll drive into Chinatown anyway. She'll get angry. They'll go back and forth, it'll get tiring. She'll have to get out and find another cab. It's cold outside, late.

The cabdriver adds, "It's on the way."

Claire rubs her eyes and says, "Whatever, I don't care."

"You could get something too," he says.

Claire doesn't answer him—she looks out the window. She wants him to stop talking to her and drive.

A few minutes later they are at the entrance of Chinatown. A prostitute in white boots is talking to someone in a car—Chinatown is right next to the seedy section of town, the Combat Zone. They drive past the parked car and pass a restaurant with an aquarium in the window. There are two giant cement dragons on each side of the street. Even though the dragons have their mouths open, they look sad to Claire, not angry.

They stop in front of a restaurant called the Golden Peacock. The cabdriver says, "We're here," as if he thinks Claire has been sleeping. He gets out of the car and opens her door so that she can get out. "Ready?" he says.

Claire looks at the door. Cold air is coming in and she pulls her coat tighter around her neck. She says, annoyed, "Ready for what?"

"Aren't you hungry?" he asks. He is bending down so that she can see him through the window. He is younger than she expected, forty maybe, and he is smiling.

Claire grabs her bag and gets out of the cab. She is going to walk and walk, she thinks, walk down this street, back past the dragons and hookers, to Tremont Street where she can try to hail another cab. But then she hears the cabdriver shut the door behind her and realizes he still believes that she is going to go in there with him and eat. She turns around facing him. "I never fuckin' said I would go in there with you." She points at him accusingly. "I never said that." Claire is screaming.

The cabdriver has his mouth slightly open and his eyes are going back and forth across her face like he can't believe it, how angry she is. Claire is breathing hard, the condensed air coming out of her mouth like smoke. "I'm not going to go in there with *you*," she says, and glares at him as if he is nothing, as if he is completely beneath her.

He looks down at the sidewalk and swallows. "I just thought—"

"I don't give a shit what you thought." She puts her hands up, exasperated. "I know what you thought. We'd go in there, talk a little talk, and then, and then, go to your place, maybe mine." She laughs bitterly. "Take a bubble bath!"

The cabdriver stands there. A car honks in the distance. The cabdriver opens his mouth like he is going to say something, but doesn't. Watching him, Claire notices how tall he is, and thin. He has his arms wrapped around himself and he keeps rubbing his elbow with one hand. He doesn't have gloves on and there is something about seeing his bare hand rubbing against the wool of his coat—so nervous—which makes her see what she has done. She has made a fool out of herself. She can still hear in her mind the way that she was screaming at him—the words "bubble bath." In the window of the restaurant, there are six Chinese men folding napkins at a giant round table. They are looking at her too.

She puts her hand over her mouth and then lets it rest on her chin. "I'm sorry," she says. Claire's so embarrassed that she can't look directly at him—she looks to the left of him at the wheel of the cab. "I'm such a mess," she says softly. "I'm such a fuckin' mess." A single tear falls down her cheek, but her face remains tight and wooden as if she is still angry. The driver is standing in front of Claire, shifting his weight. She can hear the sand crunching under his shoes. Finally he reaches behind him for the cab door. He fumbles a bit and opens the front door. "Claire, just get in, please. *I'm* sorry."

Claire wipes her face with her hand. She looks past him, past the cab, down the street. It is very dark—the streetlights are out. Slowly, Claire walks back to the cab and gets in. She waits for him to get in on his side so that he can drive her home. But he doesn't get in the car; he goes into the restaurant. Sitting there in the passenger seat, Claire doesn't know what to do. It seems to her at that moment that no matter what she decides, it will be, as always, the wrong decision. So Claire does nothing; she just sits there.

The meter in front of her is off. On the driver's side, attached to the visor, there is a picture of the cabdriver, his license. He is tan in the picture, or appears so. His name is Dean McCarthy.

The cabdriver comes back a few minutes later with a big brown bag. "It's already cold in here," he says. He puts the key in the ignition and turns the heat on. Claire's not sure what to say to him, so she doesn't say anything. She just looks at the windshield—there are flecks of dirt on the glass.

"I got you a Vegetarian's Delight." He hands her a white box that has a drawing of a palace on one side and the word "enjoy" on the other. She takes it hesitantly, and he says, "I wasn't sure if you ate meat, so . . . " He doesn't finish his sentence, instead he hands her a few napkins and a plastic fork.

"No," she says, not looking at him, "this is fine." She bends the wire over the box and opens the flaps. Steam rises against her fingertips. She looks at him out of the corner of her eye. He has his box open too and he's blowing on what appears to be a piece of chicken. She turns to him and says, "I'm sorry about—"

He puts up his hand. "You don't have to explain." He

touches the napkin on his leg. "I shouldn't have . . . I don't know why I . . . " He shrugs his shoulders. "I'm having a weird night, I guess." He shakes his head. "You just looked so unhappy, and I thought, I don't know what I thought." Claire looks down at her food and then back at him. He smiles and says, "But you looked like a calm sort of unhappy, one where I didn't think you might get upset and try to physically attack me or anything."

She laughs, not looking at him. "I didn't try to attack you."

He is still smiling. "You were on the verge, I could feel it."

"It's just my job," she says, shrugging her shoulders. "It's getting to me." She takes a bite of broccoli. It's still too hot. She puts her napkin to her mouth. "It's like you were saying, I guess, about the people. I'm surrounded by such . . . assholes that I don't know how to act around normal people." She rubs her forehead. "I need a new job, one where I don't have to talk to anyone."

"People are everywhere." He pauses and swallows. "Everyone deals with them."

"Yeah, but in jobs like ours we get the ass end of the spectrum."

He laughs and so does she. They are quiet for a minute or two, and then he says, "Do you want a wonton?" He puts the white container between them on the seat. "They're good."

Claire takes one. "I never used to yell at people before like I do now," she says. "I used to be normal. I mean, tonight I was mean to a woman who wanted a water, a water." She shakes her head.

"Nothing's wrong with you," he says. "You need a vacation maybe, something to happen to you, something fun."

"Right, Dean." Her voice is sarcastic.

He makes a face like he's trying to remember when he told her his name. She points at the license. "See," he says. He takes the license off the visor and hands it to her. "Don't I look tropical there? I went on vacation the week before. Yucatan Peninsula."

Dean starts telling her about his trip, about hammocks, flamingos, and reef diving. He talks about other places that she could go: La Selva, Tortola, Belize, the Turquoise Coast, Lahaina. He knows the airfare, the hotels, what to eat there, when's the best time to go.

"Anywhere with a beach would be nice. I like the beach," Claire says, and looks out the window. The Chinese men are still at the table in the restaurant—the folded napkins are stacked high in front of them.

Dean says abruptly, "I know what you mean, though, about work." He rubs his eyes. "It gets to me too. Tonight when that guy slapped that girl, the one that was throwing up, I didn't do anything. I didn't care about her, the fare, nothing, I just wanted out of the situation. I drove away. I left her there. . . . " He shakes his head.

"It's not your fault." Claire shrugs her shoulders. "You weren't the one slapping her."

"I should have done something. Wouldn't you have done something?"

"I would have kicked his ass," she says, and smiles.

He doesn't laugh.

Claire shifts in her seat. "You can't help everyone, you can't."

"Yeah, but some people you can." He's looking out the window, not at her.

"Right," she says, and stares at him until he looks at her. "Some people you can."

Claire picks up the box of Chinese food in front of her and folds the flaps shut.

Dean rolls up his napkin and puts it in his box. He reaches down for the bag.

"Oh, I forgot," he says. "They gave us tea to go." He takes a paper cup out of the bag and takes the lid off. Claire stares at the paper cup, thinking of the owner, of Lee. She almost says something, but doesn't. "They gave us extra cookies too," he says, with his hand still in the bag. "I think that's because they heard you screaming."

"Shut up," she says, and takes a sip of her tea.

He drinks his tea too. "It's not that hot," he says.

"That's OK."

He looks at his watch. "It's almost four o'clock. Tell me when you want to go."

Claire is leaning back in the seat with her head against the headrest. She says, "Let's wait until we finish our tea. Then we can go." He nods, and they are quiet again. There is only the sound of the heat coming out of the vents. Claire looks out the window at the men from the Golden Peacock. They are no longer folding napkins. They are smoking cigarettes and laughing.

Claire

A Train Trip

THE AMTRAK CONDUCTOR WAS WEARING little silver bells around his hat. He shouted, "How many times can I say it? How many times? If you have extra baggage, extra baggage includes scarves and hats and gloves as well as more obvious items like giant boxes, shopping bags," he pointed at a woman with a potted plant covered in red foil, "poinsettias." Then he pointed at another person behind me, "hideously large stuffed animals." I turned in my seat, there was a man holding a four-foot-tall giraffe with a red bow around its neck. "All of these things are baggage," the conductor continued, his voice growing louder. "Baggage is stored in the overhead compartment, folks. That means in the place above your head." He waited a moment, looked around the train, and then rolled his eyes.

I smiled at him. He was checking our tickets. "Springfield," he announced in this overly declarative voice, as if he thought he had to remind us where we were going.

My friend Mia nodded, and said, "Springfield, unfortunately." She was sitting across from me looking at the tips of her dark brown hair, examining split ends. She and I were sitting in those four passenger seats that are in the front of each train car. We liked those seats because we could sit across from one another and look out the window; as we talked to one another we gazed out at the stream of dilapidated houses, telephone wires, bicycles against fences, broken-down hoodless cars. It was calming somehow, soothing, to see all those things ease past us.

But today Mia was in a bad mood. She was annoyed that we had waited until Christmas Eve to take the train. It was my fault: I wanted to bartend an extra night in the nightclub I worked in, make an extra two hundred dollars.

I said to her, "You didn't have to wait for me. You could've went alone."

She said sharply, "I know that, Claire."

To make it worse, we were on the 4:15 train instead of the 2:00. We had missed the 2:00 by three minutes. In South Station we waited for the next train, sitting Indian-style on the muddied floor. For about a half hour, a woman in a white fur coat with a matching muff stood near us; she was using one of the pay phones. She kept shouting, "I know you don't give a fuck, I know that!" When she finally hung the phone up, she left the receiver dangling dramatically on its silver cord.

I said to Mia, "Do you think that woman was really talking to her imaginary boyfriend?"

Mia looked away from me. She said dryly, "I don't actually want to talk to you. I just want to blame you." She was joking, of course; that was her way of being funny, to act mean. That's how she often was, a little bit bitter—it covered up the sensitivity, the softness, of who she was.

On the train, Mia said to me, "You know that someone's going to sit next to us. Some freakazoid, no doubt." She shook her head, disgruntled.

I acted like I didn't hear her. Behind us, all around us, there was the loud rustle of paper bags being crushed, of stretched Saran Wrap, of things being opened, then closed, then opened again. The train itself smelled sweet, like sugar-coated cookies and apple pies and pumpkin muffins and opened jars of jelly.

Mia began powdering her face, staring at her reflection in the train window. She was making her mirror face, which involved wide-open eyes and pouty lips. I said, "Whoever sits with us could be the man of your dreams, you know. You'll give him your number, you'll fall in love. Move to Egypt."

"On this train?" She rolled her eyes. "I'd rather light myself on fire."

I smiled. "Well, maybe that would be the best thing for you."

The first "freakazoid" to sit with us was Gwen. She got on at Back Bay station and Mia immediately recognized her. Gwen was from Springfield too; when she saw Mia, she said, "Oh what a small world!" But she said it in this sarcastic way, as though she did not think it was a small world, but instead a very large, ridiculous one. That made me like her.

Mia said to me, "Gwen used to live on Brookside." That was a street which was in Mia's neighborhood, in the neighborhood my mother now lived in.

I said, "Oh," and nodded at her. Gwen was tall, very tall, taller than Mia or me. She had long straight blonde hair, bony wrists, curves. She stood above us, putting her things in the overhead compartment. The Amtrak conductor with the bells on his hat came over and smiled at her. He stood very close and said, "Thanks."

When Gwen sat down, she kept fixing her collar. She had on a long, gray sweater that tied at the waist, a knee-length skirt, and black boots that had intricate stitching along the sides. She looked like something out of a magazine. If I had known her when I was younger, I probably would not have liked her. Her beauty was too much. It went beyond the type of prettiness Mia and I and other girls possessed; it went into a realm in which her face seemed precise: the nose, the eyes, the jaw—like a drawing. She was the type of a girl that when you were young, you might look at and feel sorry for yourself, feel eternally cheated: Why don't I look like that? Why?

Gwen said to Mia, "How's Tanya? I heard she got married."

I looked at Mia. "Tanya got married?" Tanya was a girl from our hometown—she was younger than me. I said, "She's like twelve!"

Mia said matter-of-factly, "She's twenty and I told you that she got married."

I didn't remember anything of the sort. "I told you," she said again, and then looked at Gwen, smiling. "She looked beautiful at the wedding."

"Oh, you went?" Gwen asked.

Mia nodded. "Yeah."

Gwen looked down at her hands in her lap. She apparently wasn't invited, and it appeared to bother her; Mia didn't seem to notice. She kept talking about the wedding—the ivory lace, the butter-cream cake, baby's breath mixed with pink tulips. I looked out the window—I didn't know Tanya that well and weddings didn't interest me much.

Mia was telling Gwen about Tanya's husband. "He's so nice. And he's funny." She paused. "He has a glass eye, though."

I made a face, and then Gwen said, "Gross."

"No." Mia shook her head and smiled. "She likes it. She says at night he takes it out and wears this mask thing and she pretends he's Zorro." Mia started laughing. "Tanya's married to Zorro."

Still gazing out the window, I said, "I think I prefer men with two eyes."

Mia lightly kicked my foot. She said, "I think you would be better off with a man who didn't have any eyes."

At the Framingham stop, a swarm of people got on the train. They bumbled their way through the narrow aisle, carrying heavy shopping bags, ones that crackled as they bumped seated people in the face. "Hey, watch yourself, OK?!" this man screamed somewhere behind me. He had been hit, no doubt.

The person who had hit him said, "Calm down, guy. Just calm down." It was the loud bellowing voice that I so recognized. The voice of a drunk.

The drunk said, "I'm looking for a seat." He paused or possibly hiccuped and then shouted, "I'm going to Meriden. Are there any fellow Meridians around?" He was moving down the aisle, toward us. The seat next to me was, of course, empty. "Anyone who will let me sit on their lap?" he asked. "I weigh very little." Then he lowered his voice, as if he were talking to someone in particular. "I weigh the same as that stuffed orange horse up there."

Someone shouted, "That is a giraffe!"

"It's still orange," the drunk said, slurring a little. He was moving steadily forward toward us. I didn't look at Mia, I didn't look at Gwen. I just waited. Someone sneezed, another person coughed, then he appeared. He had his hand on the back of the seat's headrest. His face was fortyish, unshaven, a sweaty sheen across his cheeks. He was smiling—whether it was at the three of us or the brown-striped seat, I could not tell. He had on a red ski jacket and army pants; the pants were brown-and-beige, Desert Storm–like. He also had on a white angora hat, a woman's hat, something he might have found on the floor of the train station. He looked at us and said, "Before I sit down, I have to know," he put his hand on his forehead, "are you three twins?"

The drunk's name was Sheldon, or at least that's what he told us. It took him a good ten minutes to sit down. He had a lot of struggling to do with his large puff of a jacket—it had a sticky zipper and a dizzying number of snaps.

Once he sat down, a bit of tension erupted. There wasn't much room between the seats that faced one another and Sheldon ended up brushing his legs up against Gwen's.

She looked dead in his eyes and said, "Don't touch me."

Mia looked sideways at Gwen as if she thought she was being unnecessarily rude, but I didn't think so. I had already noticed something about Gwen, about Gwen and men: Earlier, when the conductor came over to take her ticket, I saw his deep, meaningful smile; I heard the way he said the word, Springfield, it became longer, the *r* rolled; and when he gave her her ticket stub, he didn't put it in her extended open-palmed hand; instead, he placed the piece of paper on her lap, on her left leg. She didn't say anything to him—she was in the middle of talking to us—but she did look down at the stub, at his hand, irritated. And it seemed to me from that one gesture that Gwen was probably the type of girl that men were always trying to trick, trying to rub up against, and for that reason I didn't blame her for being a little wary, a little hostile.

Sheldon, however, ended up handling the situation fine. He moved his legs so far away from Gwen that they were practically in the aisle. "I'm sorry," he said. "Very sorry. I didn't mean . . . "

Gwen shook her head. "It's OK, it's fine."

Afterward, there was lingering awkwardness, but then Sheldon asked abruptly, loudly, "So where are you *chicas* coming from?"

"Boston," I said, and he nodded his head for longer than he needed to. He said, "The big city." From his breath, I knew he was drunk off of whiskey. It was probably bourbon—he had the bourbon drinker look: big forehead, thick brown eyebrows, mustache. He said, "Do you girls go to school there?"

Mia and Gwen nodded. I didn't. He looked at me, expectantly, and I said, "I'm a bartender."

"Oh my dear," he said gravely, "I'm so sorry to hear that."

I laughed. I liked that.

"Where do you work?" Gwen asked, leaning forward.

"The Red Room."

Both Gwen and Mia frowned, as if the very name brought up some unpleasant picture in their minds. Perhaps they were envisioning the cheap ceramic lawn-ornament statue of Venus de Milo that was out front of the club, blinking red Christmas lights wrapped around her neck.

I said defensively, "I'm quitting The Red Room. I'm moving to New York."

Mia added, "To be a writer." She liked telling people that; she was proud.

But I didn't like telling anyone—it brought out a certain mean streak in people. They'd snicker or snort. They'd say, "Yeah, but what are you *really* going to do?"

Gwen and Sheldon didn't say anything, though. Which made me more uncomfortable, self-conscious. I looked at Sheldon. "And what do you do?"

He smacked his lips. He said, "I . . . am . . . an observer, a feeler, a man with no boundaries. I assemble rockets."

I was paranoid that he was making fun of me. I said, a little irritated, "Oh yeah?"

Mia smiled at me. "What kind of rockets?" she asked him.

He said, "I actually specialize in the M-6-12-L-O-V-E rocket." He waited a moment, and then burst out laughing.

* * *

Shortly afterward the train conductor came over to get Sheldon's ticket. He did not make eye contact with Sheldon—he simply broke off the ticket and said, "Meriden."

Sheldon said to me, "This guy looks like the one from *Fantasy Island*, doesn't he?" There was a faint resemblance. Sheldon asked, "Are you Mr. Rourke?"

The conductor did not smile. He said, "Yes, I am Mr. Rourke, your host." He adjusted one of the bells on his Amtrak hat. "And if you get too disruptive, my friend, you will be kicked off the island."

Two of the passengers sitting on the other side of the aisle, a white-haired couple who were wearing the same candy-cane sweatshirts, nodded at one another. They had been glancing nervously at Sheldon ever since he sat down.

Sheldon caught their gaze and said to them, "But will I be able to get my fantasy first? That's what I want to know."

Sheldon kept going into the bathroom every fifteen minutes or so. Each time he got up, he said, "I am off to the laboratory." He was of course drinking in there. Whether he had a pint stashed in the waistband of his pants or in some silver cubbyhole in the rest room, I do not know.

On his way back from his third trip, he found a catalog on the floor. It was one of those catalogs that has all those ridiculous Christmas gifts that no one wants. He picked out a gift for each of us: for Gwen, a gold duck that had a twig in its mouth; for Mia, a pen which was shaped like a long-faced Indian; and for me a clock shaped like an alligator's head.

Sheldon also picked out a jewelry box from the catalog and showed it to us. "Do you guys like this?" It wasn't half bad; it was heart-shaped and there was a black satiny material inside.

Mia said, "I don't like jewelry boxes."

Gwen said, "Oh, I do."

Sheldon was no longer holding the picture up. He was look-ing between me and Mia, out the window. It had gotten dark out, and if you weren't close enough there wasn't anything to see, just your own train-lit reflection. "I'd like to get something for my daughter," he said.

"Will she be waiting for you at the train station in Meriden?" Gwen asked.

"No," he said. "She won't be coming. She can't." The cat-alog was back in front of his face. Shortly afterward he went into the laboratory.

Right before we reached the Worcester stop, Mia and I decided to get something in the café car. I wanted a bottled water, Mia wanted a Pepsi, Sheldon wanted honey-roasted peanuts. We told Sheldon to stay in his seat—he wasn't having such a smooth time walking. Besides, his drunkenness had turned into some-thing else: He was no longer funny. He had veered into a dark-er place, one where he was very quiet and sad-eyed.

We asked Gwen if she wanted to come with us to the café; she said, "No," shrugging her shoulders. Her hostility toward Sheldon, her distrust, had apparently faded—she didn't seem to mind being alone with him. We went without her.

When Mia and I came back from the café car, we were able to locate our seat by the rising sound of Sheldon's voice. He was talking about Vietnam.

As the sliding spaceship doors of our train car opened, I heard him saying to Gwen, "I was eighteen, I was a fucking moron. I didn't know how to spell 'bird.'" We stood in front of our seat, waiting for one of them to get up so we could sit. Neither one of them acknowledged our presence. Sheldon screamed loudly, "B-i-r-d, bird, I did not know how to spell bird! I saw a letter that I wrote to my mother and I spelled it with an e. B-e-r-d." He laughed in this exasperated, bitter way.

"I had a fucking moon," he said, pointing to his shoulder. "I had one of those cheap, homemade tattoos of a moon on my shoulder when I left." He leaned forward toward Gwen. Her eyes were glassy and she was staring right at him. He said, "That moon's gone, honey." He shook his head. "I'm not going to go into how it got burned off, but just know this: No, it doesn't change or go away or get different. Time comes in and shuffles shit around, but where you've been is all over you. It's here," he pointed to his eye. "It's here," he pointed at the palm of his hand. "And it rumbles around, silent," he pointed at his chest, settled his finger on one of the brown buttons of his shirt, "right here."

Gwen nodded. Her eyes were soft and glassy, moving up and down his face. He seemed to have touched something, to have earned something. His knees were against hers.

When we arrived in Worcester, the candy-cane couple moved out of their seats. I heard the woman say, "There's gotta be some other ones up there." She looked at Sheldon. "There's gotta be."

There was a layover of about fifteen minutes, and a number of people were moving on and off the train. A young woman, about Mia's age, twenty-five, and a little girl came and sat in the candy-cane couple's seats. The little girl had on a white dress, with pleats—it was stained across the front from something she had apparently just eaten. She was probably about five years old and her patent leather shoes were very small—I kept staring at them. I noticed the buckle to the strap of one shoe was missing its peg—every once in a while the little girl would pull on the strap absently.

"Mommy," the little girl said, "look, it's Barbie." She was pointing at Gwen.

Gwen said, "Hi," in that big bubble way that people talk to children.

The girl's mother was brushing a Barbie's hair with a small pink brush that was no bigger than a pinkie. She kept brushing the hair and then, noticing that her daughter was still pointing and staring at Gwen, she said, "Put your arm down, don't be an idiot."

Sheldon turned in his seat. He had been looking at the gift catalog again, but now he noticed the little girl and her mother. He said, "Don't talk to her like that."

The mother froze for a moment and stared at him. She had orangy, dyed hair pulled back in a tight ponytail, and her eyes, which were now angry and wet, were outlined with smudged eyeliner. She said to Sheldon, "Excuse me? Who the hell are *you*?"

"I am Sheldon McCrory," he said, adjusting his angora hat, "and I don't like the way you're talking." He paused. "It's fucked-up to talk to your little girl like that."

I could hear the people behind us rustling. An older woman's voice said, "Oh, my God."

"Oh yeah?" the mother said. "Why don't you have another drink, Sheldon?"

He glared at her. He screamed, "You don't even know what you are, do you?!"

The little girl's mother was still holding the pink Barbie brush between her index finger and thumb. It loosened, fell onto her lap.

Sheldon licked his lips and then screamed as loud as he could, "YOU ARE A PIECE OF SHIT, LADY! A PIECE OF SHIT!"

It took about ten minutes before the police came onto the train to arrest Sheldon. We had not left Worcester yet, the train was quiet, and in those few minutes that we all sat there, stiff and nervous, we knew with a certainty that the police were coming—it was as if we could hear their buzzing walkie-talkies distantly approaching.

Sheldon did not say anything to us before they arrested him—his face was still, expressionless, as though he was suddenly tired. Once the police came they handcuffed him, which seemed unnecessary in his catatonic state. Then they pushed him down the aisle to the exit. The police officer who walked behind him held his big red jacket in one hand, the sleeves dragging on the floor.

Once the train left Worcester, the conductor, Mr. Rourke, asked us if we were OK. Mia and I said yes, Gwen didn't answer. The conductor gave us each a voucher for ten dollars off our next trip. When he handed one of the vouchers to the little girl's mother, she was outraged. "That guy tries to attack me and you give me a ten-dollar voucher. Bullshit!" she screamed, "This is bullshit!"

The conductor sighed; one of the silver bells on his hat had fallen, it hung at the back of his neck. He said, "If you would like to discuss this, let's go to the front. This particular car full of passengers has heard enough screaming for the night. Don't you think?"

They argued a little bit more, and then the mother ended up following the conductor to another car. The little girl stared after her mother, and then said to Gwen, "That guy you were with was bad."

"He didn't mean it," Mia said, leaning in. "He was just drunk."

The little girl got out of her seat and sat next to me where Sheldon had been. She played with the strap of her shoe, pulling it, then letting it go, then pulling it again. She didn't appear all that shaken by what had just happened: the police, the handcuffs, the drunkenness. Even when Sheldon was yelling at her mother, she had not flinched. She just stared at him, brown eyes wide open—she didn't cry or crawl into her mother's lap the way other children might. She was motionless, as if she knew from experience that that was the best way to be—it incited less anger.

She told us her name, Lina. Then she said, "I'm going to Springfield for Christmas. To visit my first father." The three of us just looked at one another and then at the strap of her shoe, which she was still pulling on. "He's gonna take me to Seussland," she said.

Lina's father, from what she told us, had said that he was going to take her to some sort of amusement park called Seussland, where she could ride twirling red-and-white-striped hats and fire water guns at miserable, present-stealing Grinches. There was of course no real amusement park like that, just a house, small and brown, with a sign in front of it that said Dr. Suess had once lived there—there were no Cat in the Hats, no green eggs and ham.

After telling us all about Seussland, Lina got quiet for a moment or two. Then she said to Gwen, "Were you always pretty? Or did you get pretty?" She pointed at her Barbie that was on the seat where she had been sitting. "You're like her."

Gwen smiled faintly, and then reached down at her feet and pulled a book out of her bag. Inside of the book there was a postcard of a flamenco dancer in a fuchsia dress. Gwen showed Lina the postcard. She said, "See how pretty she is. She's just like you." Lina had the same olive complexion, the brown downcast eyes, the curly black hair. She took the picture in her small hands, stared at it. Then she said, wrinkling her nose, "I don't think she's pretty." She shook her head. "No."

At 6:30 we arrived in Springfield. Inside of the train station on the wall there were two cardboard posters of *The Grinch Who Stole Christmas.* In one he was holding a swollen bag of stolen toys over his shoulder; there was an X-ray picture of his heart: It was black and shrunken. A few feet away, in the other poster, the Grinch held an empty maroon bag, children were holding toys all around him—his heart was bright red, glittery.

Gwen's father was standing in front of the good-hearted poster. He was tall, in a wool coat, a golfer's cap low on his fore-head. When he saw Gwen, he said, "Hey, critter."

Quickly, politely, Gwen said good-bye to Mia and me and then went over to her father. They hugged. Her father's eyes were squeezed shut, his two hands flat on her back. Mia and I watched from a few feet away, people bumping all around us. "Santa Baby" was playing.

Mia and I walked downstairs to where my mother would be waiting for us—Mia's mother and my mother took turns picking us up. As we walked down the steps, I saw a pink angora hat on the floor and I thought of Sheldon. I thought of him spending Christmas Eve in a jail cell, the angora hat still high on his fore-head, the peanuts I bought him in his pants pocket.

At the foot of the long staircase, Lina was with her mother. Her mother was on a pay phone, and Lina was leaning against the yellow cinder-block wall. We walked past them and stopped in front of two glass doors. My mother's blue car wasn't there yet.

We looked over in the direction of Lina. Her mother's back was to us and Lina was eating a cookie shaped like a Christmas tree. Some of the green sugar was on her face. She waved at us and we waved back. I heard her mother say into the phone, "Well, how long is it going to take you?" She paused. "What do you mean you don't know?"

I pictured the two of them being there for hours, Lina falling asleep on the trash-littered floor.

Mia said, following my gaze, "So are you going to write a story about our train ride?"

"No." I shook my head. "I only write humor." I was lying, of course. But standing there among the silver garlands and strung popcorn which hung pathetically in loops above the exit, I didn't want to talk about Lina or Sheldon. Or think about them. But I knew I would. Much later, driving along in my mother's car, listening to my mother's Christmas chatter, I'd sit there nodding my head, and beneath everything that was happening, everything I saw outside—the snow-capped cars, the houses wrapped in lights, blinking reindeers on lawns—I'd think about Sheldon and Lina, dwell on them, as if they were long-lost friends of mine.

The emotion of talking to them, of sitting so close to them, would only leave me days later, and at that point, their faces, their voices, would become all blurred up, a dream; and somehow, standing in that train station, knowing that this would happen made me angry, angry with myself for not being to able get permanently upset about anything that did not directly involve me and also irrationally angry with them, Lina and Sheldon—didn't they know what they did to people? Didn't they see?

Thinking all of this, I stared at the glass doors in front of me. I was not looking at cars in the street, but at Mia, who was standing next to me; her reflection was like a picture—her face illuminated by the train station's fluorescent lighting and the still darkness outside. After a long pause, she said to me, "You're not going to write humor."

"Yes, I am," I said, irritated.

Behind us, Lina was jumping hopscotch fashion from one square of tile to the next. I could hear her shoes.

I looked at Mia, who was looking at Lina in the reflection of the glass: her white tights and pink jacket. I said, with my arms folded, "I'm going to be funny."

Mia shrugged her shoulders, her face expressionless and still. She said softly, "Well, if you can, please do."

Claire

WHAT IF
DAVID LETTERMAN'S
OBSESSED WITH ME?*

I FIRST MET HIM IN AUGUST. It was hot, I was cranky. Everything in New York smelled bad; it was like I was trapped in a giant monkey house. On my way to work, I went into this deli on Fifty-fourth and Broadway to get a bottled water. I was already late; it was past six. When I got to the register, I couldn't find my money. I can never find my money. So I had to empty everything in my purse on the counter, including my uniform, which was this little black slip dress. It was rolled up in a ball; the spaghetti straps dangled off the side of the counter. The cashier looked at it strangely, as if it was a piece of underwear or some sort of nightie. When I found my money (it was in my pocket), I left in a hurry.

*This is a work of Claire's imagination. It is not intended to upset or disturb anyone—including Claire's mother. It is simply a story.

On the corner, I was ready to cross, when a man came out and said, "Excuse me, Miss, you forgot this." He had my dress in both of his hands like he was presenting me with long-stemmed flowers. He was apparently the man behind me in line. At first he was just a guy with a sweaty face and weird patchy hair, but then I realized he was David Letterman.

"What exactly . . . what exactly . . . is this little thing?" he asked, as he handed the dress to me.

I just stared at him. He had on khaki shorts, a T-shirt, and these sneakers that made his feet look enormously large. I said to him, "It's a dress."

"Doesn't look like a dress."

"It's my uniform."

He raised his eyebrows. "And what do you do? If you don't mind me, don't mind me asking?"

I said, "I work in a bar. I make drinks."

He smiled. "I knew it was you. You work at The Whiskey Den, don't you?"

That was the name of the bar I worked in—I didn't know what to say. We were still on the corner. There were people passing us on all sides. A man came by with a pretzel cart; I had to move out of his way.

"Yuh," he said. "I saw you in the window over there at The Whiskey Den."

There were these big windows where I worked which were meant for people inside to look out at Central Park, but what really happened was that people on the street looked in and made finger gestures or they mouthed dirty words.

David Letterman kept looking at me and smiling. I was beginning to realize that our meeting was not necessarily by chance. For a brief moment I thought: What if David Letterman's obsessed with me?

"Would you mind if I walked you to work?" he asked.

Now . . . normally I am not nice to people on the street. I don't make conversation or tell anyone the time. But it was unacceptable, it seemed, to be mean to David Letterman. So I said, "Yeah, OK," and we walked together. Up Broadway and then down Fifty-ninth. There were people, there were cars. We walked around them.

Throughout our silent, awkward walk, I was thinking: I am walking with David Letterman. I am in New York. I have lived here for a year and now I am walking with David Letterman. Which was OK because before that I was thinking: I have lived here for a year, I am almost done with my MFA, and still I suck—I can't get published. I had just opened my mailbox and found four rejected manuscripts. Four of them. One was from, of all places, the *Brown Dog Review*. What a dumb name. They even had this dumb drawing of a dog—it was a brown beagle or something—on the corner of the rejection slip. For the rest of the day, I couldn't even look at a brown dog on the street without feeling fitful and angry.

But now I was with David Letterman and everything I wanted suddenly seemed possible. So I admit for the record that I was nice to him, I smiled and stuff. I even entertained the idea of us going out for dinner together—it would be fun, exciting, public.

When we got to my work, he said, "I would, uhh . . . come in for a . . . drink, but I don't have time." He seemed nervous. His forehead was shiny and he kept rocking back and forth on his heels. I looked away from him at the park, which was right in front of us. People were jogging and it smelled like horse.

"I'll see you later," he said.

I tried to say, "OK," but it didn't come out right. I said, "Oh."

The following day he appeared in my bedroom window a little before midnight. He was on this giant crane and there was a cameraman with him. On his show, David Letterman was doing this thing where he showed up at people's apartments to see if they would let him in. Somehow he got my address. When we were walking, I did tell him my name, but I didn't tell him where I lived—and my number was unlisted. He must have used detectives.

When I first saw him in the window, I screamed. My Korean roommate, Won-Jeong, heard me and came into the room. She pointed at David Letterman and shouted, "Who he?!"

I said, "This guy I met yesterday. He's famous." I swallowed. "It's David Letterman."

He said, "Hey kids, I'm comin' in." Slowly he crawled through the window, which was already open because we didn't have air conditioning. Won-Jeong and I watched from a distance, as if he was a mouse coming out of a hole in the wall. When he finally got inside, Won-Jeong recognized him. She covered her mouth and kept saying over and over, "Of course, of course."

David Letterman sat on my bed—he was wearing jeans and a baseball hat. I became nervous—as I often do when new and unexpected people show up in my bedroom. My room was a mess: books everywhere, drawers open. The Peruvians next door were playing a loud, unhappy song.

Paul Shaffer came through the window next after the cameraman. He had these dark glasses on. He said to David Letterman, "This is the girl you like?" He had a disgusted expression on his face. I knew I didn't look that good. I had no makeup on, my hair was in a ponytail, and I was wearing boxer shorts. Dave said, "Look at her legs, look at her legs, she's got ballerina legs."

Paul was unimpressed.

Won-Jeong said, "I make dumplings in kitchen. Do you want some?"

We all went into the kitchen. Paul Shaffer stood in front of the sink full of dishes, eating with chopsticks. He had on a red tight shirt, and he was really sweating. The cameraman was eating too, and David Letterman said to him, pointing at me, "This is my girlfriend." I didn't know what he meant by girlfriend— some people use the term loosely. I let it go.

When he left, I walked him back to the window. He sat there on the sill for a moment making weird awkward faces. I was afraid he was going to try something funny. But he didn't—he just shook my hand. There was some twinkling business going on in his eyes, but I ignored it.

David Letterman was my friend, I decided, my new New York friend.

For the next two weeks, he was always bumping into me on the street by chance. We went for long silent walks. Then September came and he began appearing at Grand Central on the train I took to school. He always had a picnic basket. Sometimes there was food in it, sometimes there was just two cans of Coke. We didn't talk; we looked out the window together. One time, he said, "Riding this train must really remind you of back home." For a moment I thought, "Oh my God, he's been following me all of my life." But then I realized he was probably just making awkward conversation.

It became hard to concentrate at school. During my writing workshops, I felt like David Letterman was watching me somehow, peeping through the window, or worse, closer: somewhere under the classroom's big round table. Still I tried to participate. About this one story I said to the class, "I feel as though . . . I feel like . . . the scene where the main character falls in the ditch and finds the treasure chest . . . it didn't really . . . belong there. To me." No one said anything and I wondered if I had been too harsh.

The teacher looked at me crossly. "We finished discussing the ditch story an hour ago."

Then the ditch-story writer shouted from across the table, "I don't care what you think anyway!" He was gripping his water bottle. "All you ever write about is your goddamn mother."

I looked away from him angrily. That was a bold-faced lie.

The next day I was talking to my mother on the phone—she called me, OK, I didn't call her. Anyway, I tried to tell her about "this guy" who wouldn't stop following me around. I thought she could help. My mother was retired, bored, and single. Ever since I moved to New York she was always calling me, telling me what I needed: more locks on the door, echinacea, a giant butcher knife. She was good like that. This time she said, "A restraining order. Get a restraining order against this man."

"I can't do that," I said.

"Yes, you can, it's easy. All you do is wait in a line, fill out some papers, and it's done. They always believe you over him, always."

"But Mom, he's not a regular guy." I paused—I really didn't want to tell her. "It's David Letterman."

"The one with the show," she said. I could tell that wherever she was she had suddenly sat up straight, and like a cartoon there were money signs floating all around her head. "I like David Letterman," she said. "He's dashing."

"He is not," I said sharply.

"Yes, he is. You will like him," she commanded.

I knew what she was up to—she was picturing a house in Martha's Vineyard. She had been looking through a real estate catalog of Vineyard houses last time I saw her. She was obsessed, reading aloud certain amenities each one had: steep-pitched roof, decorative gable shingles, raised turret, spindlework, a veranda. It was all she ever dreamed of—she couldn't contain her excitement. "Now you actually have a reason for being in New York. To meet David Letterman, the man of your dreams."

"I came here to be a writer."

"Save it for somebody else." She made this awful noise into the phone. "All you want to do is write horrible horrible stories about me that aren't even true. Makes no sense." There was a pause after that. She was in the Vineyard again, moving through her new home: through the triple French doors into the parlor, the Palladian windows all around her, the distant sound of waves crashing. She said, almost breathlessly, "I could come and visit. I could help you with him."

No," I said, "you can't come. I have a lot of work—I really have to write."

She sighed. "You just remember, this is an opportunity of a lifetime. Don't screw it up." Then she added, right before she hung up, "And stay away from that other one, that ridiculous Blockbuster Boy."

Blockbuster Boy was this guy I had a crush on. He lived three blocks away from me on Forty-seventh. He worked at the Blockbuster Video on Ninth and he made movies of his own, which were up for rent. I saw one and liked it. There was a certain use of ants as imagery that I didn't understand, but the actual story was about a guy freaking out in his apartment—it was fabulous.

I thought about telling David Letterman about Blockbuster Boy, using him as an excuse, lying and saying he was my boyfriend—I wanted to make it clear to Dave that he couldn't actually touch me. But I was afraid of how he might react. It had been two months since I first met him, and he was becoming increasingly territorial. He showed up at my work one night and kept trying to pull the velvet curtains over the windows. He said, "No fiancé of mine is going to be seen in the window dressed like that."

I myself was getting a little tired of the uniform. It was October now and I was starting to get cold. Plus, the slits on the sides of the dress were so high that sometimes when I dug in the cooler for a beer, I felt like I was showing a bit more than leg.

The girl I worked with behind the bar was named Maria. She had this thick Brooklyn accent. She said, "Who's that fuckin' guy over there? Why's he messin' with the curtains?"

I put my hand on my forehead. "He's David Letterman." She looked at me and then at him. He was arguing with the busboy, who kept pulling the curtains back. She said, "That ain't him. He's fuckin' lyin'."

The customer we called Snake was at the bar. He said to Maria, "Looks like him to me."

"What are you guys, stupid?" she said. "Everybody looks like somebody."

Snake smiled. We called him Snake because his bottom teeth, the front four, were missing—it looked like he only had fangs. He was constantly moving his tongue back and forth as if he were checking to make sure those teeth were really gone. He also couldn't stop smiling at Maria. He loved her.

Maria looked at me with her hands on her hips. "You might be gettin' your master's, but I'll tell ya what I got, I got a Ph.D., a Ph.D. in drunk fuckin' bastards and," she pointed at David Letterman, "he's a drunk bastard." She looked around the dark, candlelit room. "All of them are."

David Letterman came up to the bar. "Who *are* these Mexican kids? You're not allowed, not allowed, to pull the curtains? What if someone was vomiting right outside the window—then you could pull the curtain, then you could." He was shouting.

Snake said to him, "I like your show."

Dave ignored Snake and took his glasses off. "I don't think you should work here anymore. It's not the place for you." He looked over at Snake, who was moving his tongue back and forth between his fangs. "Gross, OK."

I started to laugh. Then Paul Shaffer walked in. He had this crazy-looking spangle shirt on, and he started yelling at David Letterman. He said he was supposed to be on the set.

David Letterman ignored him. He said to me, "Don't your feet hurt standing there like that. Your little toes must be killing you."

I said, "I'm fine."

Paul was still standing there being ignored. His shirt flashing candlelight everywhere. David Letterman looked at him and snapped his fingers. "Hey, I got an idea. You can work for us."

Paul stared back at him, and then squeezed his eyes shut as though he had a headache. Then he smacked his hand on the bar. He said, "OK, just do it. Please. We'll find you something to do, I don't know what." He shrugged his shoulders. "Do you have any skills?"

I shook my head. "No, not really."

"That's OK. We'll find you something." He leaned in closer so that Dave couldn't hear him. "He's not at work when he's supposed to, he's following you around, he's lingering outside windows, he's on trains." He shook his head. "Really, man, you're ruining the show."

In the distance, I heard Maria say again to someone else, "I got a Ph.D. in drunk fuckin' bastards, that's what I got."

I myself did not want a Ph.D.—it seemed unnecessary.

Paul said, "We'll pay you a lot."

Dave was just sitting there, staring at me dreamily.

"All right," I said hesitantly, "I'll work for the David Letterman show."

My job was to hold the cards that Dave read from—you know the ones that you see when the camera flashes to the studio audience. He doesn't actually say all those things off the top of his head—somebody writes them. But anyway, it seemed like an all right job at first. The studio was closer to my house than The Whiskey Den, they paid me more, and I worked less hours, two-hour shifts instead of ten-hour ones. Less time at work meant more time that I could write. By the time I graduated, I'd have the best short story in the world. I could get published! I'd get an agent, an advance. I wouldn't have to work anymore, I would just shop all day at Century 21—so many black shoes! I'd get a bigger apartment, matching bath towels, a maid. Everything would be great and happy.

But if you remember correctly, David Letterman didn't want me to work at The Whiskey Den because of the dumb dress. Well, guess what? I had to wear a dress when I held the cue cards for him; even when they're obsessed with you, they lie. For each episode, the dress I wore had to match the color of the Magic Marker they used to write the words on the card. The dresses weren't slutty or anything but they were just . . . bad. Most of them had sequins, they were backless, they were tight.

Before and after the show we had this Special Room that we hung out in: me, Dave, and, of course, Paul. Paul wouldn't leave us alone because he thought I was going to do something horrible to Dave. I heard him once when I was on the other side of the room, saying quietly, "Why do you even like her? I mean, really? Why? I think she's sort of . . . sort of . . . I don't know, flat-chested."

Dave pushed him off the couch with one shove, and said, "She is everything I've ever wanted. And you can get out of here if you don't like it."

Paul pushed himself up onto a neighboring chair. He said, not looking at David Letterman, "Fine. She's not flat-chested. She's great, just great."

If it wasn't for Paul, I would've actually liked the Special

Room—it was sort of fabulous. It was huge, bigger than my entire apartment. The walls were beige, everything was beige, it felt calm. There were two couches, some chairs, a stereo, and a giant, glistening bar. Paul designated himself Mr. Music-man and he wouldn't let me near the stereo. He was always playing Jefferson Starship. In order to get him back, I made Dave make me the official bar person, and so Paul wasn't allowed to make his own drinks. I had to make them. When he asked for a drink, I would make him wait, or sometimes I wouldn't make him a drink at all. He always wanted Cosmos—he never said the full word Cosmopolitan, he thought he was too cool. Whenever I made him one, he complained that it wasn't pink enough. I don't understand how he could even tell, though, seeing that he never stopped wearing those ridiculous darkened glasses of his.

We worked together like this for weeks. Needless to say, me and Paul were always fighting and Dave just sat there pulling anxiously at his tie. Sometimes Dave got drunk and unbuttoned his shirt and sat there with his legs wide open, leaning back into the couch. Paul would sit there in front of the stereo, his little chicken head twittering. He'd say, "I'm in the room, Dave. Come on now, don't get weird." Often I stood behind the bar for safety purposes. Dave would shout out at me from the couch. He called me his wife. He said I was Mrs. David Letterman. I didn't want that, I didn't want that at all.

Everything was going wrong.

My mother was talking about her house in Martha's Vineyard all the time. She wanted to buy a plot of land now and design the house herself. "I'm thinking a 12-foot octagon-shaped ceiling and a marble staircase," she kept saying.

Blockbuster Boy didn't work on Ninth anymore either. I went looking for him in that big blue-and-yellow room and this guy, this salesclerk, told me he had gotten a promotion. He was now corporate director of all the Blockbusters in the greater

Manhattan area. The salesclerk told me that he could help me, though, if I would just let him. I did not respond. We were standing in the "action adventure" section and the fluorescent lights were blaringly bright. Suddenly, without warning, the guy started trying to kiss me—this salesclerk was pushy and insistent. His name tag said: David. Slowly but surely, I was coming to realize that there was something intrinsically wrong with the people in New York named David.

I made it out of that video store, though, and then I ran blindly down Ninth.

School was equally as nightmarish. The people in workshop said that I described too much and had no sense of time. I lacked structure. My teacher said, "What concerns me is the main characters' motivations. They're never clear. What do they want?"

I said, "They want to be main characters in a published story."

He shook his head grimly.

Outside of class, the students were talking about me too. There were these rock formations on campus, and I knew that that was where they went to lie on their backs like lizards and bash me. This guy—the one who wrote the treasure-chest-in-the-ditch story—said all I ever wrote about were things that really happened to me. Someone else agreed. "She doesn't have any *real* imagination."

All of this, I knew, was David Letterman's fault. If I could just get him out of my life, things would get better. He wasn't what I wanted.

I waited until after Thanksgiving to break the news. We were in the Special Room and Paul wasn't there yet. First I made him a drink. I had to put it in his mug. He was drinking Ouzo and he smelled like a big licorice stick. Once I gave him his drink, I said, "Dave, I have to talk to you."

He said, "What is it, pumpkin?"

"I'm not happy," I said and then Paul walked in. He had a

shirt with glitter moons and stars all over it. He said to me, "Make me a Cosmo now."

Dave got up from the couch. "Is it Paul? Is he making you unhappy?" Dave walked closer to Paul. He looked like he was about to strike him.

"No," I said. "I can't stand him, but that's not it."

"Is it your mother in Czechoslovakia?" he asked.

I made a face. "What are you talking about?"

Paul shouted, "Finally, here we go!" He slumped down in a chair, staring at David Letterman and then me, his little lips quivering. "This is what Dave does," he said, shaking his head bitterly. "He sees a girl from a distance and he gives her some stupid personality and whatever else. Then he becomes obsessed with her, with the person he thinks she is."

Dave looked at me. "Your mother is in Czechoslovakia. You're Czechoslovakian."

"No, I'm not."

Paul laughed. "I suppose you're going to tell us now that you were never a ballerina?"

"No."

Dave said, gritting his teeth, "Yes, you are. Yes, you are." He was pointing at me angrily. "I saw you in the window of that bar and you are from Czechoslovakia. You moved here to be a ballerina but you broke some of your toes, and so you started working in that bar. Half the money you make you send back home to your mother."

"I would never send my mother money!"

Paul shouted, "She's cheap, Dave, she's cheap!"

"I'm not cheap!" I screamed defensively. "My mother's just a fool when it come to money."

Paul turned to David Letterman. "You're pathetic!" Paul was yelling so loud his lips were wet. "You're just obsessed with being obsessed and you don't even know what you're obsessed with!" He turned to me. "And you're no better. Obsessed with being published!" Spit came out of his mouth when he said the *p* in published.

I said, "How do you know that? How do you know that about me?"

"You've got rejection slip written all over your face!" Paul shouted. "Besides . . . I was in your apartment. I saw all of them, the rejections, posted on your refrigerator with those gaudy butterfly magnets." My heart sank. I guess it wasn't the best place to put them, but I thought it motivated me.

"And, really, what do you think is going to happen if you do get published?" he asked. "You're still going to have to wear a dumb dress." I looked down at myself, at the red gown I was wearing. "You'll still live in that unkempt apartment of yours. You'll still make bad Cosmos. Nothing will change. Nothing." He turned to David Letterman. "I told you she wasn't what you wanted." He gave Dave a long, angry look. Then he stormed out of the Special Room.

"Ouch," Dave said, and shook his head. "What the hell's gotten into him." He was standing in front of the stereo, the mug in his hands.

"He's right," I said.

"No, he's not." David Letterman took a sip of his drink. "Look, I could grow to like you whoever you . . . are."

I said, "No."

He was pacing. "We just have to get out of New York, that's all. I've got a place in Connecticut. We'll go there."

I said, "I hate Connecticut. There's nothing there. Except my sister, she lives there."

His face brightened. "You have a sister?"

I said, "Yes, yes I do," and smiled. Then I gave him her address.

*　　　*　　　*

One week later, I got my job back at The Whiskey Den. I had to wear the dress again, but I didn't care—it wasn't that bad. Everything was the same. Maria was still there. Snake was on the same bar stool; his fang teeth were still intact. The only difference was that it was snowing and the park, through the window, almost looked pretty.

Maria said to me, "You didn't really think that you weren't gonna come back."

I said, "I don't know what I thought. My motivation wasn't clear."

Maria looked at Snake, who was jiggling the ice in his glass. "It's not that fuckin' easy," she said to me. "You don't just show up and have things happen to you. You gotta stay here. You gotta be tortured by all these fuckin' freaks first."

I nodded. I understood this; I just didn't like it.

Later that night, I decided to write a top-ten list of the things I wanted. But then I reduced the list to three things, because ten seemed too many—I might go berserk. What I wanted was this:

I wanted Blockbuster Boy. I called him and left a message.

I wanted my mother to get off my back. That was actually happening. My sister and David Letterman were already getting along nicely and my mother had just recently met a dashing man of her own named Hank. Hank was taking her to the Vineyard for the week—special off-season rates.

I wanted to be published—but not because it would drastically alter my life. I just wanted it to happen. I decided to write more. I put together a special color-coded schedule for writing and tacked it on the wall in my bedroom. I was going to write all day in three-hour intervals. I also allotted moments when I could eat and talk to people.

I showed Maria the cocktail napkin my list was on. She said, "You wrote this shit down. What are you, stupid?" I shrugged my shoulders. Snake smiled. She turned to him and shouted, "What are you lookin' at, guy?"

I laughed—I liked Maria a lot. She was an actress. She was from Panama; English wasn't even her first language. She did voice-overs for extra money and her specialty was the Brooklyn accent. She was always practicing at work.

Maria glanced at my list again and said, "What are you so fuckin' worried about anyway? It's gonna happen." She stretched her arms out dramatically. "This is New York."

ACKNOWLEDGMENTS

For their constant encouragement, I thank my teachers: Peter Cameron, Mary LaChapelle, Joan Larkin, Fenton Johnson, Elizabeth Searle, and Bill Holinger, as well as my readers and friends: Francine Almash, Elizabeth Lane, Jessica Powers, Tara Steketee, Kenny Switzer, Paul Schaeffer, Michelle Sanchez, Maria Torres, and Carl Indrisano.

I thank the girls at Whiskey Park—and the boys too.

I thank the city of New York for making me nervous and desperate, for pushing me so hard.

I thank my favorite priest in the whole wide world: Rev. Gary Seibert.

I thank God.

I thank my agent, Wendy Weil, her assistant, Emily Forland, and my editor, Trena Keating, for their enthusiasm and hard work.

Special thanks also goes to my roommate, Won-Jeong Han, for being able to stand me and my constant presence in our apartment. Without her tolerance and friendship, I wouldn't have been able to write all that I have.

Lastly, I owe my deepest and most urgent thanks to my family—their support and humor can get me through anything. Specifically, I would like to thank my mother and father, my sister Eileen and her boyfriend Patrick, my brother Sean and his wife Joanne, my Auntie Jo and her best friend Debbie, my Aunt Mare, my Aunt Dot and Uncle Ray, and last but not least, my nephew **MR. JOSEPH PRATT** (it was calmly requested that his name be illuminated in this fashion).